THE
TAKING
OF
LIBBIE, SD

Also by David Housewright

FEATURING RUSHMORE MCKENZIE

Jelly's Gold

Madman on a Drum

A Hard Ticket Home

Tin City

Pretty Girl Gone

Dead Boyfriends

FEATURING HOLLAND TAYLOR

Penance

Practice to Deceive

Dearly Departed

THE
TAKING
OF
LIBBIE, SD

—

David Housewright

MINOTAUR BOOKS

NEW YORK

This is a work of fiction. All of the characters, organizations, and events portrayed in this novel are either products of the author's imagination or are used fictitiously.

THE TAKING OF LIBBIE, SD. Copyright © 2010 by David Housewright. All rights reserved. Printed in the United States of America. For information, address St. Martin's Press, 175 Fifth Avenue, New York, N.Y. 10010.

www.minotaurbooks.com

Library of Congress Cataloging-in-Publication Data

Housewright, David, 1955–
    The taking of Libbie, SD / David Housewright.—Ist ed.
      p. cm.
    ISBN 978-0-312-55996-0
    1. McKenzie, Mac (Fictitious character)—Fiction. 2. Private investigators—Fiction. 3. Kidnapping—Fiction. 4. Ex-police officers—Fiction.
5. Swindlers and swindling—Fiction. 6. South Dakota—Fiction. I. Title.
    PS3558.O8668T35 2010
    813'.54—dc22

2010008712

First Edition: June 2010

10 9 8 7 6 5 4 3 2 1

For Reneé Marie Valois,
forever

ACKNOWLEDGMENTS

I want to acknowledge my debt to Roxanne Cardinal, Gary Dyshaw, Keith Kahla, Eric Odney, Alison J. Picard, and Reneé Valois.

THE
TAKING
OF
LIBBIE, SD

CHAPTER ONE

They shattered my front door with a metal battering ram at exactly four forty-seven and twenty-three seconds A.M. That's when my alarm system began whooping and a forced-entry message was dispatched to both my security company and the City of St. Anthony Police Department. The siren shook me awake, but I didn't react to it the way I should have. Instead, I remained in bed during those first crucial seconds and wondered what was wrong with my alarm clock and why in hell I had set it in the first place. By the time I realized what the siren meant, they were already on the stairs. I swung myself out of bed and made for the door. They reached it first, two men dressed for combat, one tall, one short. The short one carried an M26 Taser gun—I recognized the black body and vibrant green nose in the soft gray light filtering through my open window. I drifted back into the bedroom, my hands raised to shoulder height. The tall one said, "Rushmore McKenzie?" I lunged for my bedside lamp. It was the only weapon within reach. The short intruder pointed the Taser and squeezed the trigger. One barbed electrode hit me high in the upper shoulder, and the other imbedded itself just above the waistband of my blue shorts. My body was immediately flooded with fifty thousand volts. The electrical charge told every muscle to move at once, which caused them all to contract against each other. My body locked up. I hit the floor like a bag of sand tossed from the back of a truck.

They waited until the Taser ran through its five-second cycle, and then it was gloved hands yanking the electrodes out of my naked skin, rolling me onto my back and grabbing my arms. I was still twitching, still moaning from pain as the taller man slipped a double-loop restraint over both my wrists and pulled hard on the locking mechanism, securing my hands in front of me. The disposable cuffs were made of high-tensile-strength nylon that was just as effective as stainless steel. The tall man grabbed one shoulder. After he holstered the Taser, the short man took the other, and together they dragged me from my bedroom and down the carpeted stairs. A moment later we were out the front door. My bare feet scraped against the hard wood porch planks; my heels bounced on the concrete steps leading from the porch. I felt the pain, and it jolted me out of my stupor. I began to struggle. I yelled for help. My captors didn't seem to mind. They hustled me to a four-door sedan parked in front of my house. The trunk was already open; the trunk light had been removed.

"I got north," a voice said. The smaller man released my shoulder and grabbed both of my legs. I tried to kick myself free and failed. They lifted and swung me toward the opening of the trunk. "One, two, three." On three they let fly. My head skimmed the lid of the trunk, and my knee hit the rim as I tumbled inside.

"The battering ram," the shorter man said.

"Leave it," his partner answered.

He slammed the trunk lid shut, enclosing me in darkness. I heard car doors opening and closing, the engine starting; I felt the car lurch forward and pick up speed. I pressed my back against the trunk lid and pushed. It didn't budge. I found myself breathing harder than the exertion demanded. I caught my breath when I heard the distant wail of police sirens. Even in my befuddled condition, I knew it was the cavalry responding to my security alert. The car slowed as the sirens grew louder. The cops seemed to be right on top of us. "I'm here, I'm here," I shouted—but the sirens passed and the car began to gain speed. The sirens slowly faded to silence.

The inside of my mouth became dry, and it was difficult to swallow, although sweat seemed to flow from every pore. I felt light-headed. I began to tremble. My thoughts swung from utter helplessness to denial—it's just a dream, go back to sleep. "No!" I heard the word, but I don't know if it was spoken aloud or just inside my head. I lay on my back and kicked the trunk lid with my bare feet. I shouted obscenities. I screamed, "Let me out."

Time passed, yet in my panic I couldn't say how much. Finally— *Stop it,* my inner voice told me. *Just stop it.* I rested against the trunk floor; the vibration and noise of the moving car became a rumble in my stomach. *Think it through.*

I started with Why. Why was this happening to me? I couldn't answer that question without knowing Who. Who were these men who so efficiently snatched me from my bed? Professionals, obviously. Yet who hired them? I had many enemies, acquired back in my days as a cop and more recently as a kind of knight-errant doing favors for friends. Plenty of them would be happy to see me dead. Except, if that was the case, why the Taser? Why not a twelve-gauge sawed-off? Maybe it was a kidnapping for ransom—I had enough money to make it worthwhile. However, I had no family, no friends with access to my funds. There was no one to pay a ransom. Which brought me to What. I had been kidnapped, mana-cled, and locked in the trunk of a speeding car with no one to help me, that's what.

So, what are you going to do about it?

I tried to calm myself, slow my respiration, slow my pulse. It be-came easier when I realized that the kidnappers had made a mis-take. They cuffed my hands in front of me instead of behind. That allowed me to work my fingers along the edge of the trunk lid, frantically searching for a release catch. There wasn't any, but if I could find something to slip between the lid and the base . . . The compartment was large enough for me to roll over, and I began searching for a tire iron or jack. I found neither. Nor was there a spare.

I lay in the darkness. My thoughts were slanting toward despair.

There's no way out, I told myself.

There is always a way, my inner voice said.

"There's no way out," I said aloud.

Quitters never win and winners never quit.

"This isn't a goddamn hockey game."

Think it through.

"Goddamn, sonuvabitch . . . Hey."

Taillights. A car has taillights. How do you gain access to the taillights should a bulb burn out? Through the trunk.

I reached in darkness for the wall of the trunk and eagerly followed it to the corner. I continued to explore with my fingers until I located a small plastic panel. I felt a recessed tab. I dug my fingers into it and pried the panel off. Suddenly there was light. It came in the color red and filtered through the taillight lens. It allowed me to see a metal bracket and the hard plastic assembly that it held in place. Wires led to the back of the assembly and gave juice to the lightbulbs. I grabbed hold of the wires, considered yanking them out, and then thought better of it. If I damaged the taillights, the driver would know the first time he used his turn signal. Instead, I took a firm grip on the back of the light assembly and twisted counterclockwise. It was hard work at that angle, yet I finally managed to give it a half turn, popped the assembly free, and dropped it inside the trunk. I was so pleased with what I had done, I maneuvered my body around in the cramped space so that I could get at the other taillight. This one was more difficult—I was forced to use my left hand—but I eventually removed the assembly. For practical purposes, the car no longer had taillights or signal lights. Maybe a county cop or highway patrolman would notice—the car was moving at a steady pace that seemed fast to me, so I guessed we were on a highway or freeway. The lack of lights might even cause an accident. I had no real desire to be in a trunk during a rear-end collision, yet at that moment I would have settled for anything.

Now what?

I decided it would be nice if I could bust off the taillight lens, ease my hand through the opening, and wave it about. Certainly that would attract the attention of other drivers—the morning rush hour should begin soon, I reminded myself. Except I couldn't reach the lens; the metal bracket was in the way. I yanked hard; it was welded firmly to the frame of the car. If I had a tire iron I could punch the lens out through the hole in the bracket, only that took me back to where I started.

Wait . . .

I had no idea how long I had been in the trunk, but the sun had risen high enough that red-tinted sunshine allowed me to see the seams of the blue-brown floor mat that I was resting on. Of course, I told myself. The floor mat disguised a compartment beneath me. The spare tire, along with the jack and tire iron, was in the compartment. The problem was getting my cuffed hands under the compartment lid while my weight was resting on top of it. I maneuvered my backside as far into the corner of the trunk as possible and went up on my toes, even as I pressed my back against the lid. That gave me room to work with; however, with my weight on it, I couldn't lift the edge of the lid more than an inch or two. Still, I managed to slip my fingers beneath it. The lid was made of thin wood fiber covered by the carpet. I pulled upward. I was determined that if I couldn't lift the mat, I'd break it. Only it was stubborn. My first attempt failed. So did my second. On my third attempt I pulled as mightily on it as I could, ignoring the pain shooting through my fingertips. *Your life depends on this,* my inner voice warned me. "Break, you bastard," I said aloud. Every muscle in my body strained against the lid. Sweat poured off my forehead into my eyes. Then the wood fiber fractured. Then it broke. It sounded like the crack of gunfire inside the trunk, and my head and shoulders made an angry thud on the lid as I flew backward, yet my kidnappers either didn't hear or chose to disregard the noise.

The carpet remained intact, yet I was able to fold the broken piece of wood fiber on top of the rest of the lid. I uncovered a hole big enough to accommodate a hand—but only one. I rolled onto my shoulder and pressed my back and hips against the trunk wall and lid as I eased my right hand under the wood fiber while slipping my left hand over the top of it. I pushed as deeply as I could until the broken edge of the mat butted up against the strong nylon restraint. My knuckles skimmed over hard rubber but nothing else. I removed my hand and worked the disposable cuffs farther up my wrists. I got maybe an extra inch to work with, although the nylon was now cutting off the circulation in my hands. I eased my right hand back into the hole again. This time my fingertips touched metal. I flicked at it, and it moved toward me a fraction of an inch. I flicked at it some more until I was able to get a firm grip. I strained and manipulated and pulled until at last I was able to ease the tire iron through the hole. Actually, not a tire iron but a lug wrench— one end had a socket that fit over the wheel's lug nuts, the other a prying tip that was used primarily to remove hubcaps.

He shoots, he scores, my inner voice announced.

My arms and hands were aching, so I dropped the wrench on the floor while I worked the cuffs down to the narrow part of my wrists. I flexed my fingers until circulation returned. My entire body was now smooth with perspiration; I felt the sweat soaking my blue boxers.

"Okay," I said aloud.

Once I had the wrench, I turned my attention back to the trunk lid. It didn't take long to realize that there was no opening to insert the tip, no way to get leverage. So again I twisted and turned my body until I had access to the corner of the trunk. I jammed the lug wrench in the space between the metal bracket and the car frame, pressing the pry tip hard against the red-tinted lens. Nothing happened. I pressed harder. Given how many busted taillights I've seen over the years, I expected the lens to be fairly fragile. It wasn't. I pounded on it with the curled tip without creating so much as a scratch.

Put your back into it, my inner voice ordered.

Harder and harder I struck the wrench against the lens. Finally it cracked. The crack grew. A small triangle of plastic chipped off. A hole formed. The hole grew larger. I pushed the wrench through the hole as far as possible. Would anyone on the highway see it? A better question, would anyone be alarmed enough to do something about it? Probably not, I told myself. I needed something else. All I had was my shorts.

Should I dangle them out of the hole like a flag? I asked myself. Well, why not?

Before I could remove them, though, the taillights inside the trunk lit up, and the car began to slow. One bulb began to blink— a right turn. It went out. A few moments later, it blinked again— another right. The car sped up, and then the brake lights flared. The blinking light said left turn. As the car turned, I heard the squeal of tires followed by the bellow of a horn.

"Yes," I said aloud. This was going to work.

I hooked my thumbs under the waistband of my shorts and began to ease them down, trying to work them over my hips. The lights flared again; the car slowed to a halt. A stop sign? I wondered. No. Car doors opened and closed. Dammit.

I heard a muffled voice. "Look at this. Do you believe this?" An unseen hand jiggled the lug wrench and pushed it back into the trunk.

"Now we know why that asshole flipped us the bird back there," a second voice said.

I pulled my shorts up.

Knuckles rapped on the trunk lid. "Hey, McKenzie. Do you hear me?"

"I hear you," I said. What else was I going to do, pretend I wasn't there?

"We're going to pop the trunk. Don't do anything stupid, okay? We don't want to have to Taser you again." Apparently he expected a reply, because he rapped on the trunk lid again and said, "Did you hear me?"

"I heard you."

There was a popping sound, and the trunk opened. Harsh sunlight flooded the compartment. I brought my hands up to shield my eyes.

"Roll out of there." The tall one was speaking. The short one was standing off to the side. He had a clear shot of me with his Taser.

"Who are you guys?" I said.

"C'mon, c'mon, we have a long way to go yet."

"Where are we going?"

"You'll see when we get there."

"Is it a secret?"

"Get out of the trunk."

I managed to swing my legs over the edge and, as the man said, rolled out of there, using the back of the car to leverage myself more or less into a standing position—my legs were weak and uncertain. I looked around. We were in a small clearing surrounded by poplar trees. A dirt road led away from the clearing. There was another car, a Ford Taurus, parked ten yards away and facing the road. The car had South Dakota plates. There were no buildings and no sound of traffic.

"We expected you to be rolled up into a ball and weeping like a child by now," the short man said. "We underestimated you."

"I'll say," said the taller man. "Turn around, McKenzie. Go 'head."

I turned.

The shorter man pressed the business end of the Taser against the small of my back. "Don't even think of moving," he said.

"What should I call you guys?"

"Lord and Master."

"Which is which?"

"Hold your hands out," the taller man said. I did what he told me. He reached across with a tool that reminded me of small wire cutters except it didn't have any sharp edges. He hooked the cutter over the nylon straps and severed them. The cuffs fell away. "Put your hands behind your back."

"What is this all about?" I asked.

"Hands behind your back."

The shorter man nudged my spine with the Taser. "You heard him," he said.

I did what the taller man told me, and he recuffed my wrists, properly this time. "C'mon," he said.

The shorter man stepped backward, but didn't lower the Taser, as the taller man spun me around. He pushed me toward the Taurus. I nearly stumbled but managed to keep my feet. When we reached the rear of the car, the taller man popped the trunk.

"Inside," he said.

"Why are you taking me to South Dakota?" I said.

The two kidnappers exchanged surprised glances as if I had guessed a deep, dark secret.

"C'mon, fellas," I said. "You can tell me. Why are you doing this?"

"For the money, why else?" said the smaller man.

"What money?"

"The reward."

"Reward?"

"Five thousand dollars."

"Plus expenses," said the taller man.

"For what? What did I do?"

"We didn't ask."

There was about ten minutes of rough roads and me bouncing up and down, landing painfully on my hands and shoulders, before the ride smoothed out. I assumed we were on the freeway again heading God knew where at high speed. I felt the turns; they were wide and gradual.

The kidnappers had warned me to behave myself after stuffing me inside the trunk, and I said I would. Believe me, I would've given the lie to it if I could have. This time, though, with my hands cuffed tightly behind my back, there was nothing to work with. I could only hope it was a short ride. No such luck. I had no way of knowing the time, but I had the sense that hours were passing. It wasn't long before I felt the urge to relieve myself. I shouted my need to the kidnappers. Again, they either couldn't hear or chose to ignore me. Finally, I gave in to nature's call, soaking my shorts, my leg, and the floor mat. I promised myself I wouldn't be embarrassed. I promised myself I wouldn't become angry. I was both. I couldn't help myself. And soon a third emotion—the worst of all— supplanted them. Helplessness. It covered me like a heavy, wet blanket. I had never felt so utterly defeated. Eventually the car slowed, went up a steep incline, took a few turns, and came to a stop. The familiar sounds of a gas pump in use told me we were in a service station at the top of a freeway exit ramp. Yet I couldn't even muster enough resistance to kick the trunk lid or yell for help.

Then one of my captors did a foolish thing. He rapped rhythmically on the trunk lid—shave and a haircut, two bits—and laughed. What the hell was that? Trash talk? He was trash-talking me? That sorry sonuvabitch. You don't talk trash until the game is over, and this game was far from over. Who the hell did he think he was? Cretin–Derham Hall did the same crap when I was playing hockey for Central High School. We were down 6–1 at the beginning of the third period, and they started talking trash. So me and Bobby Dunston and the rest of the guys beat the hell out of them for fifteen minutes—we hit them so hard and so often their ancestors were probably still feeling it. We lost 7–6 in OT, but those elitist punks knew they were in a game. Now these smart-ass kidnappers were giving me the same business? I don't think so.

I know some people might think this reaction was silly given the circumstances, but trash talk was something I knew, something I understood. It rearmed me with anger; it filled me with indignation. If those bastards thought I had given up . . .

Think it through, my inner voice told me.

Typically bounty hunters are hired by bail bondsmen to rearrest felons who have skipped out on their bail and return them to the court system. It's entirely legal for them to go into most states and bring out an escaping felon. However, these guys switched cars. There was no reason for them to do that unless they were afraid they were spotted leaving the scene and an alert was issued on them—which meant they knew that there wasn't any paper out on me and that what they were doing was illegal. Also, bounty hunters usually are paid only a percentage of the bond for their ·work. These guys were getting expenses. That told me someone outside the court system had probably employed them. At the same time, I couldn't pretend that it was all just a terrible mistake, that they grabbed me thinking I was someone else—they had called me by name. Twice. So I was left with the very real possibility that

Lord and Master had been hired to kidnap and transport me to an undisclosed location so I could be killed at the pleasure of their employer. Possible, except the killer would have to suffer a pair of potential witnesses who could blackmail him, who could barter him in exchange for a plea bargain from the state should the need arise. No, there was something else in play. I knew that sooner or later I would be let out of the trunk. Sooner or later my hands would be freed.

Yeah, all right, I told myself. All right. There was nothing I could do for now, so I did nothing, resolving to conserve my energy for the moment when I would have use for it. The time would come, and soon. Then I would get my revenge. Shave and a haircut, two bits, my ass.

I fell asleep, for how long I couldn't say. When I woke, my body was sheathed in sweat. It was insufferably hot inside the trunk, and I knew I was becoming dehydrated—I was starting to feel both light-headed and nauseous. I yelled for relief. My head throbbed from the exertion.

Time passed. I rolled over in the cramped quarters, strained to stretch my legs, tensing my body in an isometric exercise. It took more effort than it was worth. There was a dull, throbbing ache in my shoulders, my elbows, my wrists and hands. I tried not to think. Not of Nina or Shelby or Bobby Dunston or my father and mother or of my life in general. There was no need. I had been in trouble before. Slowly roasting inside a locked trunk—that didn't even make my Top Ten list. Or so I told myself.

I continued to sleep sporadically during the long journey, and with each awakening I felt less confident. The darkness was becoming increasingly cruel, and I experienced a *Twilight Zone* moment, imagining that I was already dead and this was my hell, driving endlessly in the trunk of a Ford Taurus. Doo-doo-doo-doo, doo-doo-doo-doo . . . It was a dangerous frame of mind, and to alleviate it, I sang softly to myself, singing Gershwin, Porter, Springsteen, Dylan, even Petula Clark until the lyrics became incomprehensible. I envisioned myself as a guest on a talk show—Regis and Kelly, Ellen DeGeneres, Larry King, Bill O'Reilly, *The View,* nothing that I ever actually watched—talking aloud until the conversation became as oppressive as the heat. The slowing of the car, the multiple turns, the rolling stops and starts, the final stop followed by the quieting of the engine and the opening and closing of car doors—none of it even registered until the trunk squeaked open and the compartment was immersed in light.

"Out," a voice said.

I didn't move, couldn't move, except for my eyelids, which I sealed against the glaring light.

"I said outta there."

A hand on my shoulder prodded me.

"Hey, McKenzie. Ah, Christ. Give me a hand."

Two pair of hands seized me under my arms and dragged me from the trunk. Someone slapped my face.

"C'mon, McKenzie."

"Don't do that," I said.

I wanted to strike back now that I had the chance, throw some snap kicks at these bastards and hurt them like I had promised I would with every passing mile. Only my legs were both stiff and weak as they unfolded under me; they weren't strong enough to support my weight. I felt like every muscle and joint in my body was rusty. The kidnappers had to hold tight to keep me from falling.

"Look at this," said the shorter kidnapper. "He pissed himself."

"Well, duh," said his partner.

I opened my eyes, closed them, opened them again and blinked against the sun. We were in an asphalt parking lot, white lines painted neatly on the pavement. It burned my bare feet, and I instinctively went up on my toes. There was a street, also asphalt, beyond the lot. Across the street was a bank. First Integrity State Bank of Libbie. A display flashed time and temperature. *2:33 PM. 97° F.*

The kidnappers spun me around and dragged me toward the glass doors of a blond-stone building. There was a name spelled out in silver letters attached to the stone. CITY OF LIBBIE POLICE DEPARTMENT. The sight of it cheered me. I think I might even have smiled. I used to be a cop. I liked cops. Cops didn't murder people. Except on TV and in the movies. And in New York and L.A.

Lord and Master muscled me through the doors. A wave of cold air immediately pummeled my body. The dull throb above my ears became a slicing pain that attacked my eyes. It had to be thirty degrees cooler inside than outside, but instead of making me feel better, the abrupt change in temperature increased my nausea. I gagged, nearly vomited. The kidnappers stared at me nervously as they brought my limp body to a waist-high counter. A uniformed officer stood behind it.

"Is that him?" he said.

"Yeah."

"He don't look too good."

"He's fine."

"Put 'im in interrogation."

I was now able to put weight on my legs; probably I could have walked without help. The kidnappers wouldn't think of it. They half carried, half dragged me around the counter. They led me to a metal door, opened it, and pulled me inside as if they had been there many times before. The desk officer followed behind.

The room might have been used for interrogations, but the smell of fried chicken convinced me that it was also used as a lunchroom. It was probably the conference room as well. In the center of the room was a metal table that was secured to the concrete floor. There were several folding chairs around the table, plus one metal chair that was also bolted to the floor and facing a one-way mirror. The tall kidnapper dumped me into the metal chair while the officer pulled the other chairs away, folded them, and leaned them against the wall out of my reach.

Finished, he came over and gave the tall kidnapper a pair of handcuffs with a foot-long chain between them. "Here, use this," he said. The kidnapper secured one cuff to a steel ring welded to the table. The other he wound around my right wrist. After that, he severed the nylon restrains with his cutter.

I pulled my arms out from behind my back with a mixture of pain and relief. I stretched as best I could against the chain. The effort both exhilarated and tired me. I slumped forward and rested my forehead against the tabletop. The metal felt cool against my skin. The pain in my head became less pointed and seemed to spread to the entire back of my skull.

"You sure that's him?" the officer said. "He doesn't look the same."

"He's been locked in a trunk for six hundred miles," the tall kidnapper said. "What do you expect him to look like?"

"We should give him some water," said the shorter kidnapper. "Do you have any water?"

"Hey," the officer said. He nudged my bare foot with his shoe. "Hey. What's your name?"

I answered, but apparently he didn't hear me. He nudged me again. "What did you say?"

"Rushmore McKenzie," I said.

"Told you it was him," said the tall kidnapper.

"You got any water?" the shorter kidnapper repeated. "We should give 'im some water."

"Yeah, I'll get some," the officer said.

"When are we gonna get our money?" the taller kidnapper said.

"Don't ask me. Talk to old man Miller. He's the one put the bounty out. Far as I know, the city hasn't even charged McKenzie with a crime. The county, neither. I better make some calls." The officer left the room. The two kidnappers followed him out.

"We should get 'im some water," the shorter one said.

The water came in a plastic bottle with a blue label. I tried not to drink it too fast and failed. I asked for more. The officer gave me a kind of screw-you look, but my appearance must have changed his mind, because he quickly brought me two more bottles.

I had always been contemptuous of the bottled-water crowd, especially those good folks who always seem to have a jug with them, sometimes carried in a little pouch like a pet. The municipal water system had always been good enough for me—that's where most bottled water comes from, anyway. Also, I'd never much believed the myth, fiercely propagated by the bottled-water industry, that we should drink eight bottles every day in order to properly hydrate ourselves. I just couldn't see any health benefit in going to the bathroom seventeen times a day. Nor did I take pride in knowing that Americans have the clearest and most expensive urine in the world. Instead, I'd generally heeded the advice of my dad, who said you should drink only when you are thirsty and never pay for anything that's free. On the other hand, I didn't think Dad spent much time in the trunk of a Ford Taurus on a sweltering day in July.

I stood up, testing my legs. They seemed to work fine. I took a step in one direction and a second in the other—that was all I could manage with my wrist chained to the table, yet it filled me with confidence. I looked at myself in the one-way mirror. Red splotches on my shoulder and waist looked like large and dangerous bee stings. Half of my hair was plastered to my head; the other half stood out at awkward angles. I was in need of a shave, and despite the naps I took in the trunk, my face had the droopy look of someone who needed a good night's sleep. My blue shorts were damp, and the sour odor of urine mixed with the aroma of fried chicken. It wasn't a pretty smell, but it reminded me of how long it had been since I had last eaten, just the same.

The officer returned to the room.

"Sit down," he said.

"I'd rather stand," I said.

"Sit down."

There was an angry expression on his face, so I sat. I didn't feel strong enough to defy him.

He stepped over to the table. He took the empty water bottle and left the half-filled twin.

"What's that smell?" he said.

"Where am I?" I said.

The officer looked at me as if he thought I was putting him on. "The police department in Libbie," he said.

"Where is Libbie?"

"Are you trying to be funny?"

"Do I look like I'm trying to be funny?"

"You're back in South Dakota, asshole."

"Back? I've never been in South Dakota. Not once in my life."

"Is that right?"

"Why have I been brought here against my will?"

"Why is anyone brought here against their will?"

"Look, pal. I heard you say that neither the city nor the county had any paper on me. So either release me or charge me. If you charge me, you had better read me my rights and let me contact an attorney."

The officer smirked and gave me a slow head shake. "Not this time, chiseler," he said. "You're not walking away this time."

This time?

I asked him what he meant. He left the interrogation room without answering, closing the metal door behind him.

There wasn't much I could do except sit and wait, my elbows on the table, my head resting in my hands. I still had no idea what it was all about, why I was hustled to Libbie, South Dakota, wherever that was. Yet my natural confidence was returning. I felt sure that someone would explain it all to me soon, and eventually I would get my phone call. When I did—whom should I call? I wondered. A lawyer, G. K. Bonalay, probably. Except—does Nina know I'm missing? She's probably worried sick. Certainly I'd be disappointed if she wasn't. The cops, they must be searching for me, too. St. Anthony PD. St. Paul. Bobby Dunston. He's probably rousting every punk, every offender I ever knew. Those damn bounty hunters, they were the criminals, I reminded myself. There were no wants, no warrants issued against me. Taking me like they did, transporting me across state lines, they have a phrase for that—it's called felony kidnapping. A federal beef. Yeah, suddenly I knew exactly whom I was going to call. I was going to call Harry. I was going to call the FBI.

I was thinking how much fun that was going to be when I heard a murmur of voices behind the mirror. They sounded excited. I couldn't make out much, just a few words and phrases—"liar," "thief," "con artist," and "bastard" were all closely tied to my name. The voices quieted and then became louder. A moment later the door to the interrogation room burst open. A man stepped through. He was big, one of those guys who could fill a bus seat all by himself. He was old, too, pushing seventy at least. Only he didn't move like he was old. He crossed the floor in a hurry, raised a beefy hand, and swung down on my face. I tried to raise my arm to block the blow, only it was chained to the table and he was able to get over the top of it. He didn't hit like he was old, either—I felt a stinging thump above my ear that caused my brain to vibrate. I tucked my head and turned it away. His next punches fell on my neck and shoulders. He hit me at least six, seven times before a trio of men subdued him and dragged him from the room. The name Mr. Miller was mixed with their shouts.

"What was that?" I said to no one in particular.

No one answered.

"What the hell was that?"

A tall man attired in the uniform of the City of Libbie Police Department stepped back through the door. He was carrying a clipboard.

"I am Chief of Police Eric Gustafson," he said. "Are you Rushmore McKenzie?"

"Yes, I am."

He glanced down at the sheet of paper attached to the clipboard. "Do you live in Falcon Heights in Minnesota?"

"I do."

"When were you born?"

I told him.

He looked up. "Not in June?"

"No, not in June," I said.

"What is your Social Security number?"

I recited the nine digits.

"Are you sure?" he said.

"Positive."

He turned and left the room.

I heard more voices, this time from the hallway outside the interrogation room door. Someone said, "Big mistake." Someone else shouted, "No, no, no." A third voice said, "Lineup? Photo array?"

I heard nothing more. After a few minutes, I rested my head on the tabletop again. If I slept, I did so without noticing. There was a sharp rap on the mirror. I looked up and saw only myself. More time passed. I finished the water. I asked for more. Whoever was behind the mirror ignored the request.

Moments later the chief returned to the room. He halted at the door, a look of confusion on his face.

"Rushmore McKenzie." He said the name slowly. "You were a police officer. You know—"

"What do I know?"

"You know—"

"I know you got the wrong guy," I said. "You sent your thugs to Minnesota. They busted down my door, Tasered me, dragged me from my bed, locked me in a trunk, transported me across state lines, and now you're holding me without charges, without giving me my rights—these are all federal crimes. Right? You screwed up, and now you're wondering what to do about it. That's what I know." I rattled the chain against the metal table. "Well?"

He turned and stepped back through the doorway.

"The longer you keep me here, the worse it's going to get," I said. "For both of us," I added quietly as he shut the door behind him.

CHAPTER TWO

She swept into the interrogation room. That's an apt verb—swept. She moved quickly to the table, walking tall like a model inviting you to look but not touch. She was wearing a fitted white blouse tucked inside a flirty salmon skirt that revealed a lot of leg. Her hair was long, heavy, and blond-red, her features golden and pretty. There was a big-city sheen to her and, also, an odd kind of harshness around her eyes as if she had seen things that had hurt her. She looked around, found the folding chairs leaning against the wall, took one, unfolded it, and set it in front of the table.

"I'm Tracie Blake," she said.

She offered her hand even as she settled into the chair. I raised my own hand to give her a good look at the chain securing me to the table.

"Oh," she said.

"Oh," I repeated.

She sighed dramatically and said, "We thought you were someone else."

"Who did you think I was?"

"Rushmore McKenzie."

"What a coincidence. I thought I was Rushmore McKenzie, too."

"Yes, but not *the* Rushmore McKenzie."

She smiled as if she had told a joke and was waiting for her audience to get it.

"Who are you?" I said.

"I'm a member of the Libbie City Council."

"And you're here because . . . ?"

She stared for a moment as if she were considering various answers and then opted for the truth. "They think I have a better chance of convincing you not to sue the town into oblivion."

I glared at the one-way mirror, trying to see the faces of the men I knew were standing behind it. "They do, huh?"

"Yeppers."

"Honey, you may be the prettiest girl these guys have ever seen, but you're not the prettiest I've seen. If you think a come-hither smile is going to work on me, you're mistaken."

Tracie shrugged as if she didn't quite believe me.

"What would work?" she asked.

I clenched my fist and yanked my arm up as if I were going to punch her. I would have been about three feet short of her face even if the chain hadn't shortened my swing, yet she flinched and leaned backward just the same.

"You can start by unshackling me," I said.

"People are afraid of you, of what you might do."

"Yeah? Well, I'm afraid of what you might do."

"Like what?"

"I'm hundreds of miles from home, no friend knows I'm here, dressed only in soiled shorts, no wallet, no ID, chained to a table—think about it."

She did, for a full ten seconds before she smiled a most beguiling smile and said, "Oh, that's just silly."

"You think?"

"Of course I do."

"Then why am I still chained to this table?"

"I'm not—"

"Do you agree that I'm not the guy you're looking for?"

"Yes."

"Then why don't you apologize and let me go?"

Tracie spun in her chair and studied the interrogation room mirror as if she expected the answer to magically appear on the glass. When it didn't, she turned back to face me.

"Can I tell you what happened?" she said. "Can we just sit here, calmly, like adults, and I'll explain what happened?"

I made a big production of showing her the chain again. "Do I have a choice?"

"Rushmore."

"Only one person gets to call me Rushmore, and you're not her. My name is McKenzie. Just McKenzie, all right?"

"See, that's one difference right there—between you and the other McKenzie, I mean. He always told people to call him Rush."

I leaned back in the chair and made myself as comfortable as I could. I had a feeling this was going to take a while.

Tracie had a compelling voice, an actor's voice, and as she told her story I flashed on Scheherazade telling tales for a thousand and one nights until the king, hardened by the betrayal of his first wife, learned both morality and kindness and renounced his vow of vengeance against all women. Somewhere along the line, I gave up my plans for payback, too. Well, most of them, anyway.

According to Tracie, the man who called himself Rushmore McKenzie came in the spring. He did not look like me, but Tracie said he was the same height, weight, hair color—if you went solely by physical description, people would have thought we were the same person.

"Although you are much more handsome," Tracie said. She smiled at me, but I refused to give her anything in return.

The Imposter did not announce himself. He drove into town and settled in at the Pioneer, Libbie's one and only hotel. He took his meals alone in the hotel restaurant. During the day, he would drive the county's roads. Residents remembered seeing him parked on the shoulder at various intersections taking notes; they would wave to him, and he would wave back. He also spent time in the county assessor's office, studying abstracts, deeds, and zoning maps without once explaining why. Anyone who attempted to engage him in conversation learned his opinion on the weather, and little else. Not even thrice-divorced Sharren Nuffer, who worked behind the desk and sometimes in the hotel's restaurant, could get words from the Imposter no matter how breathlessly she asked if there was anything she could do for him.

It wasn't until several days later that the Imposter stepped into the office of the City of Libbie's director of economic development. A man named Ed Bizek—the department's sole employee—was there to greet him. The Imposter told Bizek that he was the front man for a syndicate of developers from the Twin Cities. He said he'd found the perfect parcel of land at the intersection where Highway 20 met Highway 73. Unfortunately, a dryland farmer named Michael Randisi owned the parcel, and it was zoned for agriculture. The Imposter said he wanted to meet with the county commissioners and the Libbie City Council. He wanted to be assured that the county would rezone the land for commercial use if he bought it, and he wanted the negotiations kept confidential for fear that if word of his intentions leaked out, Randisi would demand more for the land than the syndicate was willing to pay. That would kill the deal, the Imposter said. It was this fear—that the deal would be killed—that would induce so many people to do so many foolish things in the coming weeks.

"What were his intentions?" I asked.

"The Imposter wanted to build an outlet mall."

"Is that like a shopping mall?"

"A shopping mall where manufacturers sell their products directly to the public through their own stores. Mostly you see them in locations far away from major cities. That's because the rents are cheaper, which reduces overhead, and because most of these manufacturers have contracts with conventional retailers that sell their products. The malls have to be located in places where they won't compete with them."

"Okay."

"I know what you're thinking, McKenzie—a mall in a town with a population of twelve hundred, in a county with only thirty-three hundred people? But it was a good plan. The plan would have worked. An outlet mall here would have drawn customers from Prairie City and Bison, Meadow, Faith, Isabel, Timber Lake, Dupree—where else?—Lemmon, Reva, Lodgepole. You have to remember, we're five hundred thirty miles from Denver, six hundred miles from Minneapolis, and about the same distance from Omaha. The nearest decent shopping—we're nearly four hours by car from both Rapid City and Aberdeen. An outlet mall here would have been huge."

"Except he did not intend to build a mall."

"No. All he wanted was our money."

"How much did he take you for?"

She said, "Nothing from me," in a way that made me think she was lying. "The city, though, and some others—he picked us clean and disappeared."

"How long ago?"

"Tomorrow will make a week. McKenzie, can I rely on your discretion?"

"Not even a little bit."

"McKenzie, if we let you go—"

"What do you mean, if?"

"That came out wrong."

"I certainly hope so."

"I meant when we let you go—McKenzie, we need your help."

"To do what?"

"To catch Rush—to catch the Imposter."

"Call the cops."

"Chief Gustafson is working on it."

"Call the real cops. Call the South Dakota Division of Criminal Investigation. Call the FBI."

"We don't want—we're trying to avoid—our losses were severe, McKenzie. The city was forced to borrow to maintain basic services. Others were hurt, as well—the bank, some Main Street businesses, other investors. McKenzie, small towns all across America are drying up and blowing away. We were doing okay, except now—if we get the money back, a lot of people will be embarrassed, but life will go on. If we don't, if people learn the city is bankrupt . . ."

"Do you expect me to care?"

Tracie's eyes lost their harshness then. They became soft and moist, and I found myself looking away so I didn't have to see them. *You are the mushiest person I know,* my inner voice told me. It also reminded me that Libbie's problem wasn't my problem. *Your problem is getting home.*

"What do you expect me to do?" I said.

"Chief Gustafson said the only way to catch Rush, to catch the Imposter, is by finding out who he really is, where he really lives. We can do that, he said, by investigating the things the Imposter said that were true that might have slipped through all the lies he told us. Rush was here a long time and spoke to a lot of people, and the chief thinks he might have divulged information that he didn't mean to. The problem is, we have no way of knowing what was a lie he told about you and what was the truth he might have told about himself. Only you would know the difference."

It was a realistic plan, probably the only plan. We are all crea-
tures of habit and of our own experiences. Over time, even the
best-trained actor will slip out of character to reveal something of
himself. He'll start ad-libbing, remembering when he did this, or
when he went there, or when he saw that. It's only breadcrumbs
of information, and we all know what happened to Hansel and
Gretel when they tried to rely on them. Still, a guy could get lucky.
It would probably take an enormous amount of work, yet I had to
admit, I found the prospect challenging.

On the other hand, they kidnapped me from my home and
chained me to a table—my head had been aching for hours. I could
sue them for everything they had. 'Course, if the Imposter looted
the city's coffers, they probably didn't have much . . .

I stared into Tracie's eyes for a good long time, and then I beat
on the metal table with both hands—shave and a haircut, two bits.

"What does that mean?" she said.

"Let me go."

"Will you help us?"

"I'll think about it. Now let me go."

Tracie spun in her chair and looked at the one-way mirror. A
few moments later, the interrogation door opened, and Chief
Gustafson walked in. He was followed by the desk officer who had
chained me to the table and the old man who had slugged me.
Behind them was a teenaged girl with a mature body and a child's
face.

I stood as the chief walked to the table and uncuffed my hands.

"I'm sorry about this," he said.

I flexed my shoulders and swung my arms about the way people
sometimes do when they're cold and want to warm themselves. My
wrist was chafed and sore, and I wanted to rub it, but I refused,
not unlike a professional baseball player who jogs nonchalantly to
first base after being plunked with a fastball—I didn't want the

chief to know I was hurt. I didn't want any of them to know how vulnerable I felt. I had no real idea where I was, but I knew it was too far from home.

I tried to make my voice sound tough. "Where are the bounty hunters?" I said.

"The two men who brought you in?" the chief said.

"Where are they?"

"They're gone."

"Gone where?"

"I don't know. They left before I arrived."

"Who are they? Where can I find them?"

The chief shrugged a reply.

"Who hired them?"

The old man stepped deeper into the interrogation room. The desk officer sidled up next to him, ready to step between us if necessary.

"I hired them," the old man said. There wasn't a trace of regret in his voice.

"Well, I hope you at least stopped payment on the check."

He snickered at that and stepped closer. "I'm Dewey Miller. I own most of what's worth owning around here."

I recognized the look in his eye. He believed in the privileges of power. He had the most, so he demanded the most. Something else, there's an old movie that you can catch on TCM—*She Wore a Yellow Ribbon.* Whenever one of his subordinates would say he was sorry for screwing up, Captain John Wayne would tell him, "Don't apologize, mister. It's a sign of weakness." Miller was from that school.

"Excuse me if I appear less than conciliatory," I said.

"I did what I had to do," Miller said.

"I bet."

"I thought you were the man who raped my daughter."

I glanced at the teenager standing behind him. There was at least a fifty-year difference in their ages. Other differences, too. The old man wore a hooded expression of brooding anger, as if he became pissed off at the world one day and never changed. The girl's face, however, was open and filled with virtues—strength, humility, humor, and goodness. It was not something you could fake. This was a girl that you could hurt without even trying, I told myself.

"Now you know different," I said.

Miller nodded his head. He had nothing more to say. The teenager filled the void.

"How many times do I have to say it?" she said. "I wasn't raped."

Miller spun and slapped her across the mouth with a full-arm swing, driving her back so that she stumbled and nearly fell against the wall. In a sharp baritone, he shouted, "Have you no shame?"

I reached for the girl, the only one who did so, but she waved away my assistance. She regained her balance and gave her father an oddly neutral, unangered look while she touched the corner of her mouth where the blow had fallen. Satisfied that nothing was broken or bleeding, she let her hand fall to her side.

"No, I don't have any shame," she said. "At least none for myself."

She turned slowly and left the room.

Miller called to her, "Saranne." She didn't stop.

Miller gradually became aware that we were all staring at him. He saw the contempt in my eyes. I called him a bastard. His head jolted upward. There was a kind of hysterical expression on his face, and he clenched his fists, but I knew nothing would come of it. I wasn't chained to the table anymore.

"She's my daughter," he said.

"Why don't you treat her like it?"

Eventually his hands went limp, and he rubbed his face with them. He took Tracie's chair and sat looking at nothing in particular. He wasn't going to apologize for this, either.

The desk officer patted his shoulder in a forgiving manner. "It's tough," the officer said. "A man could lose his head."

So much for law enforcement in Libbie, South Dakota, I told myself.

"Mr. Miller brought Saranne here to confirm your identity," the chief said.

"Really? I thought he did it to show us how tough he was."

Miller gave me a look that he probably thought was threatening and clenched his fists again. All he did was remind me how much I wanted to hit someone, anyone.

"The bounty hunters," I said. "I want their names. I want to know where I can find them."

"You don't talk to me that way," Miller said.

"One way or the other I'll have the names before I leave. Get used to the idea." I silenced any potential argument by turning my back on him and facing the chief. "The Imposter—did he actually pretend to be me, or was it just a coincidence that he was using a name that happened to be the same as mine?"

"He had your actual address. He said he retired early from the St. Paul Police Department. He said he helped find some gold that a gangster hid in the city seventy-five years ago. He said he had numerous friends in high places. Does that sound like you?"

"Everything but the friends in high places."

"Then he was pretending to be you."

"What you told me, the Imposter could have learned that just by Googling my name on the Web."

The chief could only shrug at that.

"Car? Tracie said that the Imposter drove into town."

"Rental. Originated in Minneapolis. He used your name on a credit card to rent it."

"The Imposter stayed at the Pioneer Hotel. Most hotels demand a credit card."

"I checked," the chief said. "The card was issued in your name; it was the same as the one that he used for the car."

"I have a financial adviser who runs a credit check every month to help me avoid this sort of thing. If a guy was using a credit card in my name—you say he's been here since spring?"

"Since early April," Tracie said. "He didn't stay all that time. He came and went."

"Still, if he used my credit cards during all that time, I would have known it."

"Not necessarily," the chief said. "Apparently he stole your identity, not your cards. He opened accounts in your name, but he had the invoices delivered to a different address. He also used a birth date and Social Security number that were different from yours—at least they were different from the ones you gave me. There's no way you could have known the Imposter was pretending to be you."

"Where were the credit card invoices sent?"

"To a mail drop in Grand Rapids, Minnesota."

"Hmm."

"What?"

"I own some property near Grand Rapids. A lake home."

"Hmm," the chief said. "The Imposter rented a PO box in your name for six months. It expired last week."

"You checked it out, huh?"

"We're not completely helpless."

"Did you run the Social Security number?"

"Both that and the birth date were taken from a man who died of cancer twelve years ago."

"What was his name? Where did he live?"

"His name was Andrew Manning. He lived in Grand Rapids."

"If you knew all this, why did you send the bounty hunters after me?"

"I didn't."

The chief glanced down at Miller, who was pretending to be somewhere else.

"Are you going to help us?" Tracie said.

"I'm still thinking about it."

"What will it take to convince you?"

I spread my arms wide. "Clothes, food, a place to clean up, a telephone, aspirin."

Miller rose slowly from the chair and reached behind him. He produced a thick, worn wallet from the sucker pocket, unfolded it, and slipped out a credit card. He handed the card to Tracie.

"Anything he wants," he said.

I snatched the card from Tracie's fingers.

"It's gonna cost you, pal," I said.

I could read the startled expression on the face of the old woman behind the cash register when I entered the store. "Sir?" she said.

There was a row of wire shopping carts near the sliding glass door, and I took one.

"Sir? Sir? You can't be in here." She left the cash register and circled the counter. "Sir, the sign says NO SHIRT, NO SHOES, NO SERVICE."

I gave her a smile, which must have been pretty damn frightening considering my appearance—no doubt she thought I was an escapee from the nearest fun house.

"You do sell shirts," I said. She stopped on the other side of the cart. "You do sell shoes, and I presume you do provide a modicum of service."

"Sir?"

"So clearly the sign is inaccurate."

The woman placed both hands on the front of the cart. I pushed forward. She steadied herself and shoved back. She was a strong woman.

"Lady, you're making my headache worse."

"Sir, don't make me call the manager."

Tracie came in through the sliding doors, collapsing the cell phone that had delayed her and dropping it into her bag.

"What's going on?" she said.

I pushed hard against the cart, causing the cashier to slide backward about three inches.

"He can't come in here," she said.

"It's all right, Linnea," Tracie said.

"No, it's not. I'm calling the manager."

Linnea stepped out of the way and released the cart. I shot forward a good three feet before I regained my balance.

Linnea grabbed a red phone beneath her cash register. Her voice echoed from every corner of the store as she spoke into it.

"Manager to the front, please. Manager to the front."

I smiled at Tracie. "Now you're going to get it," I said.

"Having fun, McKenzie?"

"Take this." I rolled the cart toward her. "Follow me."

Munoz Emporium came closer to an old-fashioned general store than any I had ever seen outside of the movies. It was square with a high ceiling and hardwood floors aged by traffic and time. The shelves were high against the walls and stacked with just about everything you might want to buy—eggs, milk, cheese, meats, bakery, canned goods, packaged goods, ice cream, beer, wine, pharmaceuticals, home furnishings, appliances, yard supplies, sporting goods, toys, cell phones, MP3 players, DVDs, CDs, TVs, and even a few lower-end PCs. The selection was small, but the categories were immense. I marched up and down the aisles, Tracie trailing along.

My first stop was for aspirin. I opened the bottle, tossed the cotton on the floor, and poured three tablets into my palm. The instructions said to take only two, but my headache screamed for more. I swallowed the aspirin and tossed the plastic bottle to Tracie.

"Think fast," I said.

She caught the bottle with both hands.

"You're hysterical," she said.

I headed for the clothing racks. I grabbed shorts, socks, jeans, and shirts from the shelves and dropped them into the cart. I checked for my size, but not once did I look at the price, not even when I seized a pair of white, green, and black Adidas TS Lightswitch Garnett basketball shoes and pitched them on top of the jeans—and I haven't been a fan of Kevin Garnett or his shoes since he left the Minnesota Timberwolves.

The manager of Munoz's caught up to us in toiletries. He was wearing a blue smock with the name Chuck sewn above his pocket, and he didn't like the look of me any more than his cashier did. Tracie worked to calm him while I fired containers of shaving cream, razors, toothbrushes, shampoo, and hair gel into the cart. He didn't appreciate that, either, especially when I launched a tube of toothpaste from three-point range and it caromed off the wire rim and relocated a jar of face cream from the shelf to the floor.

"This is my store," he said.

"You're the owner?" I said.

"That's right."

"You should be pleased that I'm here, then."

"Pleased that some half-naked clown is throwing merchandise around?"

He had me there. Still, my muscles continued to ache from the hours I'd spent curled up in the trunk of a car, and my stomach, which hadn't seen a meal in nearly twenty-four hours, was making disconcerting grumbling sounds.

"Be nice, Chuck," I said. "Or I just might leave this happy hovel you all call home."

"See if I care."

"You don't want me to stick around and help catch the great Imposter?"

"It doesn't matter to me one way or the other."

"No, I don't suppose that it would." I made a sweeping gesture, taking in everything around us. "I can see why the mall might have given you a few sleepless nights, but now that it's gone south . . ."

"I would have been all right. This store has been here for over fifty years. My customers know me. They know I treat them fair, just like my father and grandfather did before me. They would have stayed loyal."

"Yeah. That's why Walmart does so poorly."

"What do you know about it?"

"I know that when it comes to money, loyalty doesn't mean squat."

Munoz quickly glanced at Tracie. She averted her eyes.

"I'm learning that," he said.

"It wasn't just me," Tracie said. "The whole town wanted the mall. The county wanted it."

Munoz pointed at the shopping cart. "You finished here?"

"Do you offer gift wrapping?" I said.

Munoz turned to exit the aisle, but Tracie blocked his path.

"Chuck," she said.

He didn't even say "excuse me" when he nudged her out of the way and moved to the front of the store.

"He's upset," Tracie told me.

"You think?"

"He's convinced we betrayed him by supporting the mall. He said so in a city council meeting."

"He was right."

"We did it for the town."

" 'Whenever A annoys or injures B on the pretense of saving or improving X, A is a scoundrel,'" I said, then added, "H. L. Mencken," in case Tracie thought I made it up.

She studied me for a moment before pushing the cart up the aisle.

"You're not what you seem," she said.

I did a quick inventory of my appearance.

"I certainly hope not," I said.

Her head swiveled left, then right, when she exited the store, as if she were uncertain which way to turn. Tracie paused for a beat and went left. Again, I noticed that she walked with gliding grace, her head high, her toes angled in slightly, her salmon skirt swishing back and forth in a most delightful manner. Men turned to look at her. She seemed to accept this as if they had always looked and always would. I followed her, enjoying the view, until she stopped so abruptly that I nearly ran into her. She brought her hand up to shield her eyes from the glaring sun.

"Must you walk behind me like that?" she said.

"It's your town, honey. I'm just following your lead."

"Must you call me honey?"

The question jolted me, serving notice that I had been behaving like a jerk ever since the chief removed the cuffs. Maybe I had cause. My head continued to throb; I was still naked except for my spoiled shorts and apparently a figure of some curiosity and amusement according to the expressions of the people who walked or drove by. Plus, I wasn't altogether sure where I was or how I was going to get home. Yet I could hear the old man admonishing me when I was a kid playing ball and I had a bad day at the plate. "That's no excuse for poor manners," he'd say.

"I apologize," I said. "I won't do it again."

Tracie blinked hard. I don't know if it was because of the sun or because she was startled by my response.

"You mentioned a hotel," I said.

"Just up the street."

"Here, let me carry those."

I took the two shopping bags filled with my purchases from her hands. Tracie blinked again.

"Something else?" I said.

"I keep comparing you to Rush. He was very polite, very considerate—he seemed like a nice man. Looking back, I realize now that it was all for show. You, on the other hand—you don't seem like a nice man at all, and yet you were angry when Mr. Miller hit his daughter, and what you said about Chuck . . . Who are you, McKenzie?"

"Well, I'll tell you. I don't know if I let a week go by when I don't ask myself that same question."

Sharren Nuffer grinned when we went through the front doors of the Pioneer Hotel, and she kept grinning as Tracie and I approached the registration desk. Her tumbled-down, chemically enhanced hair resembled raw blue-black silk, and her rich tan reached all the way to the valley between her breasts, which she displayed beneath a black sleeveless shirt. Apparently she didn't like buttons, because she used only a couple of them and they were straining to keep her shirt closed.

"How many times do I have to tell you, Tracie," she said. "We don't rent by the hour."

"You're hysterical, Sharren," Tracie said.

Sharren must have agreed, because she laughed long and hard. When she finished, she waved a slender hand at me and said, "Seriously, what is this all about?"

"I need a room for McKenzie here," Tracie said.

"McKenzie? Rushmore McKenzie? You're not Rushmore McKenzie."

"Actually, I am," I said. Sharren looked like she didn't believe me. "It's a long story."

"Tell me," she said.

I didn't, but Tracie did. Only the way she told it, what had happened to me since four forty-five that morning didn't seem like anything to get excited about.

"I knew Rush," Sharren said.

"Did you know him well?" I said.

Sharren hesitated before she answered. "As well as I could."

She's the first person you should talk to, my inner voice told me. I literally shook the thought from my head. Who said I'm staying? I asked myself.

It took some wrangling, yet Tracie managed to book a room using Miller's credit card—eighty-nine dollars a night. Sharren procured my key from a row of boxes behind the desk, a real key, not a plastic card. While they went at it, I looked around. From the outside, the Pioneer seemed almost quaint, a dignified redbrick Victorian with three floors and no elevator. Yet the inside had an air of quiet dissipation. The reception area was crammed with faded couches, armchairs, and marble-top tables with ceramic figurines, ashtrays, fake Roman busts, and lamps with shades fringed with tassels. It didn't seem old-fashioned as much as it seemed merely old.

After checking in, I carried the key and my shopping bags to the worn-carpeted staircase. Tracie tried to follow. I stopped her at the base of the stairs.

"This is where I draw the line," I said.

"But—" Tracie said.

"No buts."

"Ahh," said Sharren. "Too bad, so sad."

She said it with a smile, yet it was obvious that the two women did not like each other. It was equally obvious that they were very much alike.

Tracie frowned. "Dinner? Say in an hour?"

"Make it an hour and a half. I have calls to make."

Tracie was looking at Sharren when she said, "There's a diner down the street."

"We serve a very nice filet if you want real food," Sharren said. "Perhaps you'd care for room service."

Sharren batted her long, fake eyelashes at me, but I assumed that was for Tracie's benefit. The way I looked—seriously, not even an aging divorcée in Libbie, South Dakota, could be that hard up.

"Where is the diner?" I asked.

"Café Rossini," Tracie said. "Out the door and to the left."

"I'll meet you there."

"Ninety minutes." Tracie turned and left the hotel, but not before throwing Sharren a triumphant smirk.

Sharren smirked back.

"You won't be getting much from her," she said. "Very cold, that one. Very dry."

I was startled by the remark, and if I had been standing closer to Sharren I might have said something or done something about it. I don't know why I had become defensive of Tracie, yet I had. Or maybe it's just that my nerves were still keyed up by what had happened to me earlier; I wanted payback and didn't particularly care who suffered for it.

I said nothing, did nothing, except turn and climb the stairs.

CHAPTER THREE

My room was on the second floor. It was small and stylish with a soaring ceiling and black-and-white tiles in the bathroom. There was a double bed with a blue-green spread and a mattress that sagged slightly in the middle. The other furnishings were simple oak—a desk, a chair, an armoire, and a table in front of a window facing First Street. Inside the armoire was a TV that offered HBO; a phone sat on the desk.

I dropped the bags on the bed and went straight for the phone. There was something instantly comforting about it. It gave me a connection to the world—to *my* world—that the kidnappers had taken from me. Unfortunately, the feeling lasted only until I picked up the receiver and listened to the dial tone. I couldn't remember the numbers of my friends, of the people I wanted to call. I hadn't memorized them; I had seen no need. Instead, I programmed all the numbers into my cell or the phone hanging on the wall in my kitchen. When I wanted to make a call, I would just scroll through the memory for a name. Without my cell—I returned the receiver to the cradle. My headache became worse.

Still, there was directory assistance. The instructions attached to the base of the phone told me that local calls were free but that there was a surcharge for long distance. What the hell, I decided— Miller was paying for it. I dialed nine, followed by four-one-one.

After a mechanical voice recited the number I requested, the telephone company announced that it would dial the number for a nominal fee. Fine with me. A moment later, I was connected to the Minneapolis office of the FBI, and a moment after that I reached Special Agent Brian Wilson.

"Hi, Harry," I said.

"Jesus Christ, McKenzie, where are you? Are you all right?"

I knew he was concerned because he didn't admonish me for using the nickname Harry, which he never approved of.

"I'm fine. I'm in Libbie, South Dakota," I said.

"Why are you in Libbie, South Dakota?"

I explained. Harry interrupted several times, mostly to ask for names. Afterward, he told me that they had issued an alert in my name and that the FBI, the Minnesota Bureau of Criminal Investigation, the St. Anthony Police Department, and the St. Paul Police Department had launched a full-scale kidnapping investigation.

"Wow," I said.

"Wow is fucking right," Harry said. He demanded more names. I gave him what I had. He said heads would roll. I said as long as they didn't belong to the Libbie Police Department, I didn't care. He said, "Once a cop, always a cop." I said, "We protect our own." He said he wanted to speak to me—in person—as soon as possible. "There are people to see, paperwork to sign." I told him I would be home soon.

"Have you spoken to Bobby yet?" Harry said.

"Not yet."

"Give him a call. I know the St. Paul Police Department has put a lot of resources into this."

"Really?"

"Kinda makes you feel important, doesn't it?"

"A little bit, yeah."

"Well, they don't know you the way I do."

Victoria Dunston answered the phone on the second ring. When she heard my voice she sighed deeply. Victoria had been kidnapped for ransom a year earlier, and while it all worked out in the end, it had been a traumatic experience for her—I doubted that she had fully recovered from it, or that she ever would.

"You okay?" I said.

"I'm fine. Are you okay?"

I told her I was just swell.

"I had a few tough moments," she said. "You made me cry a little bit."

"I'm sorry."

"Somehow I knew it would be all right, though. Just like I knew it would be all right when they kidnapped me. God, McKenzie. Why do these things happen to us?"

"Just lucky, I guess."

I heard voices on Victoria's end of the phone. "McKenzie? Did you say McKenzie? Are you talking to McKenzie?" There was a muffled sound as the receiver was wrestled away from the girl.

"McKenzie?"

"Hey, Shelby," I said.

A moment later Bobby Dunston picked up a second receiver and called my name.

"Hey," I said.

They both demanded a detailed explanation, especially Bobby— I had the feeling he was taking notes. Bobby was a commander in St. Paul's newly minted major crimes division but wasn't running the investigation into my disappearance because the department had claimed he was too close to the case. We had been friends since the beginning of time. I gave him everything I had told Harry, and then some. When he was satisfied, he said he had to make a few calls and left me on the line with his wife.

"Are you really all right, Rushmore?" she said.

I met Shelby three and a half minutes before her husband did, and often I have wondered what would've happened if I had been the one who spilled a drink on her.

"I really am, Shel," I said. "A bit of a headache, some aches and pains, nothing more. I'm sorry if you were frightened, but it wasn't my fault."

"As opposed to all the other times you frightened me when it was your fault."

"Exactly."

She sighed deeply. It was the same sigh that Victoria had given me. Like mother, like daughter.

"I've given you and your family a few anxious moments over the years," I said. "I apologize."

"The good has always outweighed the bad."

"Thank you for saying that."

"What did Nina have to say about all this?"

"I haven't spoken to her yet."

That caused Shelby to pause for a few beats.

"You called me before you called her?" she said.

"No. I mean yes. I mean, I called—I knew Bobby would be working the case . . ." This time I sighed. "Yes, I called you first."

"Dammit, McKenzie."

"What?"

"You're supposed to call the woman you're in love with first."

"Sure."

She paused again.

"Be safe, Rushmore," she said. "Hurry home."

Shelby hung up before I could say anything more.

Nina was not at the jazz club she owned near the cathedral in St. Paul, named Rickie's after her daughter, Erica. Jenness, her assistant manager, said she had been too anxious to work. When I reached her at home, she shrieked my name so loudly I had to pull the receiver from my ear. After I assured her that I was "fit as a fiddle and ready for love," she told me that everyone was looking for me, including Harry and the FBI. I told her that I would call them as soon as I was finished talking to her.

"You called me first?"

"You're the only one that matters," I said.

I believed it with all my heart when I said it. I admit that on occasion I allow myself to become confused. Yet all I have to do is see Nina or hear her voice and everything becomes perfectly clear to me. I see the world in its entirety, and it is exactly the way it should be.

I told Nina what had happened in detail, even confessed to how frightened I had become, which I had not admitted to anyone else. I told her that I was tempted to help the City of Libbie because I was angry that the Imposter had used my name. I also told her that the idea made me uneasy because I would be cut off from my resources, from Bobby and Harry and from her. Nina told me she would support any decision I made, although she wouldn't have an untroubled moment until I returned safely to her. She was like that, supporting my crusades, as she called them, without entirely embracing them.

God, I love this woman, I told myself.

Then why did you call Shelby first? my inner voice said.

"I'll be home as soon as I can," I said.

"I'll be waiting," Nina told me.

After I shaved and showered, I stood naked in front of the bathroom mirror and fingered the puncture wounds in my shoulder and waist. The Taser marks seemed smaller now, yet they throbbed like first-degree burns. I would have liked some salve to soothe them, but all I had was aspirin tablets that I was starting to pop like M&M's. They hadn't done my headache any good at all.

I stared at my reflection.

"Screw Libbie, South Dakota," I said aloud. "Screw the Imposter. Screw everyone."

I finished dressing and peeked at my reflection yet again. For some reason I didn't look like myself. Certainly I didn't feel like myself.

"Go home, McKenzie," I said.

The reflection nodded in agreement.

Sharren gave me a wolf whistle from behind the registration desk when I reached the lobby. She spoke in a low, husky voice that sounded as if a lifetime of talking had taken its toll.

"My, oh my, but don't you clean up nice," she said.

"Clothes make the man," I said.

"I don't know about that, Rush. I kinda liked what you were wearing before."

"I'd rather you didn't call me that—Rush. McKenzie is just fine."

"Buy you a drink, big boy?"

I glanced up at the clock behind Sharren's left shoulder. Even if I took my time, I would probably be about five minutes early to the café, and I couldn't have that.

"Yes, you can buy me a drink," I said. I didn't mind at all that she called me "big boy."

The star attraction of the Pioneer Hotel was its cathedral-like dining room with a huge stone fireplace. It was half filled, a good crowd for a Monday night, Sharren said. Heads turned to watch as she led me through the room, and there were whispers.

"News travels fast in a small town," I said.

"Hmm?"

"Nothing."

At the far end of the dining room was an ancient bar, the kind with a long, graceful mirror. A young man with sparkling eyes and a winning smile stood behind the stick. The way he ran his fingers through his blond hair made me think he knew how to get girls. On the other hand, the way his white dress shirt strained at the buttons made me think that if he didn't start investing in some exercise, the girls wouldn't stay gotten for long. He greeted us with two coasters that he quickly set in front of us and a prediction that we'd like it there.

"Evan, this is Rushmore McKenzie," Sharren said. "McKenzie, this is Evan."

"The one and only," Evan said as he extended his hand. I didn't know if he meant me or himself. "What'll ya have?"

We ordered a double Jack Daniel's for me and bourbon and water for Sharren. I took a long pull of the liquor. It burned all the way down to my empty stomach. I heard my inner voice say, *You should eat something before you set to drinking.* In a minute, I told it, and took another sip.

"So, what do you think of Libbie?" Evan said.

"It's a nice place to visit, but I wouldn't want to live here."

Neither of them thought my answer was particularly funny.

Sharren asked if I would mind taking our drinks back to the

hotel lobby in case an errant traveler might seek lodging for the evening. I said that was fine. On the way out, I caught Evan giving Sharren a wink and the thumbs-up sign. Sharren responded by sticking out her tongue.

As we worked our way back through the dining room, Sharren told me about the swimming pool and sauna that were added in the early seventies and how people would often book rooms just to lounge around them, especially in winter.

"We added a water slide two years ago," she said. "It's become a big profit center for us."

Once again, I noted the turned heads, whispered words, and more than a few twisted smiles as we walked past. This time, though, it occurred to me that I was only peripherally the object of curiosity. It was Sharren that the diners followed. I began to suspect that I wasn't the first "big boy" Sharren had treated to drinks. I also wondered at what point her dalliances had become a spectator sport.

"Small towns," I said.

"Tell me about it," Sharren said.

Apparently this time she knew exactly what I meant.

I followed her to the lobby. We found a pair of overstuffed chairs with an uncluttered view of both the front door and the registration desk and settled in.

"Are you really going to try to find Rush—I mean—you know who I mean," Sharren said.

"Do you care?"

"I wouldn't mind seeing him get punished for what he did to the town."

"What did he do to you?"

Sharren surprised me by smiling. She waved her glass at the arched doorway leading to the restaurant.

"You saw those people giving me the eye," she said. "That's what he did to me."

"What do you know about him?"

"I know he used to be a cop in the Twin Cities and that he quit the force to collect a reward on an embezzler he tracked down—a couple of million dollars. I know he graduated with honors from the University of Minnesota, he speaks three languages, he's single, and his parents are dead, that he has a big house in Falcon Heights . . ."

I took a long pull of the whiskey.

"That's all you, isn't it?" Sharren said.

"Yeah."

"Sorry."

"Nothing to be sorry about. I like being me."

"Yes, but him using your name like that—I'm sorry."

"What else do you know about me?"

"I know you like sports. Do you like sports?"

"Yes."

"You played hockey?"

I nodded.

"And baseball?"

"Uh-huh."

"And football?"

"Football? No. He said I played football?"

"He said you lettered as a wide receiver and backup quarterback."

"Did he say who I played for?"

"Central High School in St. Paul. He said you were a Raider."

That caused me to lean back in my chair.

"You didn't go to Central High School?" Sharren said.

"I did, yes. We were called the Minutemen."

I bet you could catch him if you really wanted to, my inner voice told me. *There are probably a thousand high schools in the U.S. with the nickname Raiders, yet if you could narrow it down . . . Stop it! You're going home, remember?*

The clock above the registration desk told me if I hurried, I would be only fifteen minutes late for my meeting with Tracie. I drained my drink and stood up. The pain in my head made me wince.

"Are you okay?" Sharren said.

"I need to get something to eat."

"I'm off at ten, but I could stay later if . . ."

Sharren leaned forward. The front of her shirt fell away, as I'm sure she intended, and I could see the swell of her breasts encased in flimsy black nylon and lace. I forced myself to look away but could do nothing about the all too familiar stirring somewhere south of my belt. *Will you never grow up?* my inner voice asked. What are you talking about? I looked away, didn't I?

"I don't know when I'll be back," I said.

"If you're having dinner with Tracie Blake, you won't be out too late," Sharren said. "So if you want to chat some more, we could have another drink. Or two."

I knew an invitation when I heard one. Just in case I was brain dead, though, Sharren rose slowly from her chair, stepped in close, and rested her slender fingers on my shoulder at the base of my neck.

This is probably a good time to mention Nina, my inner voice told me. *You remember her, don't you? The love of your life?* Only I didn't want to get into it.

"Be careful," I said. "People will talk."

"People will talk anyway."

I eased Sharren's hand off my shoulder, gave it a friendly squeeze, and released it.

"I gotta go," I said.

I stepped around Sharren and headed for the door.

"Have a good time," she said.

"Don't wait up," I told her.

Café Rossini was located on the corner of First and Main, and it had two entrances. Enter from the west like I did and it looked like a neighborhood bar with plenty of worn wood and lights that discouraged reading. The entrance to the dining room was at the north end of the building, and I had to walk through the bar to get to it—you could not see the bar from the dining room.

Unlike the bar, the dining area looked like it had been built in the fifties—it was all stainless steel, Formica, and cold fluorescent lights. A long counter with a dozen round stools bolted to the floor faced the kitchen; slices of various fruit pies were set on small plates and displayed in clear plastic cases near the cash register. Each of the half-dozen booths against the wall had a metal napkin dispenser, bottles of ketchup and mustard, and shakers of salt and pepper. So did the small Formica tables arranged between them. Tinny, unrecognizable music poured from cheap speakers.

I found Tracie sitting in a booth nursing a glass of white zinfandel. The booth had a nice view—we could see the new concrete of Libbie's main drag. When I mentioned it, Tracie told me that it took the contractor one full day to pour the concrete for a single block of First Street from curb to curb. Two cement trucks at a time would dump their loads into a machine that kept edging forward, leaving a smooth and leveled surface behind it. Tracie was not only proud of the street, she was proud that she and the Libbie City Council had the presence of mind to set up a table with coffee, lemonade, and donuts for the nearly three hundred people who stopped by throughout the day to watch the work.

"You're wise to public relations," I said.

"Not wise enough to hide the fact that I'm upset that you kept me waiting," Tracie said. "Why are you so late? Was it Sharren?"

"The various law enforcement agencies that had been searching for me all day had many questions."

That slowed her down. "What did you tell them?"

"The truth."

"The truth?"

"It's always a good idea to tell the truth, especially to the FBI. They get cranky when you don't."

"The FBI?"

"When the home security people answered my alarm this morning and found the door smashed open and me gone, who did you think they were going to call? The Boy Scouts of America?"

"I didn't realize it was that big of a deal."

"Ever hear of the Lindbergh Act?"

"McKenzie, are you going to press charges? Are you going to sue us?"

Probably not, I decided. I didn't care what happened to Libbie, South Dakota, and I certainly had no love for Miller and his bounty hunters. Harry was right, though—I wasn't a guy to take legal action against cops, and that's what it would eventually amount to, me suing the Libbie Police Department. 'Course, I didn't want Tracie to know that. At least not while I could use the threat to leverage a meal. I grabbed a menu from behind the napkin dispenser.

"What's good?" I said.

"Rush was like that. Whenever someone asked a question he didn't want to answer, he'd change the subject."

"Did you spend much time with him?"

"Some."

Tracie glanced casually across the restaurant toward the front door. Of course, she had slept with him. She didn't need to say it; I could see the words written on her face.

My, my, my, my inner voice chanted. *He did get along, didn't he?* If what Miller had said earlier was true, the Imposter had bedded at least three attractive women using my name. I discovered that I was more than a little jealous.

"Tracie, what are you doing here?" I said. "How the hell did you end up in Libbie, South Dakota?"

"You make it sound like a Russian gulag."

"There are those who'd agree with me."

"Honestly, McKenzie, this is the only place I've been where I've felt completely at home, completely relaxed."

"Mayberry."

"Hardly that. Still . . . I don't know, McKenzie. Either you like small-town life or you don't. I like it."

"Were you born here?"

"No, no. My ex-husband was. Christopher Kramme. He was from Libbie. I met him in Chicago. He was taking graduate courses in aeronautical engineering at the Illinois Institute of Technology. He wanted to build airplanes. I didn't discover until much later that he was more passionate about that than he was about me. Oh, well."

"Were you a student?"

"I was a model. And an actress."

I knew it, my inner voice said.

"Really?" I said.

"Not a supermodel by any means," Tracie said. "I can't complain, though. I worked steady. A lot of advertising work—catalogs, brochures, a lot of weekly supplements for department stores like Nordstrom's, Macy's, Value City. Some TV spots, too, some video work, plays. I acted in a couple of small theater productions doing *Harvey,* Agatha Christie's *Murder Is Announced*—I once played Typhoid Mary in *A Plague of Angels.* They made me look thirty years older than I was. That was sobering. I read somewhere that the average career expectancy for a professional football player is something like four-point-four years. I bet it's the same for models. Still, it was fun. Not as much money as you'd think, but a good time. People stopping me on Michigan Av and pointing at an outdoor board, my face twenty feet high, and saying, 'Is that you?' What a rush."

Tracie took a long sip from her drink before continuing.

"Anyway, we lived in the same apartment building. At least once a week Christopher would come to my door carrying a pitcher of strawberry margaritas, and we'd sit on my balcony and get pleasantly stoned. Not once did he make a pass. Whenever the evening would start to take a romantic turn, he'd glance at his watch, jump up, and say, 'Gotta go.' For the longest time I thought he was gay. Then I discovered he was a member of an entirely different minority group."

"What's that?"

"He was a gentleman."

"Ahh."

"We finally went out on a real date—I had to ask him—and we just hit it off. He proposed, I accepted, and suddenly I was packing to go to Libbie to meet his parents. Unfortunately, his father died at the same time. Heart attack. He was only sixty-one. They say he was a great guy. They also say that it was the shock of his son settling down that killed him. They were wealthy people, the Krammes, and Christopher took advantage of that. Never held a job. Never wanted one. All he wanted to do was build and fly his airplanes, which he never actually did—build them, I mean."

"What happened to him?"

"Christopher? He went to prison."

"What?"

"The Feds got him. What happened, one day he jumped into his plane and flew off. The next day he called me. They had arrested him at the airport in a rinky-dink town called Mineral Point in Wisconsin. The Feds got an anonymous tip and asked the sheriff's department to detain him. Turned out Christopher had a hundred and fifty pounds of high-grade marijuana squirreled away in compartments in his plane worth something like seven hundred thousand dollars. Christopher never explained where he got the dope, or where he was taking it, or why he landed in Mineral Point, or who ratted him out. At least not to me."

"Why would he do a thing like that?"

"Money, of course. Mr. Kramme, Christopher's father, was partner with Mr. Miller in a lot of things. The grain elevator, for one. They had an agreement built into their contracts that if either of them died, the business would buy out their heirs for half the value of the business. That way their businesses were protected and neither of them would get stuck with a partner that they didn't want. Whether or not they added the clause to their partnership agreement because Mr. Miller didn't like Christopher I couldn't say, although Mr. Miller really didn't like Christopher. He considered him a wastrel. That's the term he always used, 'wastrel.'

"Anyway, they fought over the true value of the businesses until a court-appointed arbitrator settled the matter. Mrs. Kramme got all the money. She gave Christopher a monthly allowance, not huge money, just enough to live comfortably. She said she wasn't going to give Christopher what he thought was his fair share of the estate unless he got a real job and made something of himself. Maybe he would have. He was kind of afraid of his mother. Only she moved to Sioux Falls. She had family there. Sisters.

"Christopher and I remained in Libbie because I love it here. I love the vistas. I love the people. I even got myself elected to the city council despite Christopher's attempts to sabotage my campaign, like showing up drunk to meet-and-greets. He did it because he wanted to go back to Chicago, and he figured if I lost— Christopher and I never got along as well as we should have. I loved him to death. There was no one more charming than he was. Except it was like living with a frat boy.

"He got himself arrested before we could do anything about it. He pleaded guilty; the Feds took his plane and gave him eighty-four months. We divorced somewhere around the tenth month. It was his idea, not mine. We had a prenup when we were married—his mother had insisted—so I collect his allowance until he gets out."

"When is that?" I said.

"He has eighteen months to go, assuming good behavior. Jimmy." Tracie held up her empty glass for the counterman to see. Jimmy nodded. A moment later, he set a fresh glass of wine in front of Tracie.

"For you, sir?" he said.

"Do you brew your own iced tea?"

"Yes."

"I'll have that."

Tracie waited for Jimmy to leave before she said, "Iced tea?"

"After I eat something, I'll be happy to trade shots with you. In the meantime, tell me about myself."

"What do you want to know?"

I came *this* close to asking her if I was good in bed but managed to smother the impulse. Some people just don't have a sense of humor. Instead, I asked her to tell me about my childhood. Turned out I was a helluva kid—a superathlete, popular with the girls, good in school—all of which was true, of course. Yet going by what Tracie said, it became clear to me that the Imposter was not a St. Paul boy. If you came from there, you didn't say you played ball at "the park." You said you played at Dunning Field, or Linwood, or Oxford, or Aldine or Merriam Park, or the Projects, or even Desnoyer. You didn't say you hung out down at "the Mississippi River." It was simply the river, or more specifically Bare Ass Beach, the Grotto, Shriner's Hospital, the Caves, Hidden Falls, or the Monument. And while we have called it many things, including its given name, to my certain knowledge, no one from St. Paul has ever referred to Minneapolis as "the big city." Unfortunately, none of this gave me any indication of where the Imposter was actually from.

While we talked, the counterman took our orders, delivered our food—I followed Tracie's recommendation and tried the roast beef—and cleared our plates when we were finished. I ordered a shot of Jack Daniel's. It didn't do my headache any good, but it made the rest of me feel just fine.

"These questions," Tracie said. "Does this mean you're going to help us?"

"I haven't decided yet."

"What are you afraid of?"

"Heights, spoiled food, getting shot at—you know, the usual things." I was also afraid that one morning I'd wake up and discover that my life was boring, but I didn't tell her that. "I don't like it that I'm a long way from home. I don't like it that I'm cut off from my resources, my friends, my support systems. I don't like it that I don't have a wallet, ID, cash, credit cards—nothing to prove that I'm who I say I am. It makes me feel vulnerable. Besides, this isn't my town. This isn't my ground. Hell, I have to look at a map just to find out where I am."

"I can get you a map. I can get you everything you need."

"Not everything."

"Do you mean sex?"

"Where did that come from?"

"I bet Sharren would be happy to oblige you."

"I didn't mean sex. I meant backup. Don't be so defensive."

"Men are all alike. You only care about one thing."

"The Super Bowl?"

"You know what I mean."

"No. Tell me."

"Rush—"

"I'm not that guy."

"He was a liar and a thief."

"What does that have to do with me and all the other men you know?"

"You can't be trusted."

"Yeah, yeah, yeah. If we didn't open jars, there'd be a bounty on us. I gotta tell you, Tracie, if we're going to continue this conversation I'm going to need another drink."

"Oh, no."

"What?"

I followed Tracie's gaze to the entrance. A large man stepped into the café. There was a sneer on his lips that looked as if it had been in place for twenty years. A smaller man slipped in behind him. They were wearing cowboy hats, cowboy boots, and clothes that looked worked in. For a long moment, they reminded me of the bounty hunters who had Tasered me that morning.

"Who are they?" I said.

"Don't ask."

I didn't need to. The big cowboy announced himself by shouting, "Lookie what we got here," and walking to a small table in the center of the café. A man in his midthirties was sitting at the table across from a woman of the same age. He was eating what looked like a club sandwich and fries. The cowboy grabbed a couple of fries from the plate and shoved them in his mouth. I felt my body tense as I watched; the roast beef became a heavy, unmoving thing in my stomach.

"Whad I tell you, shithead?" he said. "I said I didn't want to see your ugly face anywhere in town again."

The man was considerably smaller than the cowboy was, yet he started to rise anyway. The woman reached across the table and grabbed his wrist, holding him in place.

"Ya wanna do somethin'?" the cowboy said. "C'mon. I'm waitin'."

The woman tightened her grip.

"See this, Paulie," the cowboy said. "Shithead wants to be brave, but the bitch won't let him."

Paulie grinned and shook his head as if he had seen it a hundred times before.

"Let me guess," I said. "Town bully."

"His name is Church," Tracie said. "He's been terrorizing people going back to high school."

"You put up with him—why?"

"A couple of years ago a man challenged him, a rancher; slapped Church in public. The next day his house was burned down. My ex-husband told him off not long after I moved here. A week later, they burned his plane. Everyone knew it was Church, but nothing could be proved, and now everyone is afraid to stand up to him."

"Who are the vics?"

"Vics?"

"Victims."

"Rick and Cathy Danne. I don't know what Church has against them except that the Dannes are nice people."

Jimmy moved quickly around the counter, putting himself between Church and the Dannes. "We don't want no trouble," he said.

Church shoved him hard against the counter.

"Ain't gonna be no trouble, ol' man, cuz shithead here is leavin'," he said. "Ain't that right?"

Again Danne tried to rise, and again the woman pulled him back down.

"I'm done eating, honey," she said. "C'mon, let's go."

The man was thinking about it when Church knocked over a water glass, spilling the contents into the man's lap. The man pushed away from the table, but the water had already soaked the crotch of his pants.

"Lookee," Church said. "He's so scared he pissed himself."

Something happened to me then that I have a hard time explaining, even to myself. I slipped out of the booth and started closing the distance between the cowboy and me. The café was suddenly very quiet. I could hear the squeaking of my new sneakers on the floor, I could hear my lungs breathing in and out, I could even hear the throbbing in my head, but precious little else except the cowboy's voice. I could hear that very clearly.

"What do you want?" he said. There was contempt in his tone.

I kept walking, my hands loose at my sides. I moved in close so I wouldn't have to fully extend my arms. Church tried to back away. I matched him step for step.

"What do you want?" he said again. This time I could hear a tinge of fear.

He put his hands on my chest to push me away, but I knocked them aside.

"Listen, shithead—"

He raised his hands in self-defense, only it was already too late. I curled my fingers into a hammerfist and drove it at a forty-five-degree angle into a nice little pressure point positioned in the neck, just to the side of the windpipe and just above the collarbone. This is where the carotid sinus nerve lives. By attacking this point, I artificially triggered a carotid sinus reflex, basically tricking Church's brain into thinking that there was too much blood pressure in the head and telling the heart to stop the supply of blood it was pumping. This should have caused Church to pass out. Only it didn't.

Church's hands went to his throat, and he made a kind of gagging sound. His face became a sickly white, and his knees buckled, but he did not fall. I pivoted so I was standing behind him. I raised my foot and stomped down hard on the inside of his knee, driving his knee to the floor. At the same time I slapped his hat off his head with my left hand, grabbed a fistful of hair, and yanked his head backward until I could look directly down into his eyes. They held both confusion and terror—I doubt anyone had ever hurt him before. I drove the tip of my right elbow down against the bridge of his nose. The blood was flowing freely when I released his hair and he crumbled to the floor.

I turned to his partner.

"Hey, Paulie," I said. "You want a piece of this?"

He didn't say if he did or didn't, just stood there with his mouth hanging open. I took two steps toward him. His mouth closed, and he backed toward the door, ready to make a run for it into the bar.

I glanced at the customers sitting in the booths and at the tables. "Does anyone want to help Mr. Church?"

No one said a word. No one moved. I nudged Church with the toe of my sneaker.

"This should tell you something about the kind of man you are," I said, "but I doubt it will."

Church reached out a hand for the leg of a table as if he wanted to pull himself up. I stomped on it. An older woman sitting in the nearest booth heard the bones crack. She winced, closed her eyes, and clamped a hand over her mouth as if she were afraid she would vomit. Church howled with pain. He brought his hand near his face and stared at it through tear-filled eyes. I had done a lot of damage.

"Oh no, oh no," he chanted, his voice low and hoarse.

I squatted next to him. I spoke softly. "You're hurting right now, but soon you'll be thinking what you can do to get back at me like you have at everyone else who's stood up to you. Better put the thought out of your head. If anything happens to me or my property, if anything happens to anyone in this room or their property, especially the Dannes—I don't care if we're struck by lightning—I will come for you. Not the cops. Me."

I stood. Everyone in the café was staring. I had a feeling that at that moment they were more afraid of me than they had ever been of Church.

"I cannot abide a bully," I said.

Probably I was smiling. All the stress and frustration and fear and confusion of the day had drained out of me. My headache had miraculously disappeared. I no longer felt vulnerable. Suddenly I was a manly man accomplishing manly feats in a manly way. It was exhilarating.

"Anyone want to call Chief Gustafson, I'll be sitting right back here."

I turned and made my way to the booth. Tracie was standing next to it and watching intently. She wore the same expression of disbelief as all the other customers.

"Oh, my God, McKenzie," she said. "My God. What you did to him. How could you do that to him?"

"It's easy if you know how."

"They'll arrest you for this. They'll put you in jail for real."

"I doubt it," I said.

I gazed around the café as I slid into the booth. I didn't see anyone on a cell phone. Not even Paulie. He had managed to regain enough courage to help Church off the floor and ease him out of the front door. Paulie paused only long enough to shout in my direction, "You're a dead man."

Like I hadn't heard that before.

Tracie reluctantly sat across from me.

"McKenzie," she said. That was all she said, but at least it was better than being called Rush again.

A moment later, Jimmy was at the booth with two fresh drinks. "On the house," he said. A party of four decided it was as good a time to leave as any. The two women smiled at me. One of the men gave me a nod of approval while the other looked straight ahead, seeing nothing, knowing nothing.

"Word will spread," I said to no one in particular. "Some

stranger took Church down. People will become more confident. They'll be more willing to stand up to him. If he pushes, they'll push back."

Tracie continued to stare. Finally she said, "Well, I guess he had it coming."

"This town should have dealt with him long ago. Tell me about your ex-husband."

"He was brave, but he didn't know how to fight. Not like you. McKenzie?"

"Yeah?"

"Why did you do it?"

I had been expecting the question, yet I hadn't been able to form much of an answer. "I guess I had just seen enough bullying for one day."

Rick and Cathy Danne paid their tab, rose from the table, and headed for the door. Neither of them looked even remotely pleased. If Church ignored my warning and decided to retaliate, it probably would be against them.

"Do me a favor," I said. "The Dannes—keep an eye on them if you can. Let me know if anyone bothers them."

"Let you know—you're leaving, then."

"I want a car outside the hotel at six tomorrow morning. A rental. Something I can return in the Twin Cities."

"I thought—I hoped—I'm disappointed in you, McKenzie."

"You wouldn't be the first."

CHAPTER FOUR

I had a long conversation with H. B. Sutton, my financial adviser, who assured me that my finances were unaffected by the Imposter's use of my name, although she ran every check she could think of to make sure. She said I wasn't a victim of identity theft so much as the credit card company was a victim of fraud, since the Imposter used my name yet nothing else that could be linked directly to me.

I had an even longer conversation with the FBI, who seemed reluctant to drop the kidnapping investigation. They wanted to prosecute the bounty hunters as an example to all the other punks out there who like to play fast and loose with the law. I told them I was all in favor of that—they could arrest Dewey Miller, too, for that matter—as long as the cops were left out of it. This precipitated a somewhat acrimonious discussion over exactly who in hell I thought I was to dictate policy to the Federal Bureau of Investigation. We decided to get back to each other at a later date.

"You're lucky they didn't throw your sorry ass in jail," Bobby Dunston told me.

"Bobby," Shelby said. She gestured with her head toward her children sitting at the picnic table.

Katie giggled. Victoria rolled her eyes. "Mom, we go to a public school," she said.

I had known the girls their whole lives; I'd greeted them while they were still in the hospital and wearing tiny pink hats. I have worked tirelessly to spoil them ever since. So far I had been only moderately successful, largely because their mother would give me that look whenever I attempted to give them something expensive and wholly frivolous. It was more than enough, Shelby insisted, that I had made them my heirs. They were still both quite young, though. Katie was eleven, and Victoria was pushing fourteen. One of these days they were going to need cars.

I buttered the corn on the cob that Bobby had roasted on the grill. The grill and picnic table were on a brick patio behind Bobby's house in the Merriam Park neighborhood of St. Paul, the house Bobby grew up in, that he bought from his parents when they retired. It was just a stone's throw from the house where I grew up, although I think I might have spent more time in Bobby's home than I did my own. I had helped Bobby build the patio—brick by brick—and I was proud of it.

"I'm surprised that the news media didn't pick it up," Nina said.

Normally she and I wouldn't get together on a Wednesday until after closing time, which was never a problem with me—one of the advantages of having a lot of money is that a guy can sleep in. She had taken the evening off for the Dunstons' backyard barbecue. Lately she had been doing things like that with increasing frequency, abandoning Rickie's to spend "normal" hours with me. I convinced myself it was solely because she had her jazz club humming like a well-oiled machine and didn't need to be constantly on-site to work the controls.

"If I were a pretty thirteen-year-old girl, the media would have been all over it," I said.

"I'll say," Victoria said.

I saluted her with my bottle of Summit Ale. She returned it with a can of orange pop.

"I guess that's the end of that, then," Nina said.

"Well . . ."

"Well, what?"

"The Imposter used my name."

"I understand, but if he had called himself Bill Smith, I'd hardly think that would be reason enough for all the other Bill Smiths in the world to be outraged."

"He didn't use Bill Smith."

"Why do you think the Imposter used your name?" Shelby said. "Do you think it's someone who knows you?"

"I doubt it."

"Don't be so sure," Bobby said. "He called himself a Raider. He could have gone to Cretin–Derham Hall."

"He could have gone to Roseville or Hastings or Norwood–Young America for that matter," said Victoria. "Nicollet, Northfield, Greenway, Fulda . . ." She stopped reciting teams when she found Bobby and me both staring at her. "What? I read the sports page."

"Geez," Katie said.

"I doubt the Imposter and I have ever met," I said. "Everyone I know is here or from here, and this guy doesn't know diddly-squat about the Twin Cities."

"Does it matter?" Nina asked. "What is it you guys like to say— no harm, no foul?"

"There was plenty of foul."

"Yes, but nothing lasting. 'Living well is the best revenge.' How many times have you quoted that at me? I thought it was your code."

I shrugged my reply and gnawed more corn. It seemed as if Shelby purposely waited until my mouth was full before she changed the topic.

"So, when are you kids going to get married?" she said.

I damn near choked to death. The expression on Bobby's face was of pure horror—he couldn't believe Shelby had said that.

"That's a good question," Victoria said. "You guys have been sleeping together since when?"

This time it was Shelby's turn to be shocked. "Victoria," she said.

Only Nina remained calm. She flicked away Shelby's question as if it were a bothersome fly. 'Course, she had practice. Her daughter, Erica, had asked the same question a few days earlier.

"McKenzie asked me," she said. "He asked a couple of times, only I keep turning him down."

"I don't blame you," Bobby said. "You could do so much better."

"After my last experience with marriage, I'm kinda sour on the institution."

"Besides, a woman doesn't need a man to complete her life," Victoria said.

"Yeah," Katie said. She usually agreed with her older sister.

"Were we speaking to you?" Shelby asked.

"You said 'kids.'" Victoria pointed at herself and Katie.

"It won't be long," I said, "before these two start dating."

Shelby and Bobby glared at me as if I'd told an off-color joke. I ate more corn.

Between bites of the corn, grilled chicken, and shrimp and sips of wine, beer, and orange pop, we talked. We talked about the president, and the weather, which seemed cooler than it had been in past summers despite fears of global warming, and the price of gas, and the Twins, who were once again in the thick of the American League Central Division race. Finally Victoria said, "McKenzie, when are you going back?"

"Tomorrow," I said.

Nina dropped her fork on her plate. Her startling silver-blue eyes became as dark as her shoulder-length black hair. She spoke very slowly.

"Back to Libbie?" she said.

I nodded.

"When did you make that decision?"

"Monday night."

"Give me one good reason."

Before I could, Victoria answered for me. "Because they broke into his house and kidnapped him and kept him in a trunk—a trunk! They kept me in a trunk, too."

Shelby tried to slip an arm around her shoulders, but Victoria slid off the picnic table and out of reach. I thought she might cry. There were no tears in her eyes, though. Only rage.

"They kept him prisoner," Victoria said. "They hurt him and they kept him prisoner and maybe it was mistaken identity like you said, but someone has to pay for that. The guy who started it all, the Imposter, he's got to pay for that. Him and everyone who helped him. Otherwise—otherwise you'll always wonder. You'll always be afraid. I'm not afraid anymore because the people who hurt me, they're dead or they're in prison. The people who hurt McKenzie, they're still out there and they'll probably hurt other people, too, unless someone stops them. If McKenzie doesn't stop them, who will?"

No one had anything to say to that except Victoria's younger sister, who filled the uncomfortable silence that followed with a simple declaration.

"Listen to her," Katie said. "She's an honor student."

Nina sat on the edge of a stool in my kitchen and held the stem of a wineglass against the counter as I filled it with pinot noir.

"What Victoria said earlier, is that why you're going to Libbie in the morning?" she said.

"Partly," I said.

"What else?"

"Curiosity. I want to know why the Imposter picked me. Unfortunately, I won't get the answer unless I find him."

"This doesn't have anything to do with the women you told me about, Tracie Blake and Sharren what's-her-name?"

"Certainly not. C'mon . . ."

Nina thought about it, then said, "Maybe we should get married."

The remark caught me by surprise, and it took a couple of beats before I could reply. "Nope."

"No?"

"You don't want to get married; you've made that clear. If you're talking about it now, it's because you're thinking about those women—you're thinking you can't trust me, and honestly, Nina, if that's true, then you'll trust me even less after we're married."

"Oh, McKenzie, don't be silly. Of course I trust you. That's not it."

"What, then?"

"If we were married, well, would you really leave me to go to Libbie?" She gave me an exaggerated wink just in case I missed her meaning.

"I don't know if it would be harder than it already is, but, yeah, I'd go, because then it wouldn't be just my name I'd be trying to protect, it would be yours, too."

"That's what it's about? Protecting your fair name? Honestly, McKenzie, when did you become Arthur of Camelot?"

"Nina—"

"Actually, you could be Arthur, or at least one of his knights, righting wrongs with a singing sword you pulled from a stone."

"Excalibur is the sword Arthur pulled from the stone. The Singing Sword is different. It belonged to Prince Valiant."

Nina glared at me as if she'd suddenly discovered that I was the dumbest human being alive.

"I just thought you ought to know," I said.

"What if I asked you not to sally forth?"

"What do you mean?"

"What if I asked you to stay here?"

"Are you asking?"

"I said if."

"If you asked, I would stay."

"You would?"

"Yes."

"Okay."

"Are you asking?"

"No."

"You can if you want."

"No. I knew who you were and what you did when we met. I don't have the right to ask you to change. If I don't like it, I can always leave, can't I?"

"I would if you asked—change, I mean."

"Oh, McKenzie. Don't start making promises that you can't keep."

"I love you."

"I know. I love you, too, but I don't always enjoy it."

Nina drained her wineglass in one long swallow and set it on the countertop.

"There's something you should know," she said. "If we got married—that's a big if, by the way—but if we got married, I would insist on keeping my own name."

"Nina Elizabeth Truhler. A lovely name. A lovely name for a lovely woman." I leaned in and kissed her gently on the lips. "Would you like to go upstairs?"

Nina slid off the stool and moved to the kitchen entrance. She found the light switch and pushed it to OFF.

"Here will do just fine," she said.

CHAPTER FIVE

I drove the Audi. My Cherokee was probably better suited for the terrain, but it didn't have a false bottom in the trunk for my stuff. Besides, the Audi got better gas mileage—even though I cranked the air conditioner to seventy-four degrees—and these days any trip from home becomes a major expense. It amuses my friends that I concern myself with such things, what with the money I have. I wasn't always wealthy, though. I was born and raised a middle-class kid in a middle-class neighborhood, and the lessons I learned stayed with me even after the insurance company handed me a check for three million, one hundred twenty-five thousand, five hundred eighty-four dollars and fifty cents.

I had set the cruise control to exactly nine miles per hour above the speed limit and seemed to be making better time than on my first trip to Libbie. Certainly the view was better. South Dakota, like all of the other Plains States, was supposed to be flat, with rangeland stretching as far as the eye could see, except it wasn't. It was rugged land, with canyons, gullies, ravines, and flat-topped hills. Cottonwood, elm, and willow trees were common near rivers and shelter belts. There were fields of alfalfa and grain and corn and soybeans. Along the way I also saw plenty of bison, deer, and pronghorn antelope. Yet one thing was as advertised—the sky was big and blue and seemed never to end.

By early afternoon, I had crossed the Missouri River, where the east ended and the west began. There were fewer farm fields, and now I saw pastures dotted with herds of shorthorn and Angus cattle. There was a saddle straddling a mailbox at the end of a long farm road. Someone had driven a Chevy van nose down into the drainage ditch along Highway 212 just outside of Faith. I stopped to take a look. No one was inside or around the vehicle.

A few miles up the road, I pulled into a Quick 66 to gas up. The smell of skunk as thick as a fog punched me in the nose when I stepped outside of the Audi, yet it didn't seem to bother a hen pheasant crouched alongside the road, taking grit. There was a cornfield on the other side of the gas station that looked like it was badly in need of water.

I filled my gas tank and checked the oil before I went inside. The Quick 66 was empty except for an old woman who sat behind the counter.

"As you can see, I'm just busier than heck," she said.

I told her about the van.

"Oh, that's just Eugene," she said. "I swear that boy got his license out of a Cracker Jack box. I 'spect he'll be along soon with his brother Al's wrecker to pull 'er out. Al is a mechanic, don't you know."

I thought that was convenient, and the woman agreed with me.

"Looks like you folks could use some rain," I said.

"Whaddaya mean?"

"The corn seems a little dry."

"You're not from around these parts, are ya?"

"No, ma'am."

"Cuz we only get about fifteen inches of rain each year, don't you know. Folks up here, if they ain't raising cattle, they're dryland farmers. Raise corn, beans, even watermelons with nothin' but a thimbleful of rain. It's an art."

I agreed that it probably was.

I was glad when I returned to the Audi, glad to get out of the heat—the AC did such a fine job, I had to turn it down after only a couple of miles. There was a purple ridge in the distance running north and south, how many miles away I couldn't say, and I wondered if that was where the Black Hills began. I didn't get close enough for an answer. Instead, I turned north on Highway 73, the ridge now on my left, with the sun looking to set behind it. I passed more fields of alfalfa, beans, and corn, although they were now spaced miles apart. There were steel bins visible from the highway, and barns and cattle in feedlots and cattle at pasture and a white silo with GO CARDINALS painted on it. A cock pheasant crossed the road in front of me, and I slowed down to avoid hitting it. A few miles later, I did the same for two hens. There were little songbirds balanced on fence rails, and killdeer, and in the distance I saw two red-tailed hawks perched on a big bale of alfalfa. The only things that blocked the view were the occasional windbreak of trees.

What I didn't see was another car—not one—on the whole way north.

It was a pleasant drive, but I was starting to get tired and cranky just the same. I had been over eight hours in the Audi, and I couldn't find a single radio station worth listening to. Finally I approached a sign set along the highway. LIBBIE, SD, 1884. RULES, REGULATIONS, AND RESPECT!

"That's the town motto?" I said aloud. "Really?"

It was the exclamation point that annoyed me the most. I was a big fan of respect, but rules and regulations—not so much. If I had been a teenager growing up in Libbie, somehow I could see myself burning that sign to the ground. With Bobby Dunston acting as lookout.

I leaned against the frame of Chief Gustafson's office door and watched him, my arms folded across my chest. He was sitting behind his desk, his feet up, and reading a two-week-old copy of *Time*. Except for the chief, the Libbie police station was empty and silent. It could have been a library, or a Christian Science Reading Room. There wasn't even a bell on the door to announce when visitors arrived. Eventually his eyes lifted upward off the magazine and saw me standing there.

"Hi," I said.

The chief tried to do everything at once—drop the magazine, lower his feet, stand, and reach for his gun—none of them smoothly. Still, it took only a moment before the fear slipped away.

"You startled me," he said.

"This is the least secure police station I have ever been in," I said.

"We're kinda informal around here."

"I noticed."

"So what are you doing here, McKenzie? I thought you went back to the Cities."

"I did. Like the man said, I have returned."

"Yeah?"

The chief motioned toward a chair in front of the desk, and I settled in. He sat behind the desk and folded his hands on top of his blotter.

"So, any complaints?" I asked.

"What do you mean?"

"I was wondering if anyone swore out a warrant for my arrest. Felonious assault, something like that."

"You mean what happened the other day at the Rossini? The way I heard it—a couple of witnesses swore Church threw the first punch and you were acting in self-defense. Least, that's what it says in my report."

"What does Church say?"

"Not a word."

"That surprises me. Usually bullies are the first to go whining to the law when things don't go their way."

"Church is one of those guys who likes to plot his own revenge, so be careful. Hear me?"

"Sure."

"What about you?"

"What do you mean?"

"I had a couple of interesting conversations yesterday, first with the FBI and then later with the Minnesota Bureau of Criminal Apprehension. They seem to think there was something improper about how you were treated the other day."

"They're right about that."

"And?"

"The last I spoke to them, we pretty much agreed that they have far more important things to do than rousting small-town police departments."

"I appreciate that, I surely do."

"How big is your department, anyway?"

"Three, plus a couple of part-timers."

"I'm surprised a town this small can afford a police department."

"We have contracts with a few local towns; that helps keep the price down. 'Course, with this other McKenzie defrauding the city, I don't know what'll happen. Tell me, is that why you came back? To help get the Imposter?"

There were several framed color photographs on the chief's desk. In one, a woman with black hair and pale skin, her head tilted just so, stared straight into the camera; her smile was bright and warm. I reached for it.

"May I?" I said. The chief nodded his approval. I took up the frame and gave it a long look. "Very pretty."

"My wife, Nancy."

"One look and I can tell she's far too good for the likes of you."

You say something like that and most husbands will tell you that they agree, even if they don't actually believe it. The chief's reply: "The photo was taken a couple of years ago."

"I can't get over it," I said. "The number of attractive women in this town. You must have more babes per capita than just about anywhere I've been."

"We hold our own."

"Gotta be something in the water," I said. I set the photograph back on the desk. "You know it's an inside job, don't you?"

The chief didn't say.

"The Imposter didn't simply show up one day and decide to fleece Libbie, South Dakota," I said. "He had an accomplice. Someone had to set it up, tell him who to talk to, who to avoid."

The chief rubbed his face with both hands.

"I don't believe that," he said.

"Yes, you do."

The chief stopped rubbing.

"No, I don't. I know there's an accomplice. It's the only way to explain how the Imposter got out of town. That doesn't mean he's from Libbie."

"What do you mean 'got out of town'?"

"We found the Imposter's rental in the lot at Lake Mataya. That's a park about seven miles outside of Libbie on White Buffalo Road, lots of trees, picnic tables—people sometimes use it as a kind of rendezvous. Which was what I first thought when I found the car, that he went off with someone and spent the night, if you know what I mean. Except he never came back for the car. Later, I checked with the Pioneer Hotel. Turned out the Imposter left Tuesday night, left about 9:00 P.M.—that was ten days ago. He was carrying one of those personal computer bags. Sharren Nuffer called after him as he headed for the door. Just to say hi, she said. The Imposter, he waved at her and said, 'It's been a slice,' and walked out. When we checked his room, we found that his bags and clothes were still there, but nothing that could identify him. That's when I put a call in to Jon Kampa, who owns the bank. Turned out that the Imposter had electronically transferred all of the cash in his account to a bank in the Caymans at about midnight."

"His account?"

"An account with First Integrity State Bank of Libbie. That's what the city and the other investors poured their money into."

"That doesn't make sense to me."

"Maybe if you had been here to tell everyone how dumb they were—"

"No, no, that's not it," I said. "I meant that him abandoning his clothes and just taking off suggests panic. It suggests that he had learned that someone was onto him and it was time to leave. If that were true, though, why park his car at the lake where it would be easily found? Why not drive to Rapid City? There are plenty of attractions, tourists, plenty of places where he could park a car and walk away—the car might not be discovered for days. That would have bought him more time to make his getaway. Why take the risk of being seen in Libbie with his shill?"

"Perhaps the shill didn't trust him. Perhaps he wanted to be there when the Imposter made the transfer. Perhaps it was fixed so that the Imposter couldn't make the transfer without the shill being there."

"Do you still have his possessions, what he left in the hotel?"

"In the back. Do you want to take a look?"

When he said "in the back," the chief meant in the room next to his small office. The Imposter's belongings had been packed away into his own suitcases, which we opened on top of a cafeteria-style table. There was nothing there that couldn't be easily replaced: razor, toothbrush, hairbrush, gel—plenty of stuff that could be matched to his DNA if it came to that—and lots of clothes, most of it fairly new. What shocked me was that all of the pants and shirt measurements were the same as mine—waist, inseam, sleeve length, collar. We seemed to prefer the same colors and manufacturers, too. If you hung it all in my closet, I probably wouldn't have known the difference. There was even a pair of black Florsheim slip-on dress shoes that retailed for about a hundred bucks that were identical to a pair I owned, down to the 10½ size.

"Damn," I said.

"What?" the chief said.

"Nothing."

I carefully examined every item, but it soon became apparent that the Imposter knew what he was doing. There was nothing unique in the suitcase, nothing that could be traced, nothing that could be used to help identify the owner.

"Do you think he's done this sort of thing before?" I said.

"My experience, a guy doesn't wake up one morning and decide to be an asshole. He works his way up to it."

"You think he has a record?"

"Yep."

"Do you have his fingerprints?"

"Yep. Sent them off to the FBI last week, ran 'em through their automated fingerprint ID system. Nothing yet."

"If they don't have a match in a couple of hours, you're probably not going to get one."

"I figured, so I sent them to the South Dakota Division of Criminal Investigation, too."

"Let me guess. They didn't get a hit, either."

"Not yet."

"Don't hold your breath."

For a moment, the chief looked as if he actually had been keeping it in and decided not to bother anymore.

"What about his car?" I said.

"A rental, like I said. I went through it three, four times before we had it towed back to the rental agency. Nothing. Not a gas station receipt. Not even a cigarette butt in the ashtray."

Oh, well, my inner voice said. *No one said it was going to be easy.*

"I don't suppose any longtime residents have left in the past week or so," I said. "Or announced that they were leaving."

"Nary a one."

"Would you know for sure?"

"There isn't much of a transient population. People move out—there's been a lot of that these past few years. Not many people have been moving in. Everybody knows everybody. If you're right, your accomplice is still here."

"With your permission, I'll be hanging around for a few days."

"Permission granted. Just keep me in the loop."

"I'll be asking a lot of people a lot of embarrassing questions. Do you have a problem with that?"

"Nope."

"Are you sure, Chief? You'll be getting a lot of phone calls. These people pay your salary, after all."

"Way I look at it, McKenzie, you don't help us find all that money, I'm going to be out of a job anyway."

The Tall Moon Tavern was far enough outside of Libbie that you couldn't see the glow of the town's lights from there. Or much of anything else, for that matter. There was a single fading arch light mounted on a high wooden pole to help patrons negotiate the gravel parking lot—and attract every winged insect in the known world. Yet beyond the yellow circle of light it cast, there was impenetrable darkness.

I parked the Audi under the light, locked it with my remote control key chain, and made my way toward the front door; the brown stones crunched under my shoes. There was a neon sign on the door that advertised a beer I had never heard of—Ringneck Red Ale—that apparently had something to do with pheasants. Before I could reach it, the door flew open, and out stepped a thin, wiry man with a shaved head that reflected the arch light and a mustache that looked like something I tried to grow when I was a kid and gave up on after much ridicule. He moved quickly, and I had to hop to the side to avoid a collision.

"I see you," he shouted.

He pointed more or less down the country road. I tried to follow his finger yet could see nothing beyond the circle of light.

"I see you," he repeated. "Bastard."

A moment later, a car engine turned over. Headlamps flared. A vehicle had been parked alongside the county road about two hundred yards from the Tall Moon's parking lot. It moved forward, slowly at first, then with greater speed. The thin man kept pointing his finger, pointing it like a gun, as he followed the vehicle's progress. It wasn't until it passed the parking lot that I could see that it was a City of Libbie Police Department cruiser. A moment later, it disappeared into the night; not even its taillights were visible.

"What was that about?" I said.

"Bastard's trying to ruin my business," the man said. "He parks out there, scaring my customers, making 'em think he'll bust 'em for DUI if they drink here."

"Why?"

"Why? Why?" The man turned to me. His eyes were bright and shiny in the light. "Cuz his fucking brother-in-law owns a joint down the road, that's why."

"Does Chief Gustafson know about this?"

"That was Chief Gustafson. I saw him cruise past just before you arrived. I don't know why he's doing me like this. I've been competing with his brother-in-law for years, and there's never been no, whatjacallit, animosity. Last few weeks, though, I see 'im out here a lot. I gotta figure a way to take care of this."

"That wouldn't be smart, messing with cops."

"How the fuck would you know? You a cop?"

"Me? Hell no."

I followed him inside the Tall Moon. He slipped behind a bar that looked as if it had been there since the invention of alcohol. Wooden booths with worn cushions bordered the near wall, and a regulation pool table, bumper pool table, foosball table, and plastic dart board were arrayed near the far wall. Between them were half a dozen tables and chairs. Someone had used folded napkins and cardboard to shim the legs of nearly all of the tables to keep them from tilting. That's because the wooden floor had become so badly warped over the years that it resembled the most treacherous putting green I had ever seen—drop a golf ball and there'd be no telling where it would roll. There was a dance floor, also warped, facing a small stage that was empty save for a handwritten sign propped on a chair that promised live music every other Saturday night. In the meantime, Hank Williams was playing on a jukebox that looked like it still accepted nickels.

Behind the bar I saw assorted bottles of liquor, spigots for tap beer, coolers for bottled beer, pig's feet in a jar, a pizza oven, beef jerky, bags of chips and pretzels, clear plastic bins filled with pull tabs, and a mirror that was badly in need of resilvering. Tracie Blake was sitting on a stool at the crowded bar. She was chatting with a bartender who seemed to only have eyes for her. I approached from behind.

"Hello, Tracie."

She turned to look at me. The expression on her face went from bored to surprised just like that.

"McKenzie, my God," she said.

I sat on the stool next to hers without asking permission. The owner hustled over as if he expected trouble.

"I got it, Jeff," he said.

He took the much taller bartender's elbow and literally pulled him away. Jeff frowned but began serving other customers without an argument.

"He bothering you, Tracie?" the owner asked.

I wondered how often men attempted to sit next to Tracie without permission and what the small man was prepared to do about it. Tracie removed the threat.

"No, Wayne," she said. "This is McKenzie I told you about."

"The real McKenzie?"

" 'Fraid so," I said.

"You're the one who fucked up Church. Well, hell, that deserves a beverage on the house. What'll ya have?"

"What can you tell me about Ringneck Red Ale?"

Wayne shrugged. "It's pretty good. Brewed down in Sioux Falls."

"I'll give it a try."

When the bartender left, I glanced over at Tracie. She was smiling.

"It doesn't take much to become a hero in this town, does it?" I said.

"I knew you'd come back."

"You knew nothing of the sort."

"Oh, yes, I knew. It's your eyes. Even when you demanded a rental car I could see it. You have tenacious eyes."

"Are you sure you're talking about me and not the other guy?"

Before she could answer, Wayne reappeared with my order. It turned out that the Ringneck was a medium-bodied ale. It poured a clear red, smelled slightly of caramel, and tasted of roasted malts on top followed by oak and chocolate at the finish.

"What do you think?" Wayne said.

"Nice," I said. "Very smooth."

"Better than anything you'll get in North Dakota, that's for sure."

"Heady praise, indeed."

"All they have up there is churches, more churches per capita than anywhere else in the country."

"Don't forget the missile silos," Tracie said.

"Blow themselves off the face of the earth and who would notice?" Wayne said.

He gave me a look as if he expected a challenge to his claim.

"I think much the same way about Iowa," I said.

"Iowa is the fucking Garden of Eden compared to North Dakota."

I wasn't prepared to go that far but let the argument lapse just the same. Instead, I spun on the stool and faced the rest of the bar. Most of the patrons were male, and nearly half of them were watching me.

"You don't get many strangers in Libbie, do you?" I said.

"They're all waiting to see what I do about you sitting here," Tracie said.

"Oh yeah?"

"If I tell you to get lost and you don't, half of them will jump to my defense."

"You have a lot of big brothers."

"No, just a lot of men who think they should be sitting here instead of you." Tracie turned to face the audience as I had done. "Hey, guys. This is McKenzie."

"The one who beat up Church?" someone said.

"I heard he sucker-punched him," said someone else.

"Chickenshit," said a third man.

"Glory is so fleeting," I said.

"It is, indeed," Tracie said.

We both spun back on our stools to face the fading mirror.

"Do you mind knowing that so many men are, what's the word—interested—in you?" I said.

"I'm used to it."

"How many of them"—I paused to choose my words carefully—"have you let sit here?"

"Damn few."

She waved her glass when she spoke, and some of the golden liquid spilled out. It was only then that I realized that Tracie was smashed.

"How long has your husband been in the jar?" I said.

"Ex-husband. It's been about five years. Why?"

"I was just thinking—that's a long time to be without somebody."

"Oh, there's been a lot of somebodies, McKenzie, but I'm holding out for that someone. How 'bout you? Is there a someone in your life?"

"Yes."

"Good for you."

"So," I said, "do you come here often?"

"What's that supposed to mean?"

"Chief Gustafson knew where I could find you."

"Eric always knows where he can find me, day or night."

Tracie emptied her glass and waved it at Wayne, who had been watching intently out of the corner of his eye while pretending not to. A moment later, he refilled the glass. Tracie was drinking amaretto and 7UP, and Wayne was being generous with the amaretto.

"What's the plan, McKenzie? Do we have a plan?"

"Tomorrow after breakfast, if you're up to it, I want you to introduce me to every man, woman, and child that the Imposter knew in this town. Everyone involved in the phony mall. We'll see if we can cut his trail."

"What about tonight?"

"Tonight, I'm going back to my room at the Pioneer Hotel."

"No, no, don't do that, McKenzie. You don't want to go back to Sharren Nuffer. Stay with me. I have plenty of room."

I wondered briefly if Tracie had made the same offer to the Imposter who called himself Rushmore McKenzie, but I let the question slide.

"I don't think my girl would appreciate that," I said.

"Do you have a girl, McKenzie?"

"I told you I did."

"Did you? I forgot. What's her name?"

"Nina."

"Do you love her?"

"Yes, I do."

"Isn't that—that's a great feeling, isn't it? Being in love."

I told her that it was. I don't think she heard me, though. Instead, Tracie finished her drink and beckoned to Wayne for another. This time he gave her only a splash of amaretto to go with the 7UP. He glared as if daring me to challenge his pour and set the drink in front of her.

"On the house," he said.

"You're always so nice to me, Wayne," she said.

"Are you good to drive home?" I asked.

"Of course."

"Hey," Wayne said. "You don't need to hang around. We have it covered."

"See, McKenzie," Tracie said. "I have someone, too."

CHAPTER SIX

I woke early, a common occurrence when I sleep in a bed that's not my own. I wasn't in any hurry, though, so I lay on my back and stared at the hotel room ceiling, waiting for the alarm clock to catch up to me. Bright sunlight slipped through the cracks between the window and the frilly shade. Still, it wasn't the sunlight that caused me finally to go to the window and look out. It was the silence. Even in my residential neighborhood in St. Paul there was noise: the distant murmur of traffic; neighbors opening and closing doors to houses, garages, and cars; a dog yapping. Yet Libbie woke quietly. There were few vehicles on First Street and even fewer people, who all seemed to move on tiptoes as if they were afraid of disturbing the peace. For a moment, I flashed on the old SF movie *Invasion of the Body Snatchers.* Show emotion and you die. I quickly shook the image from my head.

"Get a grip, McKenzie," I said aloud.

I decided to go for a walk. Usually I run in the morning, only this was more a journey of exploration than exercise. After putting myself together, I hurried down the three flights of steps and out the front entrance of the Pioneer. I hung a left and followed First, my back to the sun. On the other side of the hotel's driveway, there was a shop that sold collectibles. It was next to a store that sold discount items— damned if I could tell the difference between the two. There was an

American Family Insurance office and an H&R Block office with an alley between them that didn't seem to lead anywhere. Farther down the street was the Munoz Emporium I had visited on Monday, and next to that was a senior center. The senior center was actually open, but it wasn't a place I wanted to visit, so I kept moving.

I followed First Street until I reached a sprawling grain elevator located at the western edge of the town. The name Miller was painted in black across a row of corrugated steel bins and on a sign over an office building in front of them. Beyond the elevator, there were green-brown fields that seemed to stretch to the horizon. It was an impressive vista, just not something that could hold my attention for long. I preferred people in my landscapes.

I scanned the gravel parking lot. There were several cars, SUVs, and pickups but no drivers. I was about to walk away when a door marked AUTHORIZED PERSONNEL ONLY opened and Church stepped out. He was limping slightly, and his right hand was encased in a plaster cast except for his fingertips. He stopped, slipped a cigarette between his lips, and lit it with a disposable lighter. That's when he saw me. I gave him what Victoria Dunston called a microwave—holding my hand up and moving my fingers a fraction of an inch. He abruptly turned for the door. He slipped on his bad leg, and I thought he would go down until he managed to catch the door handle and steady himself. He gave me a hard look, spit the cigarette onto the gravel, and stepped back inside the office, pulling the door shut behind him. Chief Gustafson's words floated back to me. *Church is one of those guys who likes to plot his own revenge, so be careful.*

I kept walking, heading north, until I discovered a set of railroad tracks that served the elevator. The tracks seemed to divide Libbie in half between north and south, and I wondered which side was the wrong side. There's always a wrong side of the tracks.

After I crossed the tracks, I came upon a cemetery large enough to need three entrances. A block of large, well-kept houses bordered the cemetery, and I followed the sidewalk until I came across a man digging a grave, using a small, rubber-tracked excavator with a backfill blade on the front. I stopped to watch as he scooped out the dirt and deposited it into a bucket attached to the back of the machine. The gravedigger gave me a wave, and I waved back. There was something surreal about it all, and it made me think of the hours I'd spent in the trunk of the kidnappers' car. There had been a few moments when I thought . . . *Never mind what you thought,* my inner voice told me. I turned and followed the road north.

The road ended where the cemetery ended, and I went east. There were more homes, some of them quite ambitious, a small park with playground equipment, and a high school surrounded by a football field, tennis courts, a baseball diamond, and a parking lot. The school building couldn't have been more than a dozen years old. As near as I could tell, it was closed for the summer, and I wondered, if you were a teacher in Libbie, South Dakota, what did you do when school was out? Probably what all teachers do, I told myself, although that still didn't answer my question.

I kept moving east until I found a second cemetery. This one was considerably smaller than the first, yet its monuments seemed bigger and grander. There was a black iron fence surrounding it. The entrance was closed but not locked. The name Boucher Gardens was written in metal above it. A gated community, I thought. Out loud I said, "I bet people are just dying to get in here." I laughed at the joke. Sometimes I crack myself up.

I went south, skirting the eastern edge of Libbie, recrossing the railroad tracks. The houses were smaller now, and less impressive. There was a retirement home that seemed a hundred years older than the high school. Next to that was a lot where a man in a small shack decorated with flags and streamers sold mobile homes, prefabs, and RVs built for people who wanted to be someplace but weren't exactly sure where. Farther along I found Libbie's sewage treatment plant.

"Well, now I know which is the wrong side of the tracks," I said.

I went west again, moving past a small, relatively new industrial complex that seemed to be bustling with energy. There were plenty of vehicles driving in and out of parking lots, plenty of people walking in and out of doorways, going about their business. No one paid any attention to me. Why would they?

A coffeehouse named Supreme Bean was located on the corner, and I went inside. Along with coffee it sold assorted bakery goods, sandwiches, and soup, but I settled for a sixteen-ounce hazelnut, no cream, no sugar. While I waited, I noticed a high school boy sitting at a small table. A high school girl sat across from him. She was wearing the uniform of a waitress but didn't work there. If she wasn't the Libbie High School homecoming queen, it could not have been for lack of effort. What is it with this town and its women? I wondered. She had to frown before I recognized her—Miller's daughter, Saranne, the girl he slapped at the Libbie cop shop. She didn't notice me, probably because she only had eyes for the boy. She twisted her long red-brown hair and fluttered the lids of her blue-green eyes, only the boy didn't seem to notice. He was too busy talking about himself. I felt like slapping him upside the head and shouting, "The girl is interested in you, dummy. Pay attention to her." Instead, I snapped a lid over my drink and stepped outside. After all, I had learned the hard way what it took to impress women; why not him?

I was nearly to the street when I heard a voice calling after me, "Hey, hey." I stopped and turned. Saranne moved to within a few yards of me and no closer. Her eyes were wide and thoughtful and a little sad; she shielded them from the rising sun. Her smile was as fragile as a china cup.

"You're McKenzie," she said. "The real one."

"Yes."

"The one I saw at the jail."

"That's right."

"You're here to find Rush, aren't you, like they want."

"I'm going to give it a try."

"Why? What good will it do? Do you think it'll change anything?"

"I don't know."

"People have to live with their mistakes."

"Only the ones they can't fix."

She gave it a moment before answering. "Only an adult would say that." When she said adult, she meant old.

"Sometimes you have to be an adult before you figure it out," I said.

She gave that a moment, too.

"Whatever," she said.

I watched as she spun about and walked back into the coffeehouse.

Off in the distance, I could see the shining towers of the grain elevator—they had never been entirely out of sight—and I followed the road until I reached them. Once on First Street again, I hung a right and moved toward the hotel. When I reached the front entrance, I glanced at my watch. I had walked the entire perimeter of Libbie. It had taken me just over two hours. I didn't think it was possible to walk around the Mall of America in that short a time.

Tracie Blake was not happy. She was standing in the lobby of the Pioneer when I arrived, and she started barking before I was halfway through the door.

"McKenzie," Tracie said. "Where have you been?"

Sharren Nuffer was behind the reception desk. She seemed more concerned than angry.

"We didn't know where you were," she said. "You left without telling anyone."

"Ladies," I said.

"Well?" Tracie said. "Where were you?"

"I was taking a walk around town."

"You said you wanted to meet for breakfast."

"I said I wanted to meet after breakfast. What's the big deal?"

"We were worried," Sharren said.

Tracie looked at her as if the remark caught her by surprise.

"Worried?" I said.

"Rush, the first McKenzie, he disappeared, too," Sharren said. "Just walked away and never came back."

"He didn't walk," Tracie said. "He ran."

Sharren shrugged as if she didn't appreciate the difference.

"I'm not going anywhere," I said.

"Well?" Tracie said again, this time with a fist planted on each hip. "What are we going to do now?"

"Are you always this cranky in the morning?" I said.

Behind Tracie's back, Sharren made a gesture with her thumb and four curled fingers that was meant to mimic someone taking a drink. Tracie caught me watching Sharren and quickly glanced behind her. Sharren suddenly found something very important on the reception desk to occupy her attention.

"I don't need this," Tracie said.

She headed for the door, pushed it open, and stepped outside. Before the door could close, she spun around, grabbed the handle, held the door open, and spoke to me across the threshold.

"Well, are you coming?"

"Sure," I said.

I felt the heat on my face and arms as I stepped outside. The temperature seemed to have risen dramatically during the few minutes I had been inside the hotel. From the spot in front of the

hotel I could see several blocks up the street to the electronic display of First Integrity State Bank of Libbie alternating between
time and temperature. *87° F.*

"Is it always this hot?" I said.

"In the summer," Tracie said. "It's not unusual to have a string of
hundred-plus days for weeks at a time. Usually, though, the temperature drops to around sixty degrees at night, which makes it
comfortable."

"If you say so."

"Well," she said—I wished she would stop saying that word.
"Do you have a plan? Last night you said you had a plan."

"There's an old saying," I said. "When in doubt—"

"Yes?"

"Follow the money."

Red velvet and gold lamé wallpaper and a thick red carpet greeted
us when we entered the First Integrity State Bank of Libbie. An
L-shaped teller cage of deep red wood and etched glass stood facing the front doors. Behind the cage, an enormous brass door
stood open to reveal a small vault holding perhaps a hundred
bronze safe deposit boxes. There was an inner room that, I assumed, contained a safe where the cash and coin were stored. A
huge crystal chandelier hung from the center of the lobby. Arrayed
beneath the chandelier were a cotton sofa, wicker chairs, and a low,
highly polished table with coffee and rolls that were free to customers.

"Jon Kampa owns the bank," Tracie said. "It's been in his family
for almost a hundred years."

"Well, if things don't work out, he could always turn the place
into a bordello," I said.

Only five people worked there, including a man sitting behind
a large desk made of the same wood as the teller cage. He was

wearing a charcoal suit and a red tie that he adjusted as he came over to greet us.

"Tracie," he said. "It's always a pleasure to see you."

"Jon," Tracie said.

Kampa extended his hand toward me. "And you, sir?"

"My name is McKenzie."

"Ahh, yes. Mr. McKenzie. Well, well, well . . ."

"Well," I said. *Now you're doing it,* my inner voice told me. "Nice little bank you have here."

Kampa seemed to bristle at the remark.

"Hardly little," he said. "We have twenty-eight-point-five million dollars in assets. Given our charter, we feel that is plenty big enough."

"What is your charter?"

"To serve the good people of Libbie and Perkins County. Now, sir, what can I do for you?"

"Tell me about the Imposter," I said.

"There is very little information I can provide. Rush—Mr. McKenzie—how shall we refer to him? The Imposter, you said. He talked the city into opening an escrow account with us. The city poured money into it, and so did many of our leading citizens."

"How much money?"

"I am not at liberty to say."

"Oh, c'mon. Can't you give me a hint?"

Kampa glanced at Tracie. Tracie shrugged.

"No, sir," he said. "I do not believe that I can."

"More than a million?"

"Not so much."

"A half million?"

"I've already said too much."

I had the distinct impression that he was a man prone to saying too much if you pressed him, but I didn't.

"How did the Imposter manage to steal the money?" I said.

Again, Kampa looked to Tracie.

"McKenzie is trying to help us get it back," she said.

"Good luck with that," he said. "The money was transferred to a financial institution in the Cayman Islands, and from there God knows where it was sent. That's a bit of a cliché, isn't it—hiding money in the Caymans—yet that's what he did."

"Is there any way to trace the money?"

"Only to its first destination. After that—I suppose the FBI could do it if you convinced them that it was an act of terrorism. They seem more interested these days in chasing shadows than in solving actual crimes."

"How did the Imposter loot the account?"

"It was easy. The city set up an escrow account and transferred money into it from its general operating fund. Terms and conditions of the trust allowed the Imposter to access the account online. After that it was simply a matter of punching in account numbers. He could have made the transfer in less than a minute, anytime day or night."

"Why would you give him access to the account?"

"I didn't," Kampa insisted.

"He wanted to monitor account activity," Tracie said. "He wanted to know when funds were deposited, when checks cleared, etcetera."

"There were safeguards in place," Kampa said. "He shouldn't have been able to withdraw or redesignate funds without permission of the city."

"What safeguards?" I asked.

"A password was required. A password generated by the city and known only to designated city officials."

I turned toward Tracie. "Who knew the password?"

"The mayor, the other four of us on the city council, and the city manager and director of economic development," she said.

"Seven people."

"Six. The city manager and director of economic development are the same person."

"Okay. Now we have a place to start. Just out of curiosity, what was the password?"

"It needed to be twelve characters long with at least four of them being numbers. We wanted something everyone would remember."

"And . . . ?"

"L - I - B - B - I - E - S - D - 1 - 8 - 8 - 4."

"You picked your name and birthday? Seriously? A name and birthday that's on every sign leading into this town?"

Tracie found a spot on the carpet that demanded her attention. Kampa sighed heavily and rolled his eyes.

"You people deserved to be robbed," I said.

"I wouldn't say that," Kampa said.

"Was the bank hurt by the fraud?"

He waggled his hand.

"First Integrity doesn't normally do much commercial lending, and when we do it tends to be on a small scale," Kampa said. "Unfortunately, in addition to the city, several of our commercial customers insisted on investing in the mall despite our strenuous recommendations against it. There was a growing consensus that most of the town's retail businesses would move there, and those that didn't would experience difficulty, and we"—Kampa paused as if merely speaking the next few words gave him pain—"we loaned them the money. Now, because of their losses, a few customers might have a difficult time meeting their obligations. That doesn't help our loan portfolio. However, we'll work something out. Like I said, this is a community bank. We're here to serve."

"Where are your assets invested?"

"About thirty-five percent is in agriculture and ranching. The rest is in residential lending."

"Mortgages?"

"Mortgages and loans to developers."

"The housing market has taken an awful beating lately."

"That's true. Certainly we're not immune to that. However, our loan-loss provisions are substantial enough to cover our losses."

"Even with this setback?"

"Yes, even with this setback."

"When did the FDIC last examine your books?"

"Fifteen months ago. They gave us a two rating. What's the matter, McKenzie? You don't believe me?"

"Fifteen months. You're about due for another audit, aren't you?"

"Early next month. Why don't you come back then? Bring your pocket calculator with you."

"I meant no disrespect."

The expression on his face suggested that he didn't believe me.

"You said your customers invested in the mall against your advice," I said.

Kampa was looking directly at Tracie when he said, "I was one of the few people in town who advised caution."

"Why didn't they listen?"

"People never listen to the man who tells them they are not going to make money. They only listen to the guy who promises to make them rich."

The sign was flashing 90° F. by the time we left the bank.

"The weatherman said we might break one hundred," Tracie said.

"Geez."

I might have said more, except my cell phone began playing the old George Gershwin tune "Summertime." The caller ID said Nina Truhler was on the line.

"Hi," I said.

"You're up," she said.

Tracie and I passed under the bank sign, heading back toward the hotel. *9:57 A.M.*, it read. To most people, it was midmorning. To those of us who were rich, unemployed and spending late evenings in the company of women who owned jazz clubs, it was early.

"Libbie is an exciting, twenty-four-hour town, and I don't want to miss a minute of it," I said. "A little early for you, too, isn't it?"

"Actually, I'm still in bed."

"I like the sound of that."

"What are you doing?"

"Making a nuisance of myself."

"You do that so well."

"Practice, practice, practice."

"Any progress?"

"I just started."

"Let me know what happens. You know how I love your adventures."

That made me chuckle. "You say it, but we both know it's not altogether true."

"Is Tracie what's-her-name with you?" Nina asked.

"Yep."

"Do you love me?"

"What?"

"Do. You. Love. Me?"

"Of course."

"Say it."

"I love you."

"Did she hear?"

I glanced at Tracie. She continued walking with measured, graceful strides, looking straight ahead, her face without expression.

"Yes," I said.

"Okay," Nina said. "Have a nice day. I'll talk to you soon."

After Nina hung up, I slipped the cell phone back into my pocket.

"Was that your girlfriend?" Tracie said.

"Yes."

"Nina?"

"Yes."

"She sounds needy."

"Does she? I hadn't noticed."

We were nearly back to the hotel before Tracie spoke again. "Now what?"

"The mayor first, I think. Eventually we'll get to everyone who knew the password."

"They're all suspects?"

"Yep."

"Including me?"

"Yep."

"Why would I help Rush steal our money?"

"When does your ex-husband get out of stir? Eighteen months? What happens to your allowance then?"

"It'll go to him."

"What will you do? Go back to modeling?"

"I'm a little old for that."

"Exactly."

"My God, McKenzie, you've got a suspicious mind."

"Are you hungry? I'm hungry."

I drove. Tracie directed us west out of town and then north until we came to the intersection of Highways 20 and 73. She said the southwest corner was where the Imposter proposed building the outlet mall. A combination gas station and convenience store called Miller Big Stop occupied the northeast corner. A restaurant with a bar called Grandma Miller's was next to it. A new and used auto dealership that seemed to specialize in pickup trucks called Miller Ford was next to that.

"Some people love the sound of their own names," I said.

"Huh?" said Tracie.

"Never mind."

We pulled into the lot outside the restaurant. The life-sized head of a bison hung above the door. I was surprised when it greeted us as we approached, its cartoon voice triggered by a motion detector.

"It's awfully lonely hanging by a nail up here all day," the bison said. "If it weren't for you nice people stopping for a chat once in a while, I don't know what I would do. If only I had a female buffalo to talk to."

It started singing "Blue Moon," switching the lyrics to lament that he didn't have a dream in his heart or a bison of his own.

"Somewhere Rodgers and Hart are spinning in their graves," I said.

"I think it's cute," Tracie said.

"I'm sure that's what they were going for when they wrote the song."

"You're cynical, you know that, McKenzie?"

Cynical and suspicious, my inner voice said.

A sign just inside the restaurant door invited us to seat ourselves, and so we did, claiming a table in front of a large window with a view of the highway. The tables, chairs, and bar were all made of burnished redwood, yet they were covered by such a thick coating of polyurethane that they might as well have been plastic. A big-screen HD TV tuned to Fox News occupied each corner of the room. Thankfully, the volume was off.

I was watching what little traffic there was on the highway while paper place mats, silverware, and water glasses magically appeared before us. A young and pretty voice said, "We just closed our breakfast buffet, so you'll have to order off the menu." It was only then that I noticed our server and she recognized me.

"Small world," I said.

Saranne Miller blinked hard. "Too small," she said.

I took the menu from her outstretched hand. "How'd it go with the boyfriend this morning?"

"Boyfriend?" Her pretty lips curled into a slight grimace, as if she knew a painful secret she didn't wish to share. "He had his chance. Why? Are you looking to take his place?"

"I don't think so."

"What makes you different from every other man in this town?"

"I'm not from this town."

"That's the only thing about you I like."

Across the table, Tracie's intense eyes moved from Saranne to me and back again as if she were watching a tennis match. I opened the menu.

"What would you recommend?" I said.

"Eat at home."

Tracie laughed, but the expression on Saranne's face told me that she was perfectly serious.

The first item that caught my eye was Grandma Miller's World-Famous Third-Pound Burger with Bleu Cheese, Lettuce, and Tomato, so I ordered that, staying with potato chips instead of paying extra for the fries. Tracie ordered a salad with cottage cheese on the side—once a model, always a model, I guessed.

"What was that all about?" she asked after Saranne left.

"I met her this morning," I said. "She was flirting with a kid in a coffeehouse."

"I'm not surprised. She's becoming the town slut."

"C'mon. She was flirting with a high school kid. What's wrong with that? I did a lot of it myself."

"I hope you were in high school at the time. No, it's not that. It's—she's starting to get a reputation."

"Because of her relationship with the Imposter?"

"They were lovers."

"Miller says she was raped."

"I don't believe that."

"How old is Saranne? Sixteen, seventeen?"

"Sixteen."

"Then she was raped."

"I suppose."

"In any case, there were a lot of people taken in that were much older and wiser than Saranne." I looked Tracie straight in the eye when I spoke. "Why pick on her?"

"Convenience."

Saranne returned a few minutes later. She managed to serve us both without uttering a word, then swiftly disappeared. I took a bite of Grandma Miller's World-Famous Third-Pound Burger with Bleu Cheese, Lettuce, and Tomato and realized that her recommendation that I eat at home wasn't rudeness. Saranne had been simply warning me. The beef patty was burned along the edges yet cold in the center. The bun was dry, the lettuce wilted, the tomato this side of ripe, and the cheese tasted like something you spread with a dipper.

"I didn't think it was possible to screw up a cheeseburger," I said.

"Why do you think I ordered salad?" Tracie said. "You really don't want to eat here until the evening shift."

"Then why did you bring me?"

The answer came in a loud, braying voice. "You're back." It was followed by Miller, who appeared next to our table as if by magic. A blue sports coat over a powder blue shirt and blue jeans covered his large frame, and he might have been considered casual chic if not for the brown farm boots with leather laces.

"That tells me something," Miller said.

The expression on Miller's weathered face made it clear that he expected me to ask what that something was. I didn't. I'm not sure why. Lack of curiosity, I guess. He soon grew tired of waiting.

"I didn't appreciate having to explain myself to your friends from the FBI," Miller said.

I didn't have anything to say to that, either. My silence seemed to frustrate him.

"Have a seat, Mr. Miller," Tracie said. "McKenzie has a few questions."

I do? my inner voice asked.

Tracie must have heard my inner voice, because she quickly added, "Mr. Miller is the mayor of Libbie."

Yes, I do.

Still, I quickly recalled what he'd told me in the police station a few days earlier. Not *I'm the mayor.* Instead, he said, *I own most of what's worth owning around here.*

"That tells me something," I said aloud.

"Folks around here want someone running things that knows how to run things." He chuckled lightly, as if he were relating the punch line of a private joke.

Miller settled into an unclaimed chair, but only after he quickly surveyed the restaurant and the lawn outside the window. Probably he was looking for some small children to chase off, I told myself. Over his shoulder, I saw Saranne emerge from the kitchen, take one look at him, and retreat back inside.

"First tell me," Miller said. "Are you here to help catch the Imposter?"

"Yes."

"All right, then. I'll answer your questions. Shoot."

"What did he take you for?"

"Me? Not a dime."

"I meant the town."

"The town is fine." Miller shook his head like a Boy Scout leader about to tell his troop the proper way to tie a knot. "You doom-and-gloomers. Libbie is going to be fine. Do you know why?"

"The people," Tracie said. "The people in South Dakota, especially this part of South Dakota, are tough. If you want to live here you have to be tough. Tough and caring. People here are good neighbors. We take care of our own."

Miller looked at Tracie as if she were from another planet.

"No," he said slowly. "It's because we're the county seat. It happened back in 1921 after they carved up Harding and Butte counties. That was a few years before my time."

Just barely, my inner voice said.

"The old man told me about it. He was in on it. See, there was a convention. On the train ride to the convention, the boys from Libbie offered liquor to delegates who promised to vote for Libbie—this was at the beginning of Prohibition, and booze was hard to come by. Anyway, delegates got whiskey if they promised to vote for Libbie. That's how we got to be the county seat. Now the outlying towns are shrinking; their schools are closing, consolidating. Where do you think they are going to build the consolidated school? In the county seat. In ten years there are going to be only sixty-seven school districts in South Dakota. One for every county, plus an extra one for Sioux Falls. The same thing's happening with health care, law enforcement, the courts, social services. Same with everything. A lot of people are unhappy about it. What are they going to do? One community gets consolidated; the other communities get smaller."

Miller smiled. "I saw it coming," he said. "Saw it coming years ago. The big grain and livestock operations requiring fewer and fewer folks to operate them, crowding out the family farms, the small towns disappearing because they no longer have a reason to exist. Yeah, I saw it coming. That's why I wasn't all that surprised when Rush said he wanted to build an outlet mall here. Where else was he going to build it?"

"Except there was no mall," I said.

"We were taken, pure and simple."

"You don't seem too upset about it."

Miller smiled some more. He leaned in and spoke quietly. "If I picked you up and threw you through the window, would that prove how angry I am?" I didn't say if it would or wouldn't. He leaned back. "I'm too old to waste time crying over spilled milk. If you're asking if I hold a grudge, yeah, I hold a grudge. Anyone knows that, it should be you."

"How did it happen?"

"You mean, how did he play us?"

"Yes."

"The usual way. First he dazzled us with dollar signs, then he threatened to take them away. The rest is a little complicated."

"Does it need to be?"

"The national range for what is rated a regional shopping center is three hundred thousand to nine hundred thousand square feet. The syndicate Rush represented was seeking approximately seven hundred and fifty thousand square feet with room to expand. Parking is generally figured at three times the estimated floor area of the facility, so we were talking about eighty acres, total. Randisi—he's the one who owned the land." Miller gestured out the window toward the farmland across the highway. "Randisi refused to sell, wouldn't even consider it. Rush said he and his syndicate were prepared to go elsewhere. We insisted that we could acquire the land through eminent domain. He said he doubted his partners would be willing to wait while the case worked its way through the political system, maybe even the courts. Also, there was no guarantee that an arbitrator would fix the sales price at the amount he and his partners were willing to spend. And then there was the cost of infrastructure— sewers and the like—which was sure to escalate. To assure Rush and his partners that they would get the land at their price, we agreed to put funds matching the current cost per acre into an account in the Libbie bank and pay them the difference, if there was a difference."

"How much?"

"The average value of nonirrigated cropland in South Dakota is thirteen hundred and seventy-five dollars an acre. Eighty acres—we put up one hundred and ten thousand dollars, plus an additional one hundred thousand for infrastructure."

"That's what he stole? I thought it would be more than that."

"That's what he stole from us. I have no idea what other people in town might have put in."

"McKenzie," Tracie said, "our yearly fiscal budget is set at five hundred and forty-two dollars per resident. With twelve hundred and twenty-one residents, that works out to six hundred and sixty-two thousand dollars."

"You bet a third of your operating budget on a mall?"

"We weren't betting anything," Miller said. "We would have delivered the property at Rush's price. We wouldn't have lost a penny. Besides, do you have any idea how much income the mall would have generated for Libbie through property taxes? It would have funded most of our services. Hell, we would have been able to give folks free snowplowing."

While he spoke, Saranne emerged from the kitchen and began wiping tables and checking ketchup bottles.

"I notice that the mall would have been built across from your own property," I said.

"What of it?"

"Probably it would have increased traffic for your restaurant and service station and all the rest."

"So?"

"Property tax aside, I was just wondering if you would have been as insistent about putting up the money if the mall had been built somewhere else."

"Do you have something to say, McKenzie, or are you just talking?"

"I don't want to call you greedy—"

"Then don't."

"Only I wonder if that's why the Imposter picked this location. Because he knew he could count on your—let's call it your strong entrepreneurial spirit—to make his plan work."

"Are you saying I had something to do with this?"

Saranne moved closer to our table, obviously eavesdropping while pretending not to. I spoke a little louder for her benefit.

"If you had said no, Mr. Mayor, none of this would have happened."

"I did what I thought was best for the town."

"Everyone on the city council thought it was a good idea," Tracie said.

"The Imposter was counting on that. I wonder how he knew that he could."

When neither of them replied, I filled in the silence that followed.

"Miller, how much time did you spend with the Imposter?"

"I know where you're going with this, McKenzie. Chief Gustafson told me you thought Rush had an accomplice. Someone from Libbie. It ain't me."

From now on, let's not tell the chief any more than we have to, my inner voice told me.

"The Imposter needed a password to loot the escrow account. You're one of six people who knew the password."

"It ain't me."

"That doesn't answer my question," I said aloud. "How much time—"

"Very little. I spent very little time with him."

"Oh?"

"We spoke. We spoke a lot. It's not like we were friends, though."

"What did you speak about?"

"The mall."

"What else?"

"Just the mall."

"Did you ever have him over for dinner?"

"Yes. Once."

"Did he meet the family?"

"Leave my family out of this."

"What did you speak about then?"

"The mall."

"Okay."

"You don't believe me."

"Are you going to pay the town back for any of the money that they lost on this deal?"

"What? No. Why would I?"

"Could you pay it back if you had to?"

"What is that supposed to mean?"

"We live in uncertain economic times. Maybe you're over-extended. Maybe you need extra cash."

"I told you—" Miller stopped himself and closed his eyes. I never saw anyone actually count to ten before. When he opened his eyes, he said, "I will not be provoked."

I didn't believe him.

Miller stood slowly. Saranne was several tables behind him. She abruptly turned her back and moved away.

"You're looking for an accomplice," Miller said. "That's fine. You keep doing that. You'll tell me when you find him."

It was a command, not a question. Miller seemed surprised when I smiled disdainfully and shook my head.

"What's the magic word?" I said.

"Excuse me?"

"No, but it's close."

Miller's eyes swept from me to Tracie and back again. "Are you trying to be funny?"

"Here's the thing, Miller," I said. "I don't work for you. I don't like you. So either be polite, or fuck you."

"McKenzie," Tracie said.

"People don't talk to me like that," Miller said.

"Maybe if they did, their town wouldn't be on the brink of bankruptcy."

"McKenzie, please," Tracie said.

"I changed my mind," Miller said. "I think you should leave Libbie. The sooner the better."

"I don't care what you think," I said.

Miller stared at me as if I were an accident alongside the road. After a few moments, he shook his head slightly. "I will not be provoked." He turned and walked away.

"McKenzie, what are you doing?" Tracie wanted to know. "Mr. Miller is an important man in this town. Probably the most important."

"Who says?"

"I say. What was the point of insulting him like that?"

"Patience," I said.

Saranne didn't return to the table until Miller was long gone. When she did, she immediately began retrieving plates.

"How was the burger?" she said.

"Lousy," I told her.

"You really have to come in at night. The old man actually pays for a real cook then. He has specials, the cook. I get to sample them, so I can tell you what's good. Otherwise, you'll want to order the ribs. Our cook makes great ribs. Rush said they reminded him of the ribs you can get at Taste of Minnesota."

"He said that?"

"Uh-huh. Rush said every year around the Fourth of July he would go to Grant Park for Taste of Minnesota, and he always made a point of eating the ribs. You're from the Cities. Do you ever go to Taste of Minnesota?"

"Often."

"Are the ribs good?"

"Yes, they are."

"At least he told the truth about one thing."

"Did you spend much time with Rush?"

"Not as much time as people say I did." She glanced at Tracie. "Do you need anything else? Dessert?"

"Do you recommend dessert?" I said.

Saranne shook her head and smiled. "No."

"Well, then . . ."

"I'll be back in a minute."

Saranne was just out of earshot when Tracie spoke. "The enemy of my enemy is my friend," she said. "That's why you insulted Mr. Miller. To make an ally of his daughter."

"I have no idea what you're talking about," I said.

A few minutes later, Saranne returned with the bill. She set it in front of me. Tracie reached across the table and picked it up.

"I got it," she said.

"Whatever," Saranne said. "You know"—she was talking to me now—"you should be careful how you talk to the old man. He's mean."

"I'll keep that in mind."

"Maybe it's because he's so old."

"How old is he?"

"Over seventy."

"Must be tough for someone as young as you to have a father that old."

"His age isn't what makes it tough. It's not his time anymore,

and it pisses him off. He wishes Reagan was still president, arm-
ing the Contras in Nicaragua and firing air traffic controllers and
scaring hell out of the Russians."

"Long before you were born."

"That, too. My mother says he was a good person back then.
She says he was happy back then."

"How well did he get along with Rush?" I said.

"The other McKenzie? I don't think he liked him. Rush wore
expensive suits and real cuff links, and the old man thought that
was way too la-de-da for South Dakota. My mother liked him,
though, even liked the cuff links. When he came over for dinner
that one time, they talked up a storm, mostly about the Cities. Mom
was from the Twin Cities. 'Course, that just made it worse as far as
the old man was concerned, them liking each other. I gotta go. If
you come back for dinner, make 'em seat you in my section, okay?"

"Okay."

I watched as Saranne made her way back to the kitchen.

"How to win friends and influence people," Tracie said. "You
should give lessons."

I left my chair and made my way to the restroom.

"Leave a generous tip," I said over my shoulder.

I didn't use the facilities, yet I washed my hands just the same.
Afterward, I activated my cell phone and called a familiar number.

"Hello," Shelby said.

"Hi, Shel."

"McKenzie, where are you? Are you still in South Dakota?"

"I am."

"How's it going?"

"Not bad. Is Victoria around?"

"Upstairs."

"Can I speak to her?"

"Just a second."

A minute later, Victoria was on the phone. She spoke as if I had forced her to put her life on pause. "What is it?"

"How would you like to make a quick fifty bucks?"

"Do I have to do anything illegal?"

"Of course not."

"Dangerous?"

"No."

"What's the fun of that?"

"I want you to go online and find out if there are any high schools in Chicago that call their sports teams the Raiders."

"Do you think the Imposter's from Chicago?"

"You've been to Taste of Minnesota—"

"Where you can buy food from all those booths and they have free concerts."

"Do you remember where is it?"

"Well, yeah. On Harriet Island, down by the river in St. Paul."

"The Imposter said it was in Grant Park."

"The place in Chicago where President Obama gave his victory speech after he won the election?"

"Correct."

"I'm all over it."

"That's my girl. One more thing. What's your computer password?"

"My password? I'm not going to tell you my password."

"What I meant—if you wanted to hack into someone's Facebook account or something, what password would you use?"

"I don't know. Their name and birthday?"

"Yeah, that's what I was afraid of."

CHAPTER SEVEN

I met Tracie outside the entrance to Grandma Miller's. The bison was waxing poetic about the vistas of South Dakota.

Tracie said, "Where to now?"

The bison started singing "Home on the Range."

I pointed across the highway.

"Introduce me to Farmer Randisi," I said.

"I've never actually met the man."

"I thought you knew everyone around here."

"Randisi is a recluse. Or antisocial. I don't know what. He has no family, as far as I know. No friends. You never see him in town except for Sunday morning services, and even then he's in and out in a hurry, never stops to talk. He does his shopping—I don't know where he does his shopping, but it's not in Libbie."

My admiration for the Imposter was starting to grow.

"He picked his targets well, didn't he?" I said.

Randisi kept his property like he was expecting company. He lived in a pristine white clapboard house on a low hill at the end of a groomed gravel driveway. A rich, manicured lawn surrounded the house, and green and purple fields of alfalfa bordered that. The outbuildings were recently painted, and what machinery I could see, although well used, looked like it had just come off the dealership lot. There was a turnaround at the top of the driveway. Large stones painted white bordered a small garden planted in the center of the turnaround. In the center of the garden was a flagpole. Old Glory flapped listlessly in the breeze.

I parked the Audi between the flagpole and the farmhouse. We hadn't been in the car long enough for it to cool properly, yet it was still far more comfortable than the heat that greeted us when we left it. The sun was now high in the cloudless sky, and it glared down on us as if it were bad-tempered. The faint breeze that caused the flag to sway brought no relief. I saw large birds circling off to my left, and I wondered if they were buzzards—they felt like buzzards. Sweat trickled down my spine to my waist as I headed toward Randisi's back door. Tracie trailed behind.

I knocked once, and the door flew open.

Randisi was standing on the other side of it.

He was pointing a rust-spotted, long-barreled .38 Colt at my head and smiling as if he had played an April Fool's prank on me.

"What do you want?" he said.

I had been taking martial arts training on and off ever since the police academy. Some instructors were better than others, yet even the worst of them preached the same sermon—act without hesitation. Hesitation will get you killed.

Randisi was holding the gun in his right hand. I slid to my left even as I seized the wrist holding the gun and angled it away so I was out of the discharge line. I stepped in closer, took hold of the barrel of the gun with my other hand, and pushed it toward Randisi, rolling it against his thumb—the thumb is the weakest point of the hand. The gun was now pointing at his chest, but I kept twisting it until he let go of the butt. I released his wrist and shoved him hard backward into the kitchen. He lost his balance but didn't fall. He grabbed his thumb with his left hand and said something that sounded like "Huh?" I released the spring-loaded latch on the left side of the gun, swung out the cylinder, tilted the gun upward, shook out all six cartridges onto the kitchen floor, slapped the cylinder back in place, and handed the Colt butt first to Randisi—all in the time it took to say it.

"Hi," I said. "I hope I'm not disturbing you." I tried to keep my voice light and cheerful. I doubt I succeeded. My mouth was dry, my heart was drumming, and I suddenly felt out of breath.

Randisi looked down at the gun that he now held with both hands and then back at me. He was a short, compact man with thick shoulders and a worldly face and eyes that looked as if they had seen things. It was easy to imagine him helping to pull a neighbor's car out of a ditch in the rain.

"How did you do that?" he said.

"Practice," I told him. "Do you always draw down on people who come to your door?"

Randisi slipped the gun into the waistband of his jeans. "It's legal," he said. "State says I can carry."

"It doesn't say you can shoot people."

"What do you know about shooting people?"

"Far too much."

"You a cop?"

"In my misspent youth."

"What about this one?"

He gestured at Tracie. I had forgotten about her. She was standing six feet behind me, blinking in the hard sunlight, her face flushed. Heat—I assume it was heat—had covered her body with a mist of perspiration; her skin glistened, and her eyes held an almost giddy light.

"She's a model," I said.

"Model?" he repeated.

There's something about that word that makes men silly. It transformed Randisi from a menacing recluse into a gleeful teenager.

He quickly removed the Colt from his waistband, set it on the kitchen counter, and nudged it away. Almost simultaneously, he brushed past me, stepped outside of the farmhouse, paused, gave Tracie a slow, bold stare of appraisal, and extended his hand. "I'm Mike Randisi," he said.

Tracie smiled, only I could see that her heart wasn't in it. She shook Randisi's hand as if it were something she'd rather not touch.

"Sorry about the gun," he said. "I've been getting some threats lately, and a fellow can't be too careful."

"Threats?" I said.

Randisi gently set two fingers and a thumb on Tracie's elbow and urged her toward the door. "You don't want to be standing out here in this heat. Come inside now, where it's cool."

Tracie gave me a look as if she expected me to wrestle Randisi to the ground and pummel him about the head and shoulders. Instead, I stepped back to give them plenty of room to enter the house. She gave me an NHL-quality elbow as they passed.

Once inside, Randisi led Tracie to a chair in a living room that looked as though its furnishings had been lifted intact from a department store showroom. After proceeding down the list, offering her everything from water to Scotch, which Tracie politely declined, he stepped back against the wall so he could get a good look at her sitting in his chair in his living room.

The man definitely needs to get out more, my inner voice told me.

After a few silent moments, Randisi said, "I'm sorry. We weren't properly introduced." He crossed the distance to the chair and again offered Tracie his hand. "I'm Mike Randisi."

Again, Tracie shook Randisi's hand reluctantly. She didn't remind him that he had introduced himself just moments before, and I didn't, either.

"Tracie Blake," she said.

For a recluse, Randisi seemed awfully sociable.

"I'm Rushmore McKenzie," I said.

I was standing near the entrance to the living room. Randisi looked at me as if he had forgotten I was there.

"What can I do for you?" he said.

"Tell me about the threats," I said.

"Why? Are you going to do something about them?"

"I might."

From his expression, I don't think he believed me.

"It doesn't matter," Randisi said. "I haven't gotten any for about a week now."

Since the Imposter skipped town, my inner voice said.

"What were they about?" I said aloud.

"Ahh, people saying they were going to teach me a lesson; that they were going to run me off, burn me out, beat me up, bury me in a shallow grave. It was all talk. I got phone calls, I got letters, yet no one ever came near me and, as far as I know, no one ever set foot on my land."

"Did you never consider selling your property?" Tracie said.

There was a note of admiration in her voice. Randisi smiled broadly when he heard it.

"Oh, hell," he said. "I might've considered it if someone had actually made me an offer."

"Wait," I said. "No one offered to buy your land?"

"No." Randisi shook his head vigorously in case I misunderstood him. "I didn't know anyone wanted my land. Hadn't even heard about that shopping mall that folks wanted to build out here until I started getting the threats."

"No one calling himself Rushmore McKenzie—"

"I thought you were Rushmore McKenzie."

"Came to see you?"

"No. You want to tell me what's going on?"

I quickly explained.

"That doesn't make any sense," Randisi said.

I agreed with him.

"I wonder," Randisi said.

"What?"

"There was this fella—I remember a fella who looked a little like you. He drove up to the place a while back, got out of his car, walked around the car once, got back in, and drove off. I have no idea what that was about. I figured he was lost. Or nuts. Think it was him? Think he was looking the place over so he could claim he was here?"

"I don't know."

"Mr. Randisi," Tracie said, "why didn't you say something when you started getting the threats? Why didn't you call the police? Why didn't you come into town?"

"I don't do too good in town," he said. "I have a touch of the agoraphobia. I'm pretty good out here, in my own house, on my own land. In town, in stores and restaurants and church, places that aren't, you know, wide open, that aren't easy to escape from, sometimes I get panic attacks. I know it's silly, and I've talked to people about it. I've tried exposure therapy and cognitive therapy and cognitive-behavioral therapy, only nothing seems to work all that well. Now they have me on sertraline, but that doesn't do much for me, either. I can't even make myself go into town to get my prescription filled, so there you are."

Randisi was visibly disappointed to see us go. He suggested that he might give Tracie a call sometime to learn how this business with the mall went, and Tracie said she thought that was a fine idea.

"In a couple of days," Randisi said.

"A couple of days," Tracie said.

"Or maybe later today."

"Later today would be fine."

In the car, she said, "I like him."

"He's not the person people thought he was," I said.

"He's not the person I thought he was," Tracie said, which was more to the point. "If he doesn't call me, maybe I'll call him. If you don't mind."

"Why should I mind?"

She didn't answer, just looked out the window until we reached the end of Randisi's long driveway and hung a right on the highway.

"Now what?" Tracie said. "Do you want to meet the other city council members?"

"Who was the first person the Imposter spoke to about the mall?"

Tracie gave it a moment's thought before answering. "Ed Bizek, the city manager. He's also the city's director of economic development."

"Rural flight," Bizek said. "We're fighting rural flight. Eighty-nine percent of the cities in the United States have fewer than three thousand people, and they're getting smaller all the time. Six states, according to the numbers I last saw, six states—Nebraska, Kansas, Oklahoma, Iowa, North Dakota, and South Dakota—have lost over five hundred thousand residents, half of them with college degrees. Fighting rural flight. That's what my job is all about. At least that's what it was about."

"Was?" I said.

"I expect to be fired at the next city council meeting."

"Why?"

"Mistakes were made. Money was lost. Someone has to pay for that."

"You?"

"The council sure isn't going to blame itself."

He was probably right, I decided. Especially since City Council-woman Tracie Blake was sitting in the backseat of Bizek's car and didn't say a word to dispute his theory.

"You know, I did check him out," Bizek said. "The Imposter, I mean. I called his office in the Cities. I went to the Web site. I interviewed his references. We had a conference call with Rush's other investors. The city council was there. I even called a couple of the major retailers that Rush said were interested in becoming anchor tenants. They all said that they had a strict policy against commenting on future expansion, but no one set any alarm bells to ringing, either. There was no reason to believe, to not believe . . . Later, after Rush disappeared, I checked again. The investors were gone, and so were the references. The Web site had been taken down, the office phone just kept on ringing, and the retailers, they all had a strict policy against commenting on future expansion. Even then I couldn't believe it." He looked at Tracie's reflection in his rear-view mirror. "I guess I would fire me, too."

She didn't so much as smile in reply.

Bizek drove his car to a halt at a four-way stop. He surprised me by putting it into park and leaning back against his door.

"Of course, it was too good to be true," he said.

I glanced through the back window of the car, looking for the traffic that he was blocking. There wasn't any.

"I think I knew it was too good to be true, even when Rush was telling me about it," Bizek said. "He was projecting sales of four hundred to five hundred dollars a square foot, though. I had to listen, and the more I listened—it really would have improved our way of life. Right now people drive, some of them drive hundreds of miles, to go shopping for furniture, for appliances, for clothes and whatnot. Think of the difference it would make if people could get what they need right here. No long drives, no waste of time and gas. The revenue we've been losing to other communities, to Rapid City and whatnot, we would have kept that revenue. Everyone in town would have benefited."

"Not everyone," Tracie said.

Bizek looked at her in his rearview mirror.

"Yeah, well," he said, as if it were a topic not worth discussing. He sat straight in his seat, put the car in gear, and drove through the intersection.

"Still, the town should be all right," Bizek said. "Look."

He pointed to a blond-stone building to his left. The sign above the door read NORTHERN STAR NURSING HOME.

"We've got health care," he said. "We've got assisted living. We just finished up an expansion of the Libbie Medical Clinic down on the end of First Street, which has two full-time and two part-time nurse practitioners and roving doctors. People will move to a small town to retire if you have the medical facilities."

Bizek continued his slow motor tour of Libbie, showing me a lot more than I had seen during my hike around the town's perimeter that morning. There was a two-screen movie theater, a shoe store, a beauty parlor, a barbershop, an auto mechanic, a farm equipment dealer, a livestock sales barn, UPS—just about everything a small town needs except for a lumberyard.

"That was my biggest priority," Bizek said. "To get a lumberyard. I worked on it for years. Talked to Home Depot, Menards, just about everyone you can think of. They all said, the big chains said, they weren't interested in a town this size. Then I found a guy, a retired contractor—he was willing to build a lumberyard here. He was going to run it with his sons." Bizek glanced at Tracie in his rearview again. "Only the city council wouldn't dip into the development fund to help him out. They said it wasn't a good investment considering our limited tax base. Still, I'd like to get a lumberyard here."

Bizek made a couple of right turns and slowly drove past the industrial park I'd discovered that morning.

"I'm particularly proud of this," he said. "The middle building, that houses Frank Communications. It's a call center that handles inbound customer service calls and outbound sales calls, mostly for Fortune 500 companies. This guy, Ira Frank, millionaire, lives in Phoenix, has call centers scattered all across the country. I heard that he was from South Dakota, so I went to see him, went on my own dime, and talked him into moving a center here. It wasn't hard. Frank likes South Dakota, likes the work ethic we have here." Bizek looked into his rearview mirror again. "He said the fact that I drove down to Phoenix to talk to him without even an appointment was a good example of that."

"We don't need any more seven-dollar-an-hour jobs," Tracie said.

"Microsoft and Apple are not going to waltz into Libbie with high-paying jobs for two hundred and fifty skilled, college-educated workers," Bizek said.

Tracie had nothing to say to that.

"Would you like a tour?" Bizek said. "I'm sure we can arrange a quick tour."

"Why not?" I said.

Tracie rolled her eyes.

Perry Neske liked his job. He managed the second shift at Frank Communications, the 4:00 P.M. to 2:00 A.M. shift, and his smile became broad and his eyes shiny when Tracie asked him to give us the fifty-cent tour. That threw me a little bit, Tracie asking and not Bizek. Instead, Bizek kept his distance, like a child afraid of drawing attention to himself for fear the adults would ask him to leave.

"Business is ramping up," Neske said. "We expect it'll get even better as we get deeper into the political season, doing campaign surveys, opinion polls, trolling for contributions."

I was surprised by how open Neske was. Tracie had explained

to Bizek who I was and what I was doing in Libbie. She hadn't said a word to Neske, though. Still, he proved as forthcoming as if we were old friends picking up a conversation that had been on pause for about thirty seconds. While Neske spoke, Bizek carefully surveyed the people around him as if he were looking for someone and didn't want to be caught at it.

"In telemarketing, ninety-nine-point-nine percent of your success is the sound of your voice," Neske said. "Can you read a script, can you talk well, are you outgoing, do you sound upbeat and sincere?"

All around us was the steady hum of conversation, and for a while I thought we had caught the employees conversing with each other during a shift change.

"Oh, no," Neske said. "They're working."

Neske led us down a corridor between soft-wall cubicles and gestured at the men and women that we found there. They were all wearing headsets and talking to customers. Some of them were sitting at desks, others were standing, and still others paced while they worked. Bizek drifted away, looking over the top of some of the cubicle walls.

"We ask our employees to dress in what I call business casual," Neske said. "You might think that's odd. After all, they work on the phone. No one sees them. But I think you need to ask people to dress professionally if you expect them to act professionally. On Fridays, though—if you bring in a can of food or packaged goods for charity you can dress down on Fridays."

"I notice that most of your employees are pretty young," I said.

"They're either young or old," Neske said. "We have a high turnover. Partly it's the entry-level pay that comes with the job. It's not enough to support a family, so you get kids starting out or retirees looking to supplement pensions or Social Security. The other thing is, some people have a tough time handling rejection. You go a few days without a sale and it can get you down. Some people take it personally."

Bizek glanced over the top of yet another cubicle. Neske spun to face him.

"Are you looking for someone?" he said.

Bizek took a tentative step backward.

"She's not here," Neske said.

The hum of conversation suddenly ceased, and heads peered over the walls of the cubicles.

Bizek's eyes lowered until he was staring at the floor.

I glanced at Tracie, hoping for enlightenment. She pressed an index finger to her lips and watched the scene unfold.

"I should kill you," Neske said.

"Maybe you should," Bizek said. He raised his head. "But I don't think the lady would like that."

"I should kill you both."

Bizek took a step forward. If he had seemed repentant before, he now looked defiant. "Try it," he said.

Tracie grabbed my arm just above the elbow and squeezed. "McKenzie, do something," she said.

"Want me to go out for popcorn? Milk Duds?"

Bizek took another step forward. Neske moved to meet him. They stood like that for a long moment, reminding me of professional wrestlers giving each other the mad-dog stare. Only nothing happened, and after about six seconds I knew nothing would. The more people think about a fight, the less likely they are to start one.

"You should leave now," Neske said.

Bizek sneered as if it had been his idea all along. He spun around slowly and walked from the building, moving as if he had all the time in the world. Tracie, Neske, and I watched him go, along with all the heads peering over the cubicle walls. A moment later, the hum of conversation returned to its original volume.

Neske excused himself and disappeared into his office. I turned to
Tracie.

"I think we just lost our ride," I said.

The air was hot and hard to breathe. If that wasn't bad enough,
Tracie's shortcut back to my Audi was along a dirt road. Wind and
passing cars roiled up the dust, and the dust forced me to cough to
clear my throat.

"So what was that all about?" I asked.

"Perry and Ed?"

"No, Penn and Teller."

Tracie tilted her head and frowned; her hair was shiny in the
slant of the afternoon sun.

"Perry Neske was born and raised in Libbie," she said. "He left
several times, but he always came back. The last time he came back,
he brought a wife. Her name is Dawn. She hates everything about
Libbie."

"Except for Ed."

"Except for Ed."

"And everyone knows it."

"What can I say?"

"Where the hell is my car?"

Tracie pointed down the street. I followed her finger, only it
didn't lead me to the government building where I had parked the
Audi when we first went to visit Bizek. Instead, she was pointing
at an ice cream parlor.

"My treat," she said.

Back in the good ol' days—whenever that was—I'm told that
people would gather around the cracker barrel in the general store
and talk it over. That's something else I've never seen, a cracker
barrel. In Libbie, they gathered at U Scream Ice Cream Parlor.

There were about half a dozen people inside when we arrived, and another half dozen joined while we were there. I sat nursing a hot fudge sundae while the group discussed a number of subjects ranging from the economy to what's the matter with kids today. After a while, I said, "What about that damn mall?"

I waited for someone to ask who I was, yet no one did.

"Yeah, the mall," the man called Craig said. "Ol' Ed really screwed that one up."

"I hear that's not all he's screwing," said another man whose name I didn't know.

"Now, now, now," said Craig, who chuckled just the same.

The owner of the ice cream joint was wearing a white smock with the name RON stitched in red over the breast pocket. "Good riddance," he said. "A mall would have killed downtown Libbie."

"Nah," said a farmer sitting in the corner. "It woulda just moved it to the intersection."

"A mall would have turned the city into a ghost town," Ron said. "Instead of owning our own stores, we would have become greeters at one of theirs."

A woman named Joyce agreed. "Build that mall and we wouldn't even be a town no more," she said. "We'd be an area. The area around the mall."

"Woulda brought a lot of folks to town, don't you think, from all over," said Craig.

"It would have brought people to the mall," said Ron. "They'd never set foot inside Libbie."

"I gotta tell ya," said the man without a name. "It would have been nice to have shopping close."

Ron gave him a look that could have melted his ice cream.

"Losing the mall leaves Libbie in an awfully tough spot, doesn't it?" I said.

Heads turned. The expression on several faces suggested that they thought they knew who I was but couldn't remember my name. The fact I was sitting with Tracie probably helped, although she was staring at me as if I had broken one of the more important commandments.

"What tough spot?" Ron said.

"Some of the downtown businesses invested in the mall," said the farmer. "They were all set to move, leaving us flat."

"No," said Ron.

"It's true," Craig said. "I heard some people lost a lot of money when the deal collapsed, and maybe now they're in trouble, too."

"Not me," Ron said.

"Gotta sting, though," Joyce said. "So many businesses ready to abandon downtown for a mall."

"What businesses?" said Ron. "I don't know of any businesses. You, Tracie, you know of any businesses?"

"I'm not at liberty to say," Tracie replied.

"But there were some," the farmer said.

"Some," Tracie said.

"See?" the farmer said.

Another man—I called him Bob because of the way he continually nodded his head—said, "A mall never would have lasted here. After six months the novelty woulda worn off and people woulda gone back to their old ways."

"I don't think so," Joyce said.

"Old people, they have their habits," Bob said. "They like what's familiar."

"Old folks are like everyone else," said the man with no name. "They don't want to pay any more for stuff than they have to, and malls, they have lower prices, don't they?"

"Some do," Craig said.

"I'm telling you," Bob said. "Old folks can get kinda overwhelmed by the big stores. Kinda frightens them. They'd stay away."

From there the conversation veered to how many older people lived in Libbie, and from there to exactly how old is old. It was about then that Tracie suggested we leave. I think the ages that her neighbors were tossing about made her uncomfortable.

The air was still hot and heavy. If the sun had moved a centimeter in the past hour, I hadn't noticed. We were finally closing in on the Audi, and I was contemplating a dip in the Pioneer Hotel's pool.

"What do you think?" Tracie asked.

"I'm surprised you've been able to keep your losses secret for so long," I said. "It can't last, you know. Libbie's finances are public record, aren't they? Plus, you have so many people who seem to know exactly what's going on."

"We're hoping you can help us get the money back before we have to report our losses. Oh, for the record, Ronny Radosevich, the owner of U Scream? He invested thirty-five thousand dollars in the mall. He just doesn't want anyone to know. But that's not what I meant."

"What did you mean?"

"Do you think fifty is the new thirty, like they said?"

The question made me laugh.

"No, I don't," I said.

"Me, neither," Tracie said. "I might change my mind when I get there, though. You know, McKenzie, I don't have a problem with growing old. I really don't. Not if you have someone to grow old with. This town, it's not easy when you're alone."

"No town is."

"If you have someone, though, someone to grow old with, it's a fine place to live."

That sounded like the beginning of a conversation about relationships, probably my least favorite topic. Fortunately, Tracie didn't pursue it. Instead, she fell into a kind of wistful silence that lasted until we reached my car and I drove her to her own car parked outside the Pioneer.

"What are your plans for tonight?" she said.

"I haven't thought much about it beyond a dip in the pool."

"If you should get—restless, give me a call."

"I will," I said. Yet we both knew I wouldn't.

CHAPTER EIGHT

I don't like to eat alone in public, especially in formal dining rooms like the one in the Pioneer Hotel. I'm convinced it makes me seem like a pathetic and friendless creature. I also tend to eat too fast when people are watching—yes, I know they're not, but I *feel* like they are. I tore into my New York strip, consuming half of it in about five minutes before a woman appeared at my table. Because of her good bone structure and trim figure, she seemed taller than she was. She had brown close-cropped hair, a serious mouth, and dark eyes with little flickering lights in them that reminded me of a candle on a breezy night.

Okay, Libbie, my inner voice said. *Now you're just showing off.*

"Are you Rushmore McKenzie?" she said.

She was wearing dark blue slacks and a powder blue shirt that looked tailored and holding a baseball-style cap that combined both colors. The name Quik-Time Foods was stitched over one shirt pocket. Behind her, I could see Sharren Nuffer standing in the arched doorway that led from the hotel lobby to the dining room, her arms crossed over her chest. She was watching intently.

"I am," I said.

"May I sit down?"

I gestured at the chair opposite me. She took it.

"I apologize for disturbing your meal," she said.

"Not a problem." I couldn't help glancing at the other diners. I felt better now that the woman was there, even though I had no idea who she was. It was a problem soon rectified.

"I'm Dawn Neske."

"Mrs. Perry Neske?"

She winced a little at the title of "Mrs."

"Yes," she said.

"What can I do for you?"

"It's more about what I can do for you."

The remark made me lean back in my chair.

"What can you do for me?" I said.

"I like that you asked that question without smirking."

I had nothing to say to that.

"I'm told that you're looking for Rushmore McKenzie, the man who pretended to be you, the one who ripped off the city. I want to help you find him."

A couple of things hit me at once. The first, that she knew who I was and what I was doing in Libbie. The other, that she knew the Imposter had defrauded the town. She didn't get either tidbit from her husband. Bizek must have told her, and he must have told her within the past couple of hours.

"How?" I said.

"I know his real name. It's Nicholas Hendel."

That made me sit up. I carry a pen and a small notebook in the pocket of my sports coat—a habit left over from my days with the cops. I took both out and started writing.

"Do you have the correct spelling?"

She did.

"Do you know where he's from?"

"No," she said. "Just his name."

"How do you know his name?"

"I looked into his wallet. Everything he had in his wallet said Rushmore McKenzie except for a credit card that he had tucked into a secret compartment, although, when you think about it, there are no secret compartments in a wallet."

"The name Nicholas Hendel was on the credit card?"

"Yes."

"Which credit card company?"

She told me. I wrote it down.

"How did you get access to his wallet?"

"After we finished fucking he went into the bathroom. I looked then. Does that shock you?"

Geezus, not another one, my inner voice said.

"A big-city boy like me?" I said aloud. "Hardly."

"I'm not from a big city," Dawn said. "I'm from a town where the biggest building is two stories high. When I met Perry, we both worked at the same call center in Franklin, which is another shitty little town just down the highway from where I lived. I married him, and I swear to God, I meant to stick with him. I would have, too, if only he had told me the truth. He promised he would take me away from small-town life, from the call center. Instead, he brought me here. Different name, same bullshit."

I gestured at the name stitched to her pocket.

"You don't work at the call center," I said.

"I couldn't do it. I couldn't go back to that. Instead, I work for this company that delivers groceries to shut-ins and the terminally lazy. They call in with their lists, and we shop for them and deliver their groceries to their doors."

"At least the job gets you outside."

"That's the only good thing about it."

"Why did you take up with Rush?"

"He . . . We . . . I thought he was exciting."

"More exciting than Ed Bizek?"

"You know about that?"

"Everyone knows about that."

"Small fucking towns, small fucking minds."

"If you say so."

"I know what you think of me. Only I wouldn't be this way if Perry had kept his promise."

"If you say so."

"Look, I came here to do you a favor."

"I appreciate it," I said. "I'm just wondering why you're doing it."

"Because I don't want Ed to lose his job, okay? Because I don't want him to have to move away. Is that reason enough?"

"So it's about Ed."

"It's about me. If he left Libbie, I would just die."

"If you're so concerned, why didn't you tell him about Rush when you first learned the truth?"

"I tried. I told him that Rush couldn't be trusted. Only I couldn't tell him how I knew—I couldn't tell him . . . I didn't want him to know I had cheated on him. You're not going to tell anyone, are you? About me and Rush?"

"Who would I tell?"

"Ed."

Not her husband, I thought.

"No," I said. "I won't tell anyone."

"Thank you. I hope you find Rush. I really do."

Dawn rose from her chair and had started to move away when I stopped her with a question.

"Why did you look in the wallet?" I said.

She hesitated before answering. "I wanted to know if he was married. He said he wasn't."

"Did he tell you he was going to take you away from all of this?"

"Sure. Men always tell a girl what she wants to hear. If it'll get them what they want, they'll say anything."

I nodded as if I believed her.

Sharren Nuffer waited until Dawn had left the dining room before she approached my table.

"What did she want?" she asked.

"Who?"

"Who? Dawn Neske."

"Understanding," I said. "She wanted understanding."

"Did you give her any?"

"What are you so angry about?"

Instead of answering, Sharren sat across from me and pointed at my meal. "How's the steak?"

"Quite good," I said. To prove it, I consumed a forkful, and then another while she watched.

"I was married three times, and not once did I cheat on my husband," Sharren said. "Not once, although that didn't stop them from cheating on me. I want you to know that."

"Why?"

"I don't want you to think I'm like Dawn. Or Tracie."

"What did the Imposter tell you to get you to go to bed with him?"

"Nothing. I had an itch and I let him scratch it. Simple as that. There was nothing dishonest about it."

"Sure."

Sharren stood abruptly.

"Not all of us are lucky in love, McKenzie," she said. "Some of us have to take what we can get."

When she left, she followed the same path from the dining room that Dawn had followed. As I watched her go, I had to admit that Sharren was right. Sex between unmarried consenting adults who don't give a damn about each other isn't necessarily bad. It just isn't any good.

What I wanted to do next was illegal. That meant I couldn't call Bobby Dunston, or the sergeant in the Minneapolis Police Department gang unit that I sometimes paid for information. There was no way I was going to contact Chief Gustafson, either, the blabbermouth. That left only one contact.

"Schroeder Private Investigations, how may I help you," the receptionist said.

"Greg Schroeder, please," I said.

"Mr. Schroeder is unavailable at the moment. May I connect you with—"

"Tell him it's McKenzie."

"Oh, Mr. McKenzie. Just a moment, please."

Greg Schroeder never answered his own phone, and he rarely took calls he wasn't expecting, which was odd when you considered his line of work. Yet he always had time for me. The reason was simple. Most private investigations these days involve the use of computers, something old-school, trench-coat detectives like Schroeder disdain. I, on the other hand, have offered him work over the years that not only got him out of the office; it put guns in his hands.

"McKenzie," he said after the receptionist patched me through. "We were just talking about you."

"You were?"

"Yeah, me and some of the boys hanging around the ol' watercooler. Rumor has it you were jacked by a couple of cowboys and you didn't shoot either one of them. What's with that?"

"The boys" was what he called his operatives, men and women alike, most of them ex-cops, deputies, Feds, and at least one MP.

The number he employed at any one time was determined by the amount of business he had, and lately business had been very good. The economy wasn't what it could be, and that made everyone from housewives to corporate executives nervous. The more nervous they got, the better for guys like Schroeder.

"What can I say, Greg? I've become more conventional as I age."

"Yeah, that's what we thought, too. What do you need?"

"I need a favor."

"Favor? Is that a word?"

"I meant I need you to do a job for which I expect to pay your normal rate."

"Now we're talking."

"I want you to find a man named Nicholas Hendel."

"Okay."

"He has a credit card."

"Okay."

I told Schroeder the name of the credit card company.

"Okay," he said.

"That's it."

"What do you mean, that's it?"

"That's all I have."

"C'mon."

"No, wait. He might be from Chicago."

"McKenzie—"

"How long do you think it'll take to get a line on him?"

"This is just some damn paper chase. Ah, McKenzie. I expected more from you."

"You know, Greg, not every job can be a running gun battle."

"I appreciate that, but it's been so long."

"What do you mean? I let you stick a gun in a guy's ear just last May."

"Oh, gee, what fun."

"I promise, the next shooting I come across, I'll give you a call. In the meantime—"

"Yeah, yeah, yeah. I'll pass this off to the geeks, but it occurs to me, to get what you ask we might have to do some hacking. Might have to run a flimflam on the credit card company."

"Flimflam? Is that the new computer slang?"

"I don't know from fucking computer slang. I'm just saying it's illegal. It's dangerous."

"Your point is?"

"It's gonna cost you more than the normal rate."

"Fair enough."

"This Nicholas Hendel, is he one of the cowboys that snatched you? Cuz if he is, we have a rate for that, too, if you know what I mean."

I knew exactly what he meant. I also knew the rate—five thousand dollars. In cash.

"Call me when you have something," I said.

After dining, I went to my room. There was nothing on TV that interested me, so I turned to the clock radio provided by the hotel. The Minnesota Twins were on the West Coast, and I was hoping to pick up the game. I found a station that was part of the Twins network—KGFX, an AM station out of Pierre that called itself South Dakota's Pioneer Radio Station. Only the signal kept fading in and out. I thought I'd have better luck in my Audi, but the reception on First Street was just as iffy.

The buildings on the west side of the street cast shadows that touched the buildings on the east side. The sky was glaring yellow, and then—boom—as the sun set it became royal blue turning to purple, and stars appeared on the eastern horizon. It became perceptibly cooler, and I was glad I was wearing my sports jacket. Radio reception improved, and while I still couldn't dial in Pierre, the

signal from the ESPN affiliate out of Bismarck, North Dakota—
KXMR-AM—was steady and clear. I sat with my windows down,
listening to the pregame show, John Gordon talking up the Twins'
young pitching staff, while the town came alive around me.

The lights of the movie theater glittered in the windows of the
buildings around it. A couple of cars parked across the street from
the theater. Teenagers, an older couple, and a family of four hurried
inside. A small girl walked past my car between her mother and
father, holding hands with each of them, pulling them forward.
They, too, disappeared inside the theater. A few minutes later, a
teenager came out of the theater and changed the movie poster in
the display case out front. He went back inside and then returned
with a long pole that he used to switch letters on the marquee,
taking one down, putting one up.

Traffic grew heavier. Most of the cars came into town and parked,
and most of the drivers and passengers in them went into Café
Rossini and another tavern down the street called Thorn's Tap.
Other cars came, went, and came back again. I saw a Chevy Malibu
four times and a Ford Taurus twice. Two teenaged boys wearing leather jackets and T-shirts walked quickly past my Audi. A
pickup screeched to a stop next to them. The boys climbed into
the bed of the pickup. The tires screeched again as the vehicle
pulled away; farm boys doing what farm boys—and city boys—all
across the country do on a Friday night, cruising. A group of girls
queued up in front of the theater but didn't go in; another gathered
in front of a clothing store that was closed. The vehicles always
slowed when they drove past the girls. Two kids riding bicycles
peeled out of the alley between the American Family Insurance
and the H&R Block offices. They also slowed when they wheeled
past the girls, but the girls chased them off.

My cell phone rang. A familiar voice reminded me how far I was
from home.

"Hi, McKenzie," Nina said.

"Hey. What's going on?"

"I was just about to ask you the same question."

·"I'm just sitting in my car catching the action in downtown Libbie."

"It sounds like you're listening to the ball game."

"That, too."

Another car passed, driving slowly. It found a space farther down the block and parked. A lone female got out. Even from that distance, I was impressed by the shortness of her skirt and the tightness of her sleeveless shirt.

"How are things in Libbie?" Nina said.

"Do you mean here in sunny Sin City?"

"It can't be as bad as all that."

"The place is crawling with rascals and scoundrels."

The young woman moved slowly down the sidewalk on the far side of the street. She stopped outside the entrance to Café Rossini and looked into the window. A moment later, she turned and continued up the sidewalk. The pickup returned, and the two teenagers in the back called to her. She lifted her face, and for a moment I could see it clearly. Saranne Miller. She didn't reply to the teenagers, and the pickup drove out of town.

"What are you going to do about it?" Nina said.

"Nothing," I told her. "You know me. I'm a passive, go-with-the-flow, no-need-to-rock-the-boat kinda guy."

"McKenzie, you're passive the way Chief Little Crow was passive, and he and his Sioux warriors burned down half the state of Minnesota."

"With good cause, I might add."

"Nonetheless."

Saranne continued along the sidewalk, moving as if she were window shopping, her thighs and legs and arms hard white in the moonlight. Two men stepped out of the Café Rossini. They paused in the doorway and watched her. Their heads tilted toward each other as if they were afraid of being overheard when they spoke, and then they began moving in the same direction.

"It's not my town," I said.

"How long are you going to stay there?"

"I don't know yet."

"Are you any closer to finding the Imposter?"

"I might have a lead, but I don't know if it'll go anywhere. I have Greg Schroeder working on it."

"Oh," Nina said. She was a little afraid of Schroeder. Then again, so was I.

Saranne paused. She glanced at the men. The men kept moving toward her. Farther down the street, a man stepped out of Thorn's Tap, went to his car, started it up, and drove off. A car parked a few spaces behind him pulled away from the curve and followed. I couldn't see the driver, but I did notice the emblem of the Libbie City Police Department painted on the door. So did the two men. They turned abruptly and moved in the opposite direction. That lasted until the cop car's taillights became tiny red dots in the distance. Then they turned back. Saranne had disappeared into the mouth of the alley. The two men followed her.

"Honey," I said, "something just came up. I gotta go."

"Will you call me later?"

"Sure."

Nina might have said more, but I deactivated my phone and didn't hear.

Outside of the Audi, with the radio off, I heard church music, a choir practicing, singing sweet and clear, although I couldn't see a church. It took me back to St. Mark's Church in St. Paul, my face washed, my hair combed, Mom on one side, Dad on the other, sun pouring through stained glass, the choir sitting in pews to the right of the altar, the organ in the loft in back of the church. The image disappeared as soon as I thought about the guns I had hidden beneath the false floor of my trunk. I hurried to the alley without them. It was Libbie, South Dakota, I reminded myself, not North Minneapolis.

The alley was narrow and well lit at the front and back, but it was dark in the middle, and that's where the voices came from.

"Stop it," Saranne said. "Stop it, please."

"Whaddaya mean stop?" a male voice replied.

"No, no, please."

"Whaddaya mean, no?"

"Leave me alone."

There was a brick on the pavement that didn't seem to belong to either of the buildings flanking the alley. I scooped it up.

"I said stop it," Saranne said. "Please, don't do this."

"Don't do what?" the second man said. "I thought you wanted to party."

"No," Saranne said.

Neither of the two men saw me approach. Neither heard me until I spoke.

"Get away from her."

One of the men moved to intercept me.

"What do you want?" he said.

I spun counterclockwise, my right arm extended, and fired the brick into the man's chest, throwing almost underhanded, thinking Dan Quisenberry, the best of the submarine pitchers. The brick caught him high and drove him backward and down onto the pavement. There was a thud and a low moan.

"Jesus," the second man said.

He released Saranne and stepped back.

"She wanted it," he said.

"Then why did she say no?"

"She, she—"

He brought his arms up to protect his head, so I drove a forefist deep into his solar plexus. The blow knocked the wind from him, causing him to clutch his stomach, double over, and fall to his knees. There was retching, but he didn't vomit. Pity.

I took Saranne by the shoulder and led her toward the light at the far end of the alley.

"What are you doing here?" she said.

I glanced back at the two men. They helped each other up and retreated to the front of the alley.

"What were you thinking?" I said. "Did you want them to hurt you?"

"Does it matter?"

"Saranne—"

"People treat me like a whore. My father treats me like a whore. I might as well act like a whore."

"Why? To justify their expectations? To prove them right?"

Saranne thought that was funny enough to laugh over.

"McKenzie, you want to protect my virtue. Well, now you know I don't have any."

"Then why did you say no to those two? Why didn't you let them rape you?"

The question caused Saranne's face to freeze. Or maybe it was the word "rape."

"You don't need to be the town slut, you know," I said.

"What else can I be? If that's how people are going to treat me, what else can I be?"

"Have you ever read *The Scarlet Letter*?"

"What are you talking about?"

"Hester Prynne had a child by a man not her husband, so the people in her town—we're talking about seventeenth-century Puritans here—they shunned her and forced to wear the letter

A on her bosom. Yet she was the most virtuous character in the book. She not only refused to rat out the child's father, she protected him. Over time people began to respect her. They began to see her not as the person they thought she was but as the person she actually was; as someone they could go to with their problems, as someone they could trust."

"That's just a book."

"Hester was a hero because she refused to be the person the townspeople expected her to be."

"It's just a book, okay?"

"You have, what, another year of high school? Tough it out, Saranne. Do that, then you can leave Libbie, go where gossip can't reach you; go to college, go anywhere. Your old man, he isn't going to live forever. Who is he going to leave his businesses to, his grain elevator and restaurant and crap? When you come back, if you decide to come back, you'll be the one in charge. Or you can just sell it off."

"You make it sound easy."

"No. It's simple, but it won't be easy. Especially during that last year in high school."

"Like you know."

"Listen. I'll tell you the only thing I know absolutely for sure. Living well is the best revenge."

"Yeah, right. I'm out of here."

I didn't blame Saranne for dismissing me. I probably sounded like one of those TV phonies like Dr. Phil.

"I'll walk you to your car," I said.

"Whatever."

We walked back through the alley. Saranne didn't speak again until we were nearing the entrance.

"*The Scarlet Letter.* Who wrote that? Hawthorne? I think it's on the reading list next year."

I was pleased to hear that they still taught the book in high school.

"Read it," I said.

"Well, I have to, don't I?"

"I suppose."

We were rounding the corner of the alley onto the sidewalk when she spoke again.

"McKenzie, there's something I want you to know. No one else believes me, but I want you to know because, well, just because. I didn't have sex with Rush. He wanted me to. He tried to. He put his hands on me and he said things to convince me that it would be all right, but I wouldn't let him. The truth is, I've never—I haven't slept with anyone. Ever. Only no one believes me."

"I believe you," I said.

Saranne said something else, but I didn't hear. Her words were drowned out by a kind of swooshing sound, followed by a crunching blow against the back of my skull. The world turned a dazzling red-orange and then faded quickly to pitch black.

CHAPTER NINE

I was in a room. The room was white. A woman, also in white, hovered above me. Behind her was a brilliant light that stung my eyes. I tried to turn my head away, but the woman wouldn't allow it.

"Do you know who you are?" she asked.

"Where am I? Who are you?"

"My questions first."

I tried to rise. The woman prevented it with the flat of her hand pressed against my chest. It didn't take much effort on her part. The way I felt, a couple of kittens could have held me down.

"Do you know who you are?"

"Rushmore McKenzie," I said.

"Are you sure?"

"I don't know. What have you heard?"

"Where do you live?"

I told her. I gave her answers to a lot of questions—my address, phone number, Social Security number, and yes, I had health insurance, the card was in my wallet.

"Good," the woman said. "No apparent memory loss, no confusion. Very good."

"Who said I'm not confused? Where am I?"

"You are in the emergency room of the City of Libbie Medical Clinic. I'm Nancy Gustafson. You have a concussion."

"Oh."

"Do you remember what happened?"

"No."

"That's not unusual. People who have concussions almost always have no memory of the impact that caused the concussion."

"I remember walking in an alley—two men in an alley. Saranne. Saranne Miller was with me. Where is she? Is she all right?"

I tried to rise again. Nancy kept me down, although this time she had to put her weight into it.

"She's all right, she's okay," Nancy said. "She's outside. She's the one who brought you in. Rest easy."

Nancy patted my chest. Her smile was warm—I was sure I had seen it before.

"I was careless," I said. "I've been careless ever since I arrived in this burg. Big-city boy gonna show the local yokels how it's done. Dammit. I know better than that. Are you sure Saranne is all right?"

"Yes. You can see her in a bit. We need to do some things first."

"The cops."

"We called the cops. There are other things—"

"What things?"

"Listen to me, McKenzie. Are you listening?"

I stopped struggling with her.

"I'm listening," I said.

"The brain has the consistency of gelatin. All right? It floats in a cerebrospinal fluid inside your skull that cushions it from bumps and jolts. Now, a blow to your head can cause your brain to slap against the inner wall of your skull." For emphasis, she punched the palm of her hand with her fist. "This collision, the impact from the collision, can result in bleeding in or around your brain and the tearing of nerve fibers."

"I know all this. I've had concussions before."

"Then you know the drill."

"You're going to give me a CAT scan."

"Yes."

"The CAT scan will determine whether the blow has caused potentially serious bleeding or swelling in my head."

"Exactly."

"Are you set up for that in metropolitan Libbie?"

Turned out they were.

It didn't surprise me to learn that South Dakota was facing a physician shortage. Nancy said that at least eighteen counties didn't even have a single doctor living within their borders. To deal with the shortage, clinics relied on nurse practitioners—registered nurses that complete advanced education and training in the diagnosis and management of common medical conditions, including chronic illnesses. When patients were taken to emergency rooms, the nurse practitioners determined how serious their condition was and whether to transfer them to larger hospitals. In many cases, they relied on a complex telecommunications system that linked them with physicians in the bigger hospitals who provided assistance.

With the help of a nurse, I lay down on a narrow examination table, and the table was rolled into the large, donut-shaped CT scanner. A gantry containing electronic X-ray equipment rotated around me, taking multiple cross-sectional X-rays and combining them into detailed, two-dimensional images of my skull and brain. These images were sent directly to a hospital in Rapid City, where they apparently caused a certain amount of consternation.

Nancy returned me to the emergency room, set me on a gurney, and began asking more questions designed to test my memory and concentration, vision, hearing, balance, coordination, and reflexes. She asked if I felt dizzy, if I heard ringing in my ears, if I felt nauseous, if I was sensitive to light and noise, and seemed genuinely mystified when I kept answering no. In between the questions, she spent a lot of time on the phone.

Finally she said, "You told me that you had a concussion before."

"Not really a concussion," I said.

"What then?"

"An epidural hematoma."

"When?"

"A couple of years ago."

"Aha," she said and hurried from the room.

She was smiling when she returned.

"What's the problem?" I said.

"No problem. Your CAT scan revealed signs of the previous hematoma. It had us confused for a few moments. We have it sorted out now."

"It's not funny. I almost died."

"I know. I saw the two burr holes in your skull that they drilled to drain the fluid and alleviate the pressure. Fortunately, there's nothing like that this time."

"Am I good to go?"

"No."

"No?"

"I want to keep you overnight for observation."

"I feel good, I really do. Besides, I have things to do."

"Whatever they are, they can wait. I want you quiet for at least twenty-four hours. The docs say it's okay for you to be observed at home provided there's someone available to check on you periodically. If you sleep, you may need to be awakened every two hours to make sure you can be roused to normal consciousness."

"I understand."

"Do you have any friends?"

Proudly, I answered yes. Unfortunately, they were hundreds of miles away and could not help me.

"Do you have any friends in Libbie that can look out for you?" Nancy said.

"The only person I know here is Tracie Blake."

"She's not the nurse I would have chosen, but if you want to call her . . ."

"Do you know Tracie?"

"Everyone knows Tracie."

"I take it you're not friends."

"We used to be, until she started sleeping with my husband."

She smiled when she said that, a surprising thing to do, I thought.

"I remember you," I said. "I remember your smile."

"You do?"

"Nancy Gustafson."

"Yes."

"You're the chief's wife. I saw your photograph in his office. You were gorgeous."

The smile on her face stiffened just enough to tell me what a numbskull I was—I blamed it on the concussion.

"That didn't come out right," I said.

Still, there was little resemblance to the young woman in the photograph. The older Nancy's hair was short now and streaked with gray, her smooth face had become lined with worry, her eyes looked tired, and she had gained at least forty pounds.

"The photograph was taken a dozen years ago," Nancy said. "I asked him to get rid of it."

"Why?"

Nancy stepped back and held her hands wide. She spun in a slow circle.

"I'm never going to be a size six again," she said. "Or a size eight. Or a size ten. Maybe if I could work at it all day for half a year, but who has time? When I'm not here, I'm doing housework or cooking or shopping or—look, I just don't have the time or energy to be a model."

When she said "model," she meant Tracie.

"I apologize, Nancy. I didn't mean—"

"It's okay, McKenzie."

It wasn't okay, and I would have said so except a nurse interrupted us.

"The chief is here," she said.

"Send him in," Nancy said.

"I want to see Saranne if she's still around," I said.

A moment later, Saranne came through the door, followed closely by Chief Gustafson. She surprised me with a hug.

"Are you okay?" she said.

"I am very much okay, thanks to you."

"Me?"

"You're my hero."

"Shuddup."

"You are. If you hadn't looked out for me, who knows what would have happened."

"What did happen?" the chief said.

I was about to answer; only Saranne beat me to it, telling the story quickly and furiously, without a thought to editing her remarks to her advantage. The chief listened carefully. He had a notebook open and a pen poised to write, yet I noticed he didn't take any notes.

"The two men who followed you into the alley," the chief said. "Can you identify them?"

"Yeah," Saranne said. "Only they're not the ones who hit McKenzie."

"They're not?" I said.

"No, they were across the street at the time. The man who hit you, he was wearing a black ski mask and carrying a wooden base-ball bat."

"Wooden, not aluminum?" I said.

"What difference does it make?" the chief asked.

"Wooden bats are harder to come by these days. Unless they're playing pro ball, most people use aluminum."

"It was wooden," Saranne said. "That's all I can tell you. I didn't get a very good look at him before he started running. He wasn't tall. About my height. That's really all I can say."

"He was right-handed," I said.

"How do you know?" the chief asked.

I touched the back of the right side of my head. "He was right-handed," I said again.

"Any idea who might have wanted to club you, McKenzie?"

My first thought had been the two men in the alley. My second was Church. Saranne's statement eliminated both possibilities.

"No one comes to mind," I said.

"If it's not a revenge thing, it has to be something else," the chief said. "Think it might be connected to the questions you've been asking about Rush?"

"It would be helpful if you canvassed the area. Everyone seems to know everyone in this town. Could be someone saw something."

The chief sighed like a man who thought too much was being asked of him.

"About the two men in the alley," he said.

"They were across the street when we came out of the alley," Saranne said. "I saw them. I made them help me get McKenzie into my car so I could take him here."

"How did you manage that?" I asked.

"Blackmail."

"You threatened to call the police?"

"No, I threatened to call their wives. Chief, they won't be bothering me anymore. There's no sense to pressing charges or anything."

"Saranne—"

"That's another thing. My name is Sara Anne—two words. People have been slurring my name since I can remember, and I want it to stop. It's Sara Anne. Better yet, call me Sara. Just plain Sara."

"You go, girl," Nancy said.

The chief sighed some more. He said he wanted the names nonetheless. He suggested the two men witnessed the assault and, all things considered, could probably be encouraged to talk about it. Sara gave up the names. The chief wrote them down, closed his notebook, and buttoned it into the top pocket of his shirt. He bowed his head toward the girl.

"If you think of anything more, call me," he said. "McKenzie, I'll be in touch."

The chief turned toward his wife. She had been standing to the side with her arms crossed over her chest.

"I guess I'll be seeing you later," he said to her.

"When my shift ends," Nancy said. "If you're still up."

Sara Miller turned toward me the moment the chief left the room.

"What do you think?" she said.

"I think you are a very cool young lady."

"Shuddup. Really?"

"Really. It's getting late, though. Your parents must be worried about you."

"I already called them. I don't know why, but I feel so happy."

"You're a hero."

"That's not it. It's—I don't know what it is."

"Have you ever read Saul Bellow?" I said. *"Seize the Day?"*

"Oh, McKenzie, you and your books. Don't you know? It's all video now."

She hugged me again and announced that she had to go.

"Take care, Sara," I said.

She smiled at the sound of her own name.

"See ya around," she said.

A moment later she was gone.

"I've known that girl her entire life," Nancy said. "That's the longest I've seen her smile at one time. I have to admit, you do have a way with women."

"It's a gift," I said.

"Do you want me to call Tracie for you?"

"No. If I'm going to be awakened by a woman every two hours, I'd rather it be by you."

"Good choice."

"What are you going to do about her?"

"Tracie? Nothing."

"Nothing?"

"I have a pretty healthy self-esteem, McKenzie. Before time and work destroyed my body, I was a Ferrari; I was the sleekest sports car on the road. A dozen years later I'm an SUV. I'm not any happier about it than Eric. Yet that's the way it is, and if he can't deal with it, then he can't. Let him run to Tracie. If he'd rather be with a drunk than his wife, so be it. I'm not going to change just to please somebody else."

"That somebody else is your husband."

"Spoken like a guy."

"You might not have noticed, but you're married to a guy."

"Do you condone his behavior?"

"Absolutely not."

"Well, then."

"I don't condone yours, either."

"Mine?"

"You've given up."

"Excuse me?"

"You're letting Tracie win. Where I come from, you never let the other guy win. He might beat you, but you never let him win. It's a matter of principle."

"Is that right?"

"Or is it character? I often get the two confused."

"C'mon, McKenzie. Let's find you a room."

She pushed a wheelchair to where I was sitting on the gurney.

"Really?" I said.

"Get in."

After I settled into the chair, Nancy wheeled me out of the emergency room to a waiting elevator.

"How long have you been in Libbie?" she asked.

"One full day."

"And you already have it all figured out."

"Of course. There's one thing you should know, though."

"What's that?"

"I actually like Tracie Blake. She's been very considerate. Even so, it wouldn't bother me at all to see her run down by a Ferrari."

Nancy gave me a hospital gown to wear, and I slipped into bed, keeping my back to the wall as I crossed from the bathroom after I changed.

"You didn't strike me as the shy type, McKenzie," she said.

"You didn't strike me as a voyeur."

"That's why I took all those medical courses, so I could see the hairy butts of middle-aged men."

"Who are you calling middle-aged?"

After I settled in, Nancy gave me a bottle of water and a remote control for the TV mounted high in the corner of the room.

"We have satellite," she said.

"I'm good." I set the remote aside. "If you have time, I wouldn't mind chatting."

Nancy pulled up a chair.

"Just as long as we don't talk about me," she said.

"Tell me about Libbie."

"Let's see. It was originally settled by a couple of ex–Seventh Cavalrymen who named it after General Custer's wife, Elizabeth, who everyone called Libbie. What else do you want to know?"

"I think every town has its own personality. I'm trying to figure out Libbie's; why it's the way it is."

"What do you mean?"

"I have discovered two things since I have been here. One is that all the women are preternaturally beautiful."

"All?"

"All."

Nancy smiled prettily. "What else?" she said.

"Man for man, this is the most screwed-up community I have ever seen."

"The politically correct phrase is dysfunctional."

"Dysfunctional, hell. You guys are raving lunatics. I'm beginning to think that you're the sanest person in this burg."

"Thanks for the compliment. I'll put it in a box at home and take it out when I need cheering up."

"I just don't get it."

"This is a dying town, McKenzie. If you were dying, you'd be screwed up, too."

"Dying?"

"Have you seen the new high school?"

"Yes."

"It was built for five hundred and fifty students. We have less than three hundred going there. Next year it'll be even fewer. It's happening all over. The counties in the Great Plains have been losing population for decades, and it isn't going to stop. All the young people are moving to the cities—they should be moving to the cities. Break down the population of an average county and something like twelve-point-five percent will be sixty-five or older. That's the national average. The average here in the Great Plains is twenty percent. And growing. I know the numbers because of the way it affects the medical community. The biggest industry in most small towns today is nursing homes. When these people die out—there are several hundred thousand square miles of the Great Plains that have fewer than six people per square mile living there; in some cases it's two people per square mile. The last time that happened was eighteen ninety-something, and they declared that the frontier was closed. It might as well be the frontier again."

"I remember hearing something about the Buffalo Commons," I said.

"That was a proposal presented by a couple of sociologists twenty years ago. They claimed that most of the Great Plains was unsustainable, and they wanted the federal government to depopulate the area and turn it into a vast nature preserve. Of course, the government ignored them, but damn if it isn't coming true anyway. Look around and all you'll see is empty churches, abandoned farms, closed schoolhouses, shuttered businesses—I heard that there were six thousand ghost towns in Kansas alone. God knows how many there are around here.

"I'm telling you, McKenzie, it's all dying. Fifty years from now, I doubt that anyone will be living here at all. That's why people are the way they are. We're all desperate."

"Why do you stay?"

"It's home."

Nancy returned the chair to its spot near the wall.

"Try to get some sleep," she said. "I'll see you soon."

She wasn't kidding. Nancy woke me every two hours until her shift ended at 2:00 A.M., and she was replaced by a second nurse practitioner that was just as punctual. I wasn't happy about it, yet I kept it to myself—crankiness and irritability are symptoms of a concussion, and I didn't want to confuse anyone. I figured I could always return to the Pioneer Hotel in the morning to get some shuteye. No such luck. The second NP discovered that I had a low-grade temperature. She fed me ibuprofen and insisted that I remain in bed. I spent most of the morning on my cell phone burning minutes, talking to Nina and to Bobby and Shelby. I wondered how Victoria had fared with her research assignment. She was at a soccer tournament for the weekend, though, and wouldn't return until Sunday evening. I said I'd call later. My fever broke just before noon. I dressed in the clothes I'd worn the previous day and walked to the Pioneer Hotel.

CHAPTER TEN

It was about a half mile to the hotel—everything in Libbie was about a half mile away—and the fresh air and exercise did me good. I actually broke a sweat, which was more a result of the heat than of any exertion on my part. I walked west past the First Integrity State Bank. Its electronic sign announced that at eleven fifty-two the temperature had reached ninety-seven degrees. I would have thought that the heat would have slowed people down, yet there was an unexpected energy to the traffic around me. The citizens of Libbie all seemed to move with a deliberateness that I had not seen before. It was as if they all shared a secret that they couldn't wait to reveal to each other.

I stepped through the large wooden doors into the lobby of the Pioneer Hotel, where I was assaulted by a wave of cool air. I automatically began rubbing my hands over my upper arms the way people do when they want to warm themselves. Sharren Nuffer was sitting behind the reception desk, a pair of cheaters balanced on her nose, reading something on her computer screen.

"Hi," I said.

Her head jolted upward.

"Oh my God, McKenzie," she said.

The glasses came off quickly as Sharren rounded the desk. She came toward me, her arms flung wide.

"McKenzie," she said again. A moment later, her arms were around me and she was hugging me tight. "You're okay, you're okay."

"Why wouldn't I be? What's going on?"

"I was so worried about you. I heard what happened last night. I heard that they took you to the clinic. Are you okay?"

"I'm fine. Who told you about last night?"

Sharren paused a moment before answering.

"It's a small town," she said.

"Still, that's a pretty enthusiastic welcome."

"I thought, because of what happened, I thought—I don't know what I thought."

Sharren and I didn't have that kind of relationship, I told myself. If she was anxious about me, it wasn't because we were close. There was something else on her mind.

"What do you know that I don't?" I said.

"You mean you haven't heard?"

"Heard what?"

"It's terrible. Oh, McKenzie, it's so terrible. That's why I'm upset. Because of what happened to you last night and then this morning and Rush, the way he disappeared—"

"Sharren, you're not making any sense."

"I'm trying to, but I'm afraid. I'm afraid you'll think less of me, and I wouldn't like that."

My cell phone, safely tucked in the pocket of my sports jacket, called to me. I held up a finger while I answered it.

"Hold that thought," I told Sharren. "This is McKenzie," I said into the phone.

"This is Chief Gustafson. Are you still in the hospital?"

"No. I was discharged a little while ago. What can I do for you, Chief?"

At the word "Chief," Sharren took two steps backward and covered her mouth with her hand.

"How are you feeling?" he said. "Are you up for a little trip?"

"Chief—"

"I'm at Mike Randisi's place. Do you remember how to get here?"

"Yes."

"I need you to come out right away."

"Why?"

"He's dead. Somebody shot him."

There were so many vehicles parked on Mike Randisi's turnaround that I had to park well back on the gravel driveway and walk up the hill to his home. Most of the cars carried the emblem of the Perkins County Sheriff's Department. One belonged to the Libbie Police Department. There was also a white van with QUIK-TIME FOODS painted across its doors. Dawn Neske, wearing her tailored light and dark blue uniform, stood in front of it, waving her arms emphatically at the two deputies that were interviewing her. Her arms froze in midgesture when she saw me. Her eyes grew wide, and her mouth hung open. The deputies turned to see what had captured Dawn's attention. I gave them all one of Victoria Dunston's microwaves.

Chief Gustafson opened the door to the house as if he had been watching for me. He waved me over.

"It's not my case," he said. "We just don't have the resources for a deal like this. I handed it off to Big Joe Balk. He's the county sheriff. He might kick it up to the South Dakota Division of Criminal Investigation, I don't know."

I flicked a thumb toward Dawn. She had resumed gesturing, and the deputies had resumed watching her.

"What is she doing here?" I asked.

"She discovered the bodies," the chief said. "When she came to deliver Randisi's groceries this morning."

"Bodies?"

"Step inside. Don't touch anything."

I wasn't prepared for what I found there.

Mike Randisi, dressed only in blue boxers, was lying on the kitchen floor. The bullet hole was on the left side, just below his ribs. It was a small hole, surrounded by seared, blackened skin and a patch of powder soot. Soot also stained both of his hands. There was very little blood around the entrance wound. The exit wound in his back was a different matter. Instead of a neat hole, there was a deep, irregular gash, with tissue and bone protruding from it. There was an enormous amount of blood on his back, on the floor, and splattered all over the kitchen appliances, cabinets, cupboards, and floor. It had not yet dried. Next to him on the floor was the long-barreled .38 Colt.

I turned away, fighting the impulse to steady myself against the kitchen counter (I didn't want to corrupt the crime scene with my fingerprints) while fighting an even great impulse to vomit in the sink (I didn't want to look like a wuss). I forced myself to concentrate. The blackened skin suggested a near-contact wound, I told myself. That and the powder burns on his hands left open the possibility that Randisi and his killer had wrestled over the gun and Randisi lost. The murder weapon—it was Mike's, his name was Mike—he seemed like a nice guy. Dammit! Concentrate. If he was killed by his own gun, that likely ruled out premeditation. If it had been premeditated, the killer would have brought his own weapon; of course he would, wouldn't you? The killer came to Mike's place because, well, because there was no way Mike would have gone to see the killer. He had agoraphobia. He was taking sertraline. The orange prescription bottle was right there on the counter next to the sink.

I heard voices behind me.

"Goldarn air-conditioning," one voice said.

"Can you give me a time of death?" said another.

"Goldarn air-conditioning," the first voice repeated. "Until I get her back to the morgue, I can only guess."

Her? my inner voice said.

"I'll take a guess."

"I'm going to say she was killed between 2:00 and 6:00 A.M. Don't hold me to it, though."

She?

I spun to face the kitchen again. A knot of men, all wearing khaki and Sam Browne pistol belts and holsters, blocked my view from the kitchen into the living room. I kept staring until the group parted. Then I saw her. On the floor and facing the kitchen. Her arms and legs were spread apart as if she were making snow angels. She was dressed only in white lace panties and a man's white dress shirt that was unbuttoned and hanging open, the sleeves rolled up. In the center of her chest, just above her breasts, was a small, nearly bloodless bullet hole.

Tracie Blake.

"Oh no," I said.

The two men who had been speaking turned to look at me.

"Oh no," I repeated.

"Who are you?" said the one with the badge.

"This is McKenzie," Chief Gustafson said. "I told you about him."

"Sonuvabitch," I said.

"Get him out of here," the badge said.

The chief grabbed my arm with both hands and pulled me toward the door.

"Goddamn sonuvabitch."

For the first time since I'd arrived in Libbie, I didn't mind the heat. I pulled my arm out of the chief's grasp as soon as we exited the kitchen. He called my name, but I ignored him, walking around to the front of the house and sitting on the lush green grass. I turned my face to the sun and closed my eyes, willing the sun to burn the image of Tracie Blake's dead body from my brain. And Mike Randisi's. And all the dead bodies that came before them. Most people didn't have to deal with such things. Most people were luckier than I was. It was not something I often admitted. Most days I fought against conformity, resisted the ordinary—my greatest fear growing up was that I would one day discover that I was boring. That was most days. On this day I found myself wishing I were an accountant, or a plumber, or a poor, overworked bookstore owner, anything other than what I was so drearily—a cop. Even without a badge I was a cop.

Goddamn sonuvabitch!

I heard their footfalls on the grass before I heard their voices.

"McKenzie, this is Sheriff Balk," the chief said.

I opened my eyes. Big Joe was standing in front of me, making a large hole in the sunlight. He looked like the guy that Jack met at the top of the beanstalk.

The sheriff smiled and extended his hand. His face was wide and full of smile wrinkles, and he had a loud, penetrating voice that made me think he was good with a joke. I reached to shake his hand without leaving my spot on the grass.

"How you doin'?" he said.

"I've been better."

I released his hand and gazed across the highway, looking northeast toward Miller's properties off in the distance.

"I'm sorry about your friends," the sheriff said.

"I barely knew them," I said.

"I understand."

I glanced up at him again, this time squinting against the sun. He was younger than the chief, closer to my age, yet there was something in his face to suggest that he was wiser, that he had seen things and had learned from them.

"Chief Gustafson explained why you're here," the sheriff said. "He said you and Ms. Blake visited Mr. Randisi yesterday afternoon."

"Yes."

"What can you tell me?"

I knew the kind of information the sheriff wanted, and I gave it to him, explaining that Mike had been weary of threats, that he had met Tracie and me with a gun in his hand.

"That was his Colt on the floor?" the sheriff said.

"Yes. Last time I saw it, it was on the kitchen counter near the door."

"There was no forced entry."

"Mike knew who was knocking on his door or he wouldn't have opened it. Unless . . ."

"Unless what?"

"It was a pretty girl come to call." I gestured with my head more or less up the hill toward the Quik-Time Foods van. "Mike liked pretty girls."

"Do you believe Ms. Neske might have had something to do with this?" the sheriff said.

"I have no idea, but if she had knocked on my door, I probably would have opened it, too. Wouldn't you?"

"Not if I had Ms. Blake in the bedroom. Certainly something to consider, though."

"Tell me that you haven't already considered it."

The sheriff's smile was faint, and it didn't last long.

"That's what I thought," I said. Big Joe Balk was a crime dog, I could tell.

"How well did Ms. Blake and Mr. Randisi know each other, can you tell me?" the sheriff said.

"As far as I know, they spoke for the first time yesterday afternoon."

"Didn't take long for them to hook up."

"They were both lonely people."

"Yeah. There's a lot of that going around. Do you believe that Mr. Randisi was involved with your Imposter?"

"He said he wasn't, and I believed him. Of course, I've been lied to before."

"Haven't we all."

I was surprised when the sheriff sat on the grass next to me.

"Let me run this by you," he said. "Mr. Randisi is in on the scam. His accomplice discovers that you went to see him. The accomplice becomes nervous. He goes to Mr. Randisi's house to discuss it. They quarrel. One or the other grabs the gun. It goes off, killing Mr. Randisi. Ms. Blake hears the commotion, goes to the kitchen to see what it's about. She's shot simply because she's in the wrong place at the wrong time."

"I never liked that phrase—in the wrong place at the wrong time. It implies that the vic put herself in danger, that she was at least partially responsible for her own murder."

"I hadn't thought of it that way."

"As for the rest, it's all speculation until your people go over the crime scene."

"Very true, but I'd like to get a head start if I could. Any suggestions?"

I had to take a good hard look at the sheriff's face. It's not often that cops, even my friends, seek advice from civilians.

"Are you asking me?" I said.

"Yes."

"Thank you. I do have one suggestion. Your ME said the murders took place between 2:00 and 6:00 A.M.?"

"That's his preliminary estimate."

I pointed across the highway. Sheriff Balk followed my finger to Grandma Miller's bar and grill.

"When is closing time in South Dakota?" I asked.

"Two."

"I'd start there. Look for someone who was drinking alone."

"Good idea."

"Something else. Chief?"

Chief Gustafson was standing behind us. He now moved to where we both could see him.

"Chief," I said, "how did you know that Tracie and I came out here to see Mike?"

The chief answered in a flat, nearly monotone voice as if he were expecting the question and had already prepared an answer.

"She told me last night around dinnertime. I called to ask about your progress looking for the Imposter—"

"Why not call me?"

"She reported on everything you did."

"Chief?"

The chief said, "I know your next question, McKenzie." He was looking at the sheriff when he answered it. "Yes, Tracie and I had been seeing each other. Our affair ended a couple of weeks ago. I am the one who ended it. I ended it when my wife, Nancy, learned about the affair. We spoke about it again at some length last night or, I should say, early this morning, after she came home from work. She came home at about two fifteen, and we talked until sunrise. Nancy said she expected better from me, and I promised that she would get it. I suspect you might have had something to do with that, McKenzie, encouraging her to speak up."

God, I hope so, I thought but didn't say.

The sheriff grabbed a couple of tufts of grass, tossed them into the air, and watched the wind take them like a golfer contemplating his next shot. I had no idea what he was thinking, which was probably the way he wanted it. He stood, brushing his uniform pants with both hands.

"Well, I have work to do," he said. "In the meantime—"

"You're not really going to tell me not to leave town, are you, Sheriff?" I said.

"Nah. Being an ex-cop and all, you know I have no legal right to say that. On the other hand . . ."

"Yes?"

"You don't want to go anywhere it'll trouble me to find you."

"Fair enough," I said.

"One more thing. You can prove you were in the Libbie Medical Clinic all last night, right?"

"From about nine thirty until well after eleven this morning."

"How convenient."

"Wasn't it, though?"

Sheriff Balk turned and started walking back toward the house. He called over his shoulder, "Chief, a word?" Chief Gustafson scurried after him, leaving me alone on the grass with thoughts of Tracie Blake and Mike Randisi swirling in my head.

Sonuvabitch.

I was surprised to see the white van in my rearview mirror. Even more surprised to see that it was gaining on me. I had pushed the Audi up to ninety miles an hour, cruising the long, flat highway, my windows down, trying to blow the heat and all bad thoughts out of the car. I recognized the van almost immediately. It belonged to Quik-Time Foods. I slowed to seventy. The van soon reached my back bumper. I could see Dawn Neske behind the steering wheel. She leaned on her horn, and I pulled to the shoulder of the highway and stopped. Dawn halted behind me. She sat in the van, probably waiting for me to join her. When I didn't, she came to me. I made sure both of her hands were empty as she approached. I left the Audi in gear, my left foot depressing the clutch, just the same.

"Nice car, McKenzie," Dawn said. She placed both of her hands on the driver's side door, which was fine with me—it made it easier to keep track of them.

"Thanks," I said.

"How much does a car like this go for?"

"About fifty grand."

"Must be tough."

"It can be."

She grinned at that.

"That was something else, huh?" Dawn said. "Two dead bodies. Wow. You don't see that every day."

"You don't seem too upset about Tracie Blake."

"It's not like we were friends or anything."

"How well did you know Mike Randisi?"

"I didn't. He was just a customer."

"You knew he had agoraphobia."

"That's why he used the service, because he didn't like to leave his place."

"He never invited you in for a cup of coffee? You never spent time with him?"

"The company doesn't like employees fraternizing with customers. Get in and out, that's what the company says."

"Of course you always do what the company says."

"Of course. Geezus, McKenzie. You sound like the cops."

"Do I?"

"Yeah, but forget that. The reason I chased after you—you were really driving fast. The van started to shake and shimmy, scared the hell outta me."

"Why did you chase me?"

"I was wondering about Nick Hendel. You know, the Imposter. Have you found him yet?"

"Not yet."

Dawn seemed genuinely disappointed.

"Do you have any leads at all?" she said.

"I think he might be from Chicago."

"Nothing else?"

"Dawn, don't worry. I'm working on it."

I waited until Dawn's van was just a white speck on the highway before I activated my cell phone. I was surprised I still had coverage. The bars had been pretty low in Libbie, and out here they were nearly nonexistent. As it was, it took about five minutes before I finally negotiated my way past Greg Schroeder's secretaries.

"What the hell, Greg," I said. "Do you get paid by the hour?"

"As a matter of fact, I do," he said.

"I mean, how many Nicholas Hendels can there be?"

"From coast to coast, about a thousand."

"Really? How many in Chicago?"

"Seventeen. If you include all of Chicagoland, it's sixty-eight."

"Swell."

"The Imposter is your age, right?"

"Thereabouts."

"We're trimming the list according to age and race. I should have something for you soon."

"When you do, send a fax to the Pioneer Hotel."

"Okay."

"Sooner would be better than later."

"McKenzie, don't worry. I'm working on it."

This time when Sharren Nuffer came around the desk to hug me, I hugged her back. Her eyes were red and swollen from tears, and as I embraced her she began crying again. I led her to a chair in the lobby, the same one she used when we had shared a drink just last Monday. I asked her if she wanted a drink now, and she said she did, which gave me a chance to escape her grief. Truth be told, I felt a little like weeping myself, but it wasn't something I did or wanted to do.

I cut through the dining room to the bar in back. Evan was on duty. His only patrons were four older men sitting together at a table and playing hearts, wearing work shirts and baseball-style caps that promoted everything from farm implements to the Veterans of Foreign Wars.

"McKenzie," he said. A good bartender always remembers the names of his customers.

I stood between two stools, setting both hands on the bar top. For a moment, I forgot why I was there.

"I take it you heard," Evan said. He ran his fingers through his blond hair just like he did the last time I saw him. I could see how that might get annoying after a while.

"Yeah," I said.

"Helluva thing,"

"Helluva thing," I repeated.

"There hasn't been a murder in Libbie, or the whole county for that matter, since, I don't know, forever."

For reasons I didn't fully understand, I flashed on a verse of poetry from a long-forgotten college English class, William Dunbar's "Lament for the Makers":

> The state of man does change and vary,
> Now sound, now sick, now blithe, now sary,
> Now dansand mirry,
> Now like to die—

"Helluva thing," I said again.

"What'll ya have?" Evan said.

I ordered the same drinks as before—double Jack Daniel's for me, bourbon and water for Sharren—and told Evan to charge them to my room.

"If you don't mind my saying so, McKenzie, you look like crap."

I did mind. Still, a quick glance at my reflection in the mirror told me that he was right. I hadn't shaved or changed clothes since the day before, and my eyes were bloodshot from lack of sleep.

"I'm starting a new fashion trend," I said.

"Let me know how that works out for you."

Sharren had stopped weeping by the time I returned and was now staring out of the large window at nothing. She said, "Thank you," when I set the bourbon on the small table next to the chair and didn't speak again for a long time. I was nearly finished with the Black Jack when she turned in her chair to face me.

"You think I'm being silly," she said.

"Not at all."

"I didn't know Mike Randisi, and I didn't like Tracie Blake. So why am I crying for them?"

I had an answer that involved other English poets, only Sharren wasn't looking for answers, so I kept my mouth shut.

"I thought Tracie was an opportunistic, money-grubbing slut, and she—she thought the very same of me. So why—"

Sharren turned to gaze out the window again, and for a moment I thought she would begin weeping some more. She didn't.

"It's my fault," she said. "I can't get past the idea that it's all my fault."

"Why do you say that?"

"Do you think what happened—do you think that it might have something to do with Rush?"

"I don't know. It could have."

"It is my fault."

"What are you trying to tell me, Sharren?"

Sharren retrieved the glass from the table and drank down half of the bourbon. She took a deep breath as if it had burned her throat and then pressed the glass against her forehead with both hands while she studied the carpet at her feet. A moment later she drained the glass, studied the carpet some more, then looked at me. She was working herself up to telling me something, and I was going to let her, no matter how long it took. It took a long time. I had finished my own drink before she began to speak again.

"The Miller family keeps a room—they have a room reserved just off the swimming pool year-round with a sliding door that opens right onto the deck. Saranne uses it a lot."

That would be Sara Anne, my inner voice said. Yet I kept it to myself. There was no way I was going to interrupt Sharren now.

"I won't lie to you, McKenzie. I slept with him, with Rush—the Imposter. I told you that. Afterward, the day after, I saw him in his swimming trunks walking to the pool. First chance I got, I went to say hello. Only I couldn't find him anywhere. I walked around the pool. There were people there, not many. I thought I might have missed him until I heard his voice. He had a voice that carried, an actor's voice, you know? The voice was coming from the Millers' room. The sliding door was open, but the drapes were drawn. He was saying things—they were the same kinds of things he had said to me the night before. I pulled open the drapes, and he was sitting on the bed in his swimming trunks. Saranne was across the room. She was holding a beach towel in front of herself. It didn't do much to hide her own swimsuit, this skimpy two-piece, and Rush was trying to talk her onto the bed next to him, patting the bedspread like he was calling a pet, and I—I made a scene. I don't know why. He didn't mean anything to me. He was just, he was just—I called him things, bad things. I called her things, too, just as bad, things that she didn't deserve to be called, and everyone at the pool heard me. Rush thought it was funny. Saranne, of course, was crying. That's what I heard when I left. His laughter and her tears. It's not something I'm proud of. I'm afraid I hurt Saranne badly."

I don't often come across this degree of honesty, and it made me squirm in my chair. I felt as though I should reciprocate in some way, tell her something uncomfortably honest about myself to even the score—it would have been the Minnesota Nice thing to do. I resisted the impulse. I had no idea what Sharren's confession had to do with the murders of Tracie and Mike, but I wanted to hear it. Still, I didn't push. I figured she would get to it in her own time. After a while, she did.

"I was on duty the Tuesday evening Rush disappeared. I didn't tell the chief this, I didn't tell anybody, but the evening he disappeared, right before he left the hotel, Rush received a phone call, a call to his room. It was made through our switchboard. Our switchboard is automatic. If you know the recipient's room number, you can just punch it in and not use the operator, so I didn't hear a voice. Our switchboard, we have caller ID. The call came from Mr. Miller's house."

It made perfect sense to me. The Imposter gets a call from Miller, probably about Sara, and he panics. That's why he left town so quickly, not even bothering to pack. Perfect sense.

"Why didn't you tell the chief?" I said.

"I should have. I know I should have because now, if keeping quiet is the reason Tracie and Mike . . . I didn't tell him because, McKenzie, you should know, Mr. Miller—he owns the hotel. Also, I felt guilty about Saranne, about ruining her reputation. As for Rush, he got what he deserved, didn't he?"

"Sharren, unless you know something I don't, what Rush got was a whole lot of money and a trip to the Cayman Islands."

"Do you still believe that?"

"What do you believe?"

"I believe he's lying in a shallow grave somewhere."

CHAPTER ELEVEN

I liked it, I really did—the idea that Dewey Miller put the Imposter down for trifling with his daughter. It smacked of frontier justice. Except I didn't believe it. The problem was the missing money. If the Imposter was dead, whoever took the money must have known he was dead—probably killed him—and had to have the wherewithal to abscond with the funds. I didn't think Miller was that guy. If he were, he never would have sent two bounty hunters to track down Rushmore McKenzie. 'Course, he might have, knowing I was innocent, to prove his deep concern to the community, an alibi after the fact . . .

Stop it, my inner voice warned me. *You're thinking too hard.*

After cleaning up, I asked Sharren for directions to Miller's home. I waited patiently while she cycled through a menu of conflicting emotions. Finally, after I promised to keep her name out of it, she relented, pointing me in the direction of Boucher Gardens. I found the house just west of the cemetery. I was expecting a mansion, but the Miller home didn't even aspire to a McMansion. It was no bigger or grander than any home you might find in a first-ring suburb of St. Paul.

The woman who answered my knock was another one of Libbie's seemingly endless supply of beauties—red-brown hair, blue-green eyes, and a body that most twenty-year-olds would do anything for, except diet and exercise, of course, and she so closely resembled her daughter that I nearly asked if her father was home. Instead, I said, "I would like to see Mr. Miller. My name is McKenzie."

"I know who you are," she said. "I'm Mrs. Miller." She paused while she carefully considered my appearance. "I'm told you are a millionaire."

"I have a couple of bucks."

"Do you always go about attired in this fashion, or are you dressing down for the natives?"

I did a quick inventory of my dress—white Nikes, blue jeans, rust-colored short-sleeve polo shirt, and black lightweight sports jacket.

"If I had known it mattered, I would have put a ribbon in my hair," I said.

"I guess not everyone should have money," Mrs. Miller said.

I asked again to see her husband.

"He is unavailable at this time," she said.

"When will he be available?"

"I do not approve of your tone."

"Oh, for crissake."

"Mr. McKenzie!"

"Tell your husband I was here. Tell him that I have questions, specifically where was he the night the Imposter disappeared. Tell him he can talk to me or Big Joe Balk—I really don't care which."

I turned and started for my car. It was a fully loaded Audi 225 TT Coupe with a Napa leather interior and light silver exterior. I doubted Mrs. Miller approved of that, either. She called to me before I could reach it.

"Stop. Mr. McKenzie. Please."

I spun to face her. She was still standing at the front door, still holding it open. She gestured inside.

"Please," she said.

I hesitated.

"Please," she said again.

Unlike her husband, Mrs. Miller apparently knew the magic word.

I went inside.

She shut the door behind me.

"Make yourself comfortable," Mrs. Miller said. She pointed at a chair, and I sat. "May I get you anything? A drink, perhaps?"

"I'm fine," I said.

Mrs. Miller sat across from me.

"How is your head?" she asked.

I automatically touched the back of my head and winced, although the pain was more memory now.

"I'm fine," I said.

"I'm delighted to hear it."

"Mrs. Miller—"

"My name is Michelle. Better yet, call me Mickie. All my friends do."

"Michelle," I said, although Mrs. Miller didn't seem to notice the snub.

"I am grateful to you, of course," she said. "Grateful that you went to my daughter's defense last night. That was heroic of you. I cannot say the same, however, about the lecture you delivered afterward. It seems you have rekindled her rebellious nature. Sara Anne, indeed. Suddenly she insists on being called Sara Anne. I swear, I don't know what's wrong with that girl."

"Neither do I."

"This morning she announced that she intends to move to Hollywood and become a sound effects woman." Mrs. Miller quoted the air around the word "woman." "What rubbish. I thought we had drummed that fantasy out of her head years ago."

"What's wrong with creating sound effects? Someone has to do it. Why not her?"

"Mr. McKenzie, please. It is a pipe dream, at best. A childhood fancy."

"I remember one time when I was a kid, I wanted to become a professional water-skier. I told the old man I was going to run away and join the Tommy Bartlett Show in the Wisconsin Dells. He said if that's what I really wanted to do, I should practice first. He got me lessons with a guy who actually worked with Tommy Bartlett at one time. Turned out I lacked the necessary aptitude for the profession. Oh well."

"What's your point?"

"No point. Just telling you a story about me and my father."

Mrs. Miller smirked. "You're suggesting that we are unsupportive of our daughter," she said. "Far from it. She is being groomed to take over our numerous business concerns. One day she will thank us."

"Assuming the businesses are still here to inherit."

"What is that supposed to mean?"

"I've been told on several occasions that the Great Plains are dying. Why shouldn't your numerous business concerns die with them?"

She stared at me as if I had been the first person to suggest the possibility to her. Perhaps I was. She turned it over in her head for a few moments before smirking again.

"What utter nonsense," she said.

"When do you expect Mr. Miller?"

"Not for a few hours at least. He is meeting with our banker. Mr. McKenzie, you mentioned the evening when Rush—hmm. Should I call him that?"

"Why not?"

"You asked about the evening Rush disappeared. May I ask why?"

"The Imposter left his hotel that evening immediately after receiving a call from your husband."

Mrs. Miller thought long and hard about that bit of news before answering.

"You are mistaken," she said.

"I'm only telling you what I heard," I said.

"From that trollop who works for us, no doubt. Still, Mr. McKenzie, you are mistaken."

"We can check the phone records to make sure. When I say we, of course, I mean the cops."

"Yes, yes, but that is not what I meant when I said you are mistaken. It was not my husband who made the call. I did."

"You?"

"Yes."

"May I ask why you called the Imposter?"

"So I could kill him."

"What?"

"I didn't tell him that, naturally, when I lured him to Lake Mataya."

"I wouldn't think so."

"Instead, I gave him the impression that we would exchange sexual favors. To be honest, I was a little surprised he fell for that gambit, especially after he was just caught in a hotel room with my teenage daughter. Imagine the arrogance."

"Are you saying you killed the Imposter because you believe he assaulted your daughter?"

"Yes."

"Michelle, you must know nothing happened. Sara Anne was not assaulted."

"So she says."

"You don't believe her?"

"I knew Rush."

"You should have believed her. She was telling the truth."

"You're saying I killed the Imposter for nothing? It matters not. It is a mother's prerogative, her duty, in fact, to defend her children. I am sure that any jury that consists of at least one mother will agree with me."

I had nothing to say to that, but something in my face must have spoken to her, because Mrs. Miller said, "I feel neither regret nor remorse over what I have done. Why should I? To be honest, Mr. McKenzie, it feels good to finally tell someone about it. Liberating, in fact. Yes, liberating." She was smiling now. "What surprises me is that no one has yet discovered the body. I left it in plain sight."

"Where?"

"Would you like me to show you?"

Although I drove the Audi northwest out of town with the air conditioner on full, I kept sweating. Michelle Miller sat next to me, chatting as if we were old friends out for a ride in the country. She told me that she was twenty-five when she first met her husband; that he was thirty years her senior, yet it didn't seem to make much difference at the time—he was so alive, so vibrant, so much fun, she said. That changed as he grew older.

"Somewhere over the ensuing decades he misplaced his sense of humor," she said. "Or maybe he sold it. Do you know why he got himself elected mayor?"

"So he could be in charge."

"He's already in charge. No, he ran for office so he'd be in a position to change the town's name."

"To what?" I said. "Millerville?"

"Millertown," Mrs. Miller said.

"Ahh."

"I laughed when he told me that. It sounded like something he

might have joked about when we were first married. He was perfectly serious."

Mrs. Miller shook her head at the thought of it. We drove in
silence until she told me to take a left at White Buffalo Road. I
slowed the car and turned.

"How well did you know the Imposter?" I said as we accelerated.

"Well enough to know that he was a phony," she said. "I recognized it the evening he came to dinner; knew before we finished
the chicken. I'm from the Cities. I grew up in Edina."

"Cake eater," I said, which was the standard insult for residents
of the moneyed suburb.

"Breakfast of champions," she said, which was the standard reply.

"Yeah, you're an Edina girl."

"Only Rush wasn't a St. Paul guy. He knew all the names, yet
none of the locations and none of the slang. He didn't know Dinky-
town was practically on the campus of the University of Minnesota.
He didn't know where Uptown was, or Seven Corners."

"Why didn't you speak up? Why didn't you tell your husband?"

"I don't like my husband very much these days. It gives me pleasure to listen to him explain how his mistakes were not mistakes;
the way his voice gets serious and he says, 'I will not be provoked.'
Hysterical."

"Why don't you leave him?"

"Why bother when he'll be leaving me soon?"

"You mean dying."

"Yes, I mean dying. None of us live forever."

"When he's gone, I take it you'll inherit all he's built."

"Saranne will inherit. Excuse me—Sara Anne. I hope she will be
generous with her mother. If not, I will gain a two-million-dollar
life insurance settlement and my freedom."

"Nothing if you leave him?"

"According to our prenup, if I leave him I'll get twenty-five thousand dollars for every year that we were married for the first ten, forty thousand for the second ten, and seventy-five after that. That's a small percentage of our net worth and barely covers my mental anguish. Dewey inserted a clause stating that the contract will be nullified in case of immorality." Michelle took her time sounding out the word. "Im-mo-ral-i-ty. I presume that means adultery, and lately I've been watching Dewey very closely. Unfortunately, he will not be provoked."

"Why are you telling me this?"

"You're a stranger. It is much easier to confide secrets to a stranger. As judgmental as you might prove to be, you will soon be gone and your opinions will not trouble me."

"I might have a big mouth," I said. "I might blab your secrets all over town before I go."

"I hardly think so. Except when it comes to my husband, I am a fairly astute judge of character. You will keep my secrets. Not out of any sense of loyalty to me, certainly. Yet you seem to care about my daughter. You will keep my secrets to protect her."

Not if we find Rushmore McKenzie's dead body, my inner voice said. *I'll scream that from the rooftops.*

"We'll see," I said aloud.

I have no idea who first decided that "10,000 Lakes" should be printed on Minnesota's license plates. Yet whoever it was got it wrong. There are actually 11,842 lakes in Minnesota that measure ten acres or better and another couple of thousand that just miss the cut. Lake Mataya was smaller than all of them. It wasn't even a lake. More like a giant puddle after a hard rain. I was sure I could wade across it without getting wet above the knees.

I first glimpsed Lake Mataya when we pulled into the gravel parking lot off of the county road. I thought I was seeing just a small bay and the trees that surrounded it hid the rest of the lake.

No, that was all there was. Grass and weeds receded at the water's edge; there was no beach. The wooden planks of a T-style dock squeaked as we walked across them. I counted six signs posted on the dock. NO DIVING, they each said. Seemed like sound advice to me.

"Pathetic, isn't it?" Mrs. Miller said. "In Minnesota, they'd bulldoze this place out of principle. Here it's practically a tourist attraction."

"How's the fishing?" I said.

Mrs. Miller thought that was an awfully funny question. When she stopped laughing I said, "Where did you kill the Imposter?"

"This way."

Mrs. Miller did not hesitate at all as she led me off the dock. We followed a worn path halfway around the lake. "Here's the place," she said when we reached a narrow trail that left the path and disappeared into a stand of ponderosa pine, American elm, box elder, green ash, and willow trees. There was a clearing among the trees where someone had built a bench using the trunk of a cottonwood tree. People had come to the clearing often, leaving behind empty beer cans, food wrappers, and cigarette butts. What grasses and shrubs there were had been trampled into submission, and in most places the ground was hard-packed dirt. The clearing was invisible from both the lake and the parking lot.

As good a place for an ambush as any, my inner voice told me.

"This is where you killed him?" I said aloud.

"Yes, right there."

Mrs. Miller pointed at a spot along the far edge of the clearing. There was no body. Then again, I never thought for a moment that there would be. We do not live in an Agatha Christie world. People do not admit that they committed murder and announce, "Yes, and I'm glad that I killed him, glad, do you hear? Ah ha ha ha ha ha." I was convinced that Mrs. Miller was playing me. The question was, why? Still, just in case there was some truth to what she said, I squatted near the spot and examined the ground carefully. There were footprints, mostly the tread of tennis shoes and the impressions of boot heels.

"When was the last time you had rain?" I said.

"Last month sometime."

"Okay."

"Do you see anything?"

"Nope."

"No?" She seemed surprised.

"What did you kill him with?" I said.

"Rush? What did I use to kill Rush?"

"Yes, Rush. Unless you've killed so many people lately that it's hard to keep them straight."

"That's not funny, McKenzie."

"I apologize."

"I used a tree branch."

"A tree branch?"

"Yes."

"You lured Rush here so you could kill him with a tree branch?"

"I thought it would be better that way. Harder to trace the murder weapon."

"What did you do with it?"

"The tree branch?"

"Yes."

"I threw it into the lake."

"You walked out to the lake where people could see you and threw the branch in?"

"It was dark. No one could see me. Besides, there was no one here. Just me and Rush."

"No other cars in the parking lot?"

"No."

I examined the ground some more. There were no bloodstains and no drag marks.

"How did you manage it?" I said.

"Manage what?"

"Mrs. Miller . . ."

"I told Rush to meet me here. Here in this spot. I waited for him. When he stepped into the clearing I hit him with the branch."

"How many times did you hit him?"

"Times? Just once."

"How did you know he was dead?"

"He fell. He didn't move."

"That doesn't mean he was dead."

"I checked his pulse."

"Where?"

"Where?"

I touched my wrist and the carotid artery in my throat as I spoke. "Wrist, carotid artery—"

"Wrist."

I held out my arm. "Show me."

Mrs. Miller set all four of her fingers over the tendons that ran down the center of my wrist instead of the radial artery that's found on the thumb side between the tendons and the edge of the bone. She jumped back when she discovered that I didn't have a pulse, either.

"Feeling for a pulse in the wrist isn't always reliable," I said. "Especially if the pulse is faint, especially if you don't have much experience at it, especially if you were rattled. You were rattled, right?"

"Are you saying he isn't dead?"

"There are two possibilities. First, that you actually did kill the Imposter and someone came along and removed the body—but I don't see any blood or drag marks. Two, that you hurt him, perhaps even knocked him unconscious, and sometime after you left he got up and walked away. Or at least he recovered enough to call for help, called for someone to pick him up, his accomplice probably. That would explain why his car was still here."

There was a third possibility—that she was lying through her teeth, but I didn't mention that.

"Are you saying I didn't kill him?" Mrs. Miller said.

"You sound disappointed."

"I am, a little."

"Well, cheer up. You committed assault with a deadly weapon with intent to kill. That's a Class C felony in most states."

"I hit him extremely hard."

"As hard as you hit me last night?"

"I didn't—McKenzie. Certainly not. I had nothing to do with what happened to you. How can you suggest such a thing?"

"Okay."

"What reason would I have for attacking you?"

"The same reason you had for attacking the Imposter."

"Rush assaulted my daughter; you protected her."

"You might not have known that."

"Mr. McKenzie."

"All right."

"Surely you don't believe—"

"Just a thought."

"I have never been so insulted."

It was hard to keep from laughing at her, but I managed it just the same.

Mrs. Miller stared down at the spot where the Imposter's body should have been.

"Should we call the police?" she said.

"We could do that. They'll strap you to a polygraph and ask some hard questions, though. Are you prepared to answer them?"

She didn't say if she was or wasn't.

"Why don't we just hold off on calling the cops for now," I said.

"Until when?"

"Until we know what really happened."

"I told you what really happened."

"I meant until we have confirmation."

"What should I do in the meantime?"

"Leave your husband, challenge the prenup, divorce him for half of everything he owns, take your daughter back to Edina, and start living the life you deserve to live—or at least the life Sara deserves to live."

"I meant for right now."

"Go home and forget all this ever happened."

A puzzled expression spread over Mrs. Miller's face.

"I don't know what you're talking about," she said.

"See, it's working already."

We slowly made our way through the trees back to the parking lot. Mrs. Miller's cell phone rang—it sounded like an old-fashioned telephone.

"Uh-oh," she said when she read the display, and then, "Hello, dear," when she activated the phone.

I could hear only her end of the conversation.

"I'm at Lake Mataya . . . I'm with Mr. McKenzie. He asked if I would show him where Rush— . . . If you must know, he came to the house looking for you . . . Apparently Rush received a phone call that originated from our home just before he disappeared. Did you call Rush, dear? . . . Of course."

Mrs. Miller held the phone out for me. I took the phone and pressed the receiver to my ear.

"Yes?"

"What are you doing?" Miller said. "I said I wanted my family left out of this."

"I said I don't work for you."

There was a long pause, and for a moment I thought we had lost Miller's signal.

"I will not be provoked," he said at last.

I placed my thumb over the microphone.

"He will not be provoked," I said.

Mrs. Miller covered her mouth with her hand and turned away, afraid that her husband would hear her laughter.

I removed my thumb from the microphone.

"Mr. Miller, I'm not trying to be a pain in the ass." *Oh yeah, like he believes that,* my inner voice said. "I'm just trying to find answers, like I was asked to do, remember?"

Mr. Miller sighed heavily. "Tell my wife to bring you out to the sheds," he said. Then he hung up.

Miller Self-Storage was a work in progress. It was located north of Libbie, and from the illustration on the huge sign along the county road, it would eventually have sheds large enough to house RVs, not to mention cars, boats, and furniture. Only that was some time in the future. When I arrived there, it was little more than a huge slab of concrete surrounded by gravel, stacks of cinder blocks, bags of cement, wood, and corrugated tin. Mr. Miller and the banker, Jon Kampa, were standing near the center of the slab, where additional building supplies were also stacked. Miller wore an untucked sports shirt loudly decorated with rodeo images; Kampa wore a powder blue dress shirt unbuttoned at the collar, the shirtsleeves carefully rolled up. There were no workmen in sight, which raised the question, what were Miller and Kampa doing there alone on a late Saturday afternoon? After parking the car, Mrs. Miller and I walked toward them. The bright sunshine made Miller look much older than the previous times I'd met him.

"Explain yourself," he said.

"I was born in St. Paul to an ex-marine and his wife—"

"I don't want your fucking life's story. I want to know why you're messing with my wife."

"Actually, your wife was messing with me, but what the hell."

"McKenzie," Mrs. Miller said. She appeared shocked at my remark, but appearances can be deceiving. "I did no such thing." She turned to her husband. "Mr. McKenzie asked about a phone call that was made from our house to Rush just before he disappeared. I told him—"

"She told me that she lured Rush to Lake Mataya and killed him with a tree branch, but of course there was no sign of foul play and we couldn't find a body." I stamped the concrete slab with my foot. "Is it under here, do you think?" I stamped some more.

"What I told you was true," Mrs. Miller said.

"I believe you," I said. "Only I'm notoriously gullible. Just ask my investment counselor."

Mr. Miller shook his head, his expression an odd mixture of disappointment, amusement, and anger.

"Mickie, what were you thinking?" he said.

"She was thinking about her investment," I said.

"Her investment?"

"She was protecting you."

"I didn't make a phone call."

"Are you sure?"

"Are you calling me a liar?"

"Yep."

"Watch your mouth."

"Someone called the Imposter using your phone."

"Nonsense."

"I told you, I did it," Mrs. Miller said.

"Nonsense," her husband said.

Jon Kampa stood at a discreet distance throughout the conversation, pretending not to be there, giving the Millers the illusion of privacy while listening intently to every word. Finally he spoke up.

"I did it," he said. "I made the phone call."

"Ahh, another county heard from," I said.

Kampa moved closer, stepping between me and Miller.

"I had dinner that Tuesday night at the Millers'." He gave Miller a meaningful stare over his shoulder. "Remember?" Mr. and Mrs. Miller both nodded their heads, so I knew he must have been telling the truth. "Just before I left, I asked to use the phone. I called Rush. I called the Imposter."

"Why?" I said.

"To warn him. Dewey kept saying that he was going to kill him or have him killed because of Saranne. I couldn't let that happen. I didn't care about Rush, but Dewey and I have been friends for a long time, and I didn't want to see him do anything foolish. So I warned Rush to get out of town."

"You're a good friend," Miller said.

"Either that, or he's protecting his investment, too," I said.

"What's that supposed to mean?"

I ignored the question. Instead, I asked Kampa, "Did you arrange to meet Rush?"

"No," he said. "I just told him that he was no longer welcome in Libbie and that he should leave."

"What about the mall?"

"It didn't come up. It was a short conversation."

I turned toward Miller. "That's two versions. Want to make it three, turn it into a real *Rashomon*?"

"You heard the truth," Miller said.

"Which time? You know what, it doesn't matter. Why don't we call the cops and let them sort it out."

"McKenzie, you said you weren't going to call the police," Mrs. Miller said.

"I lied," I said. "Why not? Everyone else is doing it."

"Fine," Miller said. "Call Chief Gustafson. See where that gets you."

"I'm not going to call Gustafson. I'm going to call Big Joe Balk. I bet he asks if this has anything to do with the murders of Tracie Blake and Mike Randisi."

From the expression on the big man's face, he didn't like that idea at all. *Another reason to give the sheriff some respect,* my inner voice told me.

"I've had enough of you," Miller said. He used a big, beefy arm to nudge Kampa aside and moved close to me, a bully trying to use his size to intimidate. "You're getting out of town. You're getting out of town now."

"You remind me of Church. Remember what happened to him?"

"I'm not afraid of you."

Miller shoved hard enough against my chest to force me to take a couple of backward steps. I was surprised a man his age was that strong; it made me think that Michelle Miller's plan to wait for his demise was not all that sound.

"Do you think I'm afraid of you?" Miller asked.

He pushed again, and again I had to give ground. He followed close behind.

"Don't do that," I said.

"Get out of town."

Miller leaned on me a third time. I retreated a few steps to maintain my balance.

"Don't do that," I said. "I'm serious."

"No, I'm serious. I've had it with you, city boy."

Miller brought both hands up and lunged toward my face. This time I caught his left hand between both of my hands, his knuckles between my palms, my fingers interlocked. I squeezed hard and lifted the hand high in the air while keeping the knuckles pressed together. I pushed his hand back as I pulled his arm down. The big man came down with it, falling to his knees in front of me. He shouted, "Let me go," as I applied more pressure. It would have been easy to crumple his aging fingers, to snap his wrist.

"I do believe you need anger management therapy," I said. I squeezed his knuckles and bent his hand farther back, making him cry out in pain some more. "Get used to the idea—I'm not going anywhere until I find out what happened to the Imposter and all that money. In the meantime . . ." I leaned in close and hissed in his ear. "Say anything that you want, to me or about me, I don't care. But you lay hands on me again, they'll need tweezers to put you back together, I don't give a damn how old you are."

I released his hand. He cradled it with the other and tried to massage the pain away.

"We're having some fun now, aren't we, kids?" I said.

Neither the Millers nor Jon Kampa seemed to agree with me. I can't say I blamed them. I didn't mind hurting Miller—it wasn't long ago that he had me Tasered, kidnapped, and locked in the trunk of a car, remember? On the other hand, I had accomplished nothing except to identify a couple more liars in a town that seemed loaded with them. Worse, I was no closer to finding the Imposter than when I started.

"This is getting us nowhere," I said.

I left them there, crossing the concrete slab back to my car. Not for the first time, I wondered what the hell I was doing in Libbie, SD.

It wasn't until I was two miles down the road that I started to wonder, what if Kampa was telling the truth, as unlikely as that might be—what if he had warned Rush to get outta Dodge? I pulled to the shoulder and tried to call Chief Gustafson. I didn't have any coverage. I drove closer to town. It wasn't until I was near the outskirts of Libbie that my cell phone picked up the faintest sliver of a bar.

"Hey, Chief," I said when he answered my call. "I know you have a lot on your plate right now, but I'd like you to check something for me, if you could."

"What?"

"I've been thinking about the Imposter's car. You said you found it parked in the lot over at Lake Mataya."

"What about it?"

"You said you had it towed back to the rental agency."

"That's right."

"Why tow it?"

"We didn't have the keys."

"The Imposter abandoned the car but didn't leave the keys?" I said.

"Probably he just slipped them in his pocket without thinking about it. That would be a natural thing to do, wouldn't it?"

"I suppose. Except I keep going back to my original question. Why abandon the car in the first place? Why not just drive off? And why abandon it at the park, where it would be easy to spot?"

"What's on your mind, McKenzie?"

"Lake Mataya is on a main drag out of town, right?"

"White Buffalo Road, sure."

"I want you to call the rental agency and see if there was any trouble with the car. See if it started and drove okay."

"Do you think the car broke down, that's why it was abandoned?"

"It's a possibility."

The chief thought about it for a few beats, and I wondered if he was thinking what I was thinking. Turned out he was.

"Rush figures someone is onto him and panics, just like you thought," he said. "He fully intends to head somewhere like Rapid

City, but his car breaks down. The only person he can trust to give him a ride would be his accomplice."

"We think that the Imposter is in the Cayman Islands because that's where the money is," I said. "Except there are at least a half-dozen people with the account numbers and password that could have stolen the money. If the accomplice was one of them—"

"The accomplice would have known the bank account was as flush as it was going to get, that it was time to pull the plug—"

"Which meant he no longer needed Rush. He could have killed Rush—"

"Kept the money for himself, and because we found the car abandoned at the lake—"

"We would assume that the Imposter blew town with the money and would be spending our time looking for him instead of the real villain."

The chief gave it another beat.

"It's a good theory except for one thing—there's no body. Where is Rush?"

"I'm working on it," I said.

"You do that. I'll call the rental agency and get back to you."

CHAPTER TWELVE

Night seemed to fall quicker and more colorfully in Libbie than it did in the Cities. Out here it went from orange to red to purple to dark blue to black, and it went through this transformation in mere minutes. I found myself sitting in my car next to the Pioneer Hotel watching it, wishing I didn't have to wait twenty-four hours to see it again.

Sharren Nuffer was back behind the registration desk when I finally stepped inside the hotel. Her eyes were still red and puffy.

"Hi," she said.

"How are you doing?" I asked.

"I'm okay. It's been a tough day. I think the whole town is in mourning."

"I can appreciate that."

"Nothing like this has ever happened to us before."

I liked how she said "us." In the greater Twin Cities, which boasts a population of about two-point-eight million, us was a comparatively small group of people consisting of families, friends, and co-workers. Murders occurred with some frequency, yet they nearly always involved someone else, rarely us. Out of either indifference or self-defense, we didn't take them personally. In a small town like Libbie, which had far fewer people than your average Twin Cities high school, us was everyone. In a very real sense, what happened to one happened to all. Presumably it was the reason people in small towns looked out for each other more than we did in the Cities.

"How did it go with Mr. Miller?" Sharren asked.

"About what you would expect. Are you sure that Rush received a call from Miller the Tuesday night he disappeared?"

"That's what the caller ID said. Does he deny it?"

"Yeah, but he's the only one that does."

"I don't understand."

"Neither do I. Can you do me a favor?"

"Of course."

"I need a list of the names of all the city council members and where I can find them. Tracie was going to introduce me, but . . ."

Sharren stood perfectly still for a moment; she didn't even blink.

"Of course," she said. "I am so sorry about Tracie and Mike. It's depressing. It makes me feel old. I don't like to feel old."

"I understand."

"Oh, I nearly forgot." She reached under the desk and produced a sheet of white paper. "This was faxed to you."

I studied the sheet. Sharren did the same, looking over my shoulder.

"What is it?" she said.

The fax was from Greg Schroeder, and it listed the addresses and phone numbers of a couple of dozen men named Nicholas Hendel. Most of them lived in Chicago. There were also a few in Skokie, Oak Park, Cicero, Winnetka, Arlington Heights, Ashton, Joliet, and more.

"A needle in a haystack," I said.

A moment later, the lobby was filled with the whoop and wail of a fire truck siren. It started low, increased in volume, and then decreased as the truck passed the hotel's large windows. Seconds later, another truck passed.

"Volunteer fire department," Sharren said. She rushed to the window and looked out. As she did, Evan, the blond bartender, backed into the lobby through the front door, watching the trucks pass as he did.

"What's going on?" Sharren asked him. "Do you know?"

"It's the Dannes—Rick and Cathy—over by the high school. Their house is on fire."

By the time I reached the site, the eight-man volunteer fire department was already hard at it. I could see them clearly in the high-intensity lights that they had trained on the building. Two two-man crews were hosing down the side of the house where the fire was visible, while a third team cautiously crossed the roof. One of the firefighters powered up a chain saw. He carefully cut a hole in the roof to release the intense heat while the second gave him a steadying embrace. I wanted to help, but I didn't even know where to begin, so I stood back like a couple of dozen other gawkers, staying out of the way as best I could.

The flames licked one side of the house, but the opposite side had remained untouched. A fire ladder was set against that wall, and the two men who had used it to reach the roof now scrambled back down. A firefighter with an ax smashed a window on the ground floor, and smoke began billowing out, rising until it disappeared into the night sky. A moment later, he smashed another window.

A woman screamed. I followed the scream to the front of the house, where Rick Danne was holding tight to his wife, trying to console her. It didn't seem to do any good. She writhed in his arms as if she wanted to run into the burning building. I wondered if someone could be trapped inside until I heard a voice announce, "No one was home when it started."

The flames cast frightening orange shadows against Cathy's face and white shirt. Her sorrow and fear and rage were agonizing to watch. It reminded me of those times when I worked traffic control at fires when I was a cop in St. Paul, sometimes having to restrain residents from braving the fire to recover some cherished heirloom. I knew what she must have been feeling, what other fire victims felt—the terrific sense of loss. It wasn't just her belongings that were going up in smoke; it was the nourishing routine of her life. After all, shelter isn't that hard to come by. Clothes, furniture, appliances, the house itself—those all could be replaced. Wedding photos could not. Nor could music collections, books, childhood mementos, the little black dress that fit just so, the comfy chair that was just the way we liked it, the mug we reached for whenever we wanted a cup of joe, or the prized souvenirs of a life lived long and well. They were the things that anchored us to our lives. Without them, we were like kites cut loose from their strings.

I found myself moving far out of Cathy's sight line for fear that seeing me would cause her even greater pain—and because I wanted to spare myself the reproachful stare and accusatory oaths that I knew I deserved. There was no doubt in my mind that Church had caused this fire, as he had so many others, to get back at the Dannes and to get back at me, to make a joke of my vow to protect them. I also had no doubt that Cathy Danne would blame me for this outrage, and she would be right to do so. The fire would not have happened if I had kept my seat in the Café Rossini, if I had not insisted on standing up to Church, if I had not been so quick to impose myself on someone else's life.

There was a hole deep in my stomach now, and it was slowly filling with the black bile of guilt. I didn't like the feeling it gave me, and I wished it would go away. I wished there were something I could do to make it all right. I wished I could put out the fire and rebuild their home, and I wished I could do it in seconds. The more I wished, the angrier I became.

A moment later, the hoses were shut down. Yet the fire still burned. The flames, hot against my face from the beginning, gained in intensity. The wind—the wretched wind had not stopped blowing since I arrived in Libbie—swirled the smoke and blew it into my eyes. I blamed the smoke for the tears that came suddenly. I wiped them with the back of my hand and eased farther away from the fire until I was across the street.

"What the hell?" I said.

A red tanker truck disconnected from the pump truck and sped off. A second tanker quickly replaced it, and a firefighter worked frantically until the hoses were resupplied with water.

"What the hell?" I said again.

"It's the ol' tanker shuffle," a voice said.

An old man leaning on a cane was standing behind me on the sidewalk. He brushed his nearly nonexistent hair with his hand. I drifted back to where he stood.

"What do you mean?"

"We have only one water hydrant in this town that works properly," he said. "We call it the sacred hydrant, down on Main. So what we hafta do, we hafta shuttle our water tankers back and forth from a fill site to the pump truck, kinda like a bucket brigade. One's got twelve hundred and fifty gallons; the other holds fifteen hundred. Luckily, the fill site is less than a mile from here, so it won't be much of a problem. If it were outside of town, this fire, we'd be fucked. As it is . . ." The old man lowered his head, gave it a slow shake, and raised it again. "Eight-man crew to cover a whole town— it's ridiculous. Should have fifteen at least. I'd lend a hand, but . . ." He raised his cane for me to see.

Like everyone else, I kept staring at the fire. It was tragic, yet also quite seductive, almost beautiful. *An enraged elemental beast slaking a hunger so old only stones and gods remembered.* The mystery writer Nevada Barr wrote that. Now I knew what she meant.

I watched the fire crawl up the outside wall of the Danne home. Flames started venting in the open window on the second floor.

"Huh," the old man said. "That shouldn't be happening."

"What?"

"The flames in the window. This here is an exterior fire; fire is burning mostly on the surface, not burning through the wall, you can tell. To spread so rapidly to the second floor like that, it must be feeding off an accelerant of some kind."

"An accelerant?"

"Yeah. Look. You got black smoke coming off the wall, there. See it? Black smoke, usually that means petroleum-based products. The rest of the fire—that's white smoke. Even the roof where you have tar paper and oil-based shingles, that's white smoke."

"Do you think the fire was set?"

"Looks like," the old man said. " 'Course, I could be wrong. These throwaway houses, the way they're built now, using all them lightweight construction materials. Used to be, back in my day, builders used dimensional lumber to make your wood frames, had masonry walls, wood floors—there was mass to resist the heat; the building's support system had a longer life expectancy. That woulda given you time for an interior attack. Go inside to get at the fire without worrying about the damn roof comin' down on your head. Now, hell, the cheap crap they use cuz they wanna keep the cost down—your plywood and fiberboard and plastics and crap; walls built to carry only as much load as you need to meet code—you just can't risk it. No, sir.

"Ten years ago, I woulda been the first to say you can't put out no fire standing outside shooting through windows and holes in the roof. Now, now you gotta use them blitz attack nozzles to overpower the fire, cool the exterior and then go interior. 'Course, if you got someone inside that needs rescuing, you forget all that crap and just go get 'im."

I stood silently and watched the firefighters go about their business. The old man said the boys knew what they doing, and I guess it must have been true because they managed to knock down the blaze in just over a quarter of an hour. After that it was all about cooling hot spots. My impression was that the water damage would be far greater than the fire damage.

Once the blaze was extinguished to their satisfaction, the firefighters used giant fans to help vent the house of smoke. The old man moved forward, and I went with him. The firefighters and a few neighbors began carrying belongings from the ground floor onto the lawn, where they were covered with a tarp. No one was allowed to go upstairs until an engineer determined if it was safe to use the staircase, although from the look on Rick Danne's face, I knew that as soon as someone's back was turned, he would give it a try. A man carrying a large overstuffed chair by himself became lodged in the doorway, and I helped him out. He and I made a few more trips in and out of the house, rescuing furniture, before I actually bumped into Cathy. Her face was smudged with soot, and her hair appeared singed. Her eyes held a kind of wild expression that I had never seen before, as if they were trying to convey too many emotions at once. She stared, and for a moment I thought she did not recognize me. A single word told me otherwise.

"McKenzie," she said.

"I am so, so sorry," I told her.

I took a deep breath and waited for the angry words, even blows, that I felt I deserved—I promised myself I would accept them all without complaint or defense. They didn't land. Long moments passed before Cathy spoke.

"It's terrible," she said.

"Yes, it is."

"He'll probably get away with it, too, just like he did all those other times."

She was staring so intently that I found myself taking a backward step.

"The police can't help," she said.

In that instant, I knew exactly what she was doing. Cathy Danne was reminding me of the promise I had made Church in the Café Rossini: *If anything happens to anyone in this room or their property, especially the Dannes—I don't care if they're struck by lightning—I will come for you. Not the cops. Me.*

"I'm not the police," I said.

"I know."

"Good luck to you, Mrs. Danne."

She bobbed her head purposefully. "McKenzie," she said.

Cathy retreated into her home without a backward glance. The old man was still watching from the sidewalk. I thanked him for his courtesy and turned away from the house. That's when I saw Church's pal Paulie. He was sitting on the hood of a car down the street and drinking beer from a longneck bottle. I walked up to him. He smiled.

"Guess someone was careless with matches," he said. "Tsk, tsk, tsk."

"Tell Church to meet me at the Tall Moon Tavern tomorrow night at nine," I said. "Tell him not to keep me waiting."

"I ain't your nigger," he said.

I grabbed both of Paulie's legs and yanked hard. His entire body slid off the car and fell straight down. His head banged off the bumper, and the rest of him bounced hard against the asphalt. The bottle shattered and splashed him with beer and glass.

I kept walking, not even bothering to look back.

Sharren was behind the registration desk when I entered the Pioneer Hotel. I asked her if she ever went home. She said a fellow employee was on vacation so she was working double shifts.

"I don't mind," she said. "I don't have anything else to do."

"Why do you stay here?" I asked.

"What do you mean?"

"In Libbie. Why do you stay here?"

"Where would I go?"

"Anywhere. Anywhere with a future. There's no future here. It was used up years ago."

"You're upset because of the fire."

"Am I?"

"It's not your fault."

"Who said it was?"

"Everybody knows what happened at the Café Rossini, McKenzie."

"What is everybody going to do about it?"

"What do you mean?"

"How many fires has that sonuvabitch set over the years? A dozen? More? Guys like Church get away with their bullshit because the people they hurt insist on following the rules even when the rules work against them, and he's going to get away with this, too, unless—"

"Unless someone breaks the rules just like Church," Sharren said.

"Yes."

"What are you trying to talk yourself into?"

I flashed on the look in Cathy Danne's eyes.

"Not a thing," I said.

"I hate to think that you would stoop to Church's level."

"There would be a difference."

"Doing wrong for the right reason, is that the difference?"

"Something like that."

"Are you hungry?"

"Excuse me?"

"The kitchen's closed. Everything in town is closed at this hour except for a couple of bars. I bet I could rustle something up for you in the kitchen if you wanted. When was the last time you ate?"

"I had something at the clinic this morning."

Sharren glanced at her watch and shook her head.

"I'll be right back," she said. "Watch the desk for me. Give a shout if someone comes in or calls."

I made myself comfortable in an overstuffed chair when she left. No one did come in, and I was starting to doze when Sharren returned with a club sandwich and a tap beer.

"Evan was just closing the bar, but I got him to pour this for you," she said.

I thanked her profusely for both the sandwich and the beer and dug in. I didn't know how hungry I was until I started to eat. She sat in the nearest chair and watched me. After a while, she said, "I thought about leaving, only I don't know where I would go or what I would find there. It frightens me. If I were younger . . . Could you just up and leave your home?"

"It would be hard," I admitted.

"What would make it hard?"

"Leaving the people I love."

"That's the thing, isn't it?"

"Is there someone in Libbie you can't live without?"

Sharren looked up and to her right as if she were remembering something. "Yes," she said. "Finally, at last, yes, I think there is."

Her answer surprised me, and I said, "Oh?"

"You're thinking about Rush," she said. "You're thinking about the times I flirted with you."

"More than flirted," I said. "You opened the door pretty wide."

"I suppose I was testing myself, making sure I was making the right decision. Have you ever done anything like that?"

I thought of Nina. I thought of a red-haired beauty named Danielle Mallinger, the police chief of a small town in southwestern

Minnesota that I met months later. I thought of how I didn't fully and truly commit to Nina until after I spent time with Danny.

"Sounds kind of juvenile," I said.

"I guess, but you need to be sure, don't you? It's about peace of mind. Peace of mind is hard to come by for most people."

I told her that was probably true.

CHAPTER THIRTEEN

Sunday morning, and the window to my antiquated hotel room was open—when was the last time you were able to open a window in a hotel? Through the window I heard three sets of church bells calling to each other from different corners of the city. Through the window I could smell the lingering smoke and ash from the Danne house fire. Or maybe it was just the clothes I had worn last night and tossed on the floor.

I lay in bed, my hands tucked beneath my head, and stared at the ceiling. I thought about Tracie Blake. She had been a lonely woman. She asked me to help chase the alone feeling away. I understood the alone feeling; I knew about waking up alone and going to bed alone and all the lonely hours in between with the phone not ringing and the e-mail in-box coming up empty. I believed we all knew it at one time or another. Yet I had turned her down, just as I had turned down Sharren Nuffer. I did it for honorable reasons. I did it for Nina, the woman who had chased the alone feeling away for me. That didn't make me feel any less guilty about it.

I thought about Mike, another solitary soul. He and Tracie found each other. Together they had chased away the alone feeling, if only for one night. But who knows? One night could have become two. Then a week. A month. A year. Maybe it would have been permanent if they had time.

I liked Tracie. I liked Mike. In my neighborhood, they both would have been labeled "good guys"—high praise indeed. Now they were both gone, and there wasn't anything I could do about it. I didn't even know where to start; not that Big Joe Balk would tolerate my kibitzing. He didn't know me. This was his ground, not mine. My only thought was to keep after the Imposter and see if one thing might lead to another.

Church, on the other hand, was a different matter.

I listened to the bells. When they finally fell silent, I spoke aloud—"Brothers and sisters, the subject of today's homily is"— and stopped. The Old Testament God spoke of an eye for an eye and a tooth for a tooth—proportional justice. The New Testament God preached forgiveness—"Turn the other cheek," He said.

So which is it? Justice or forgiveness?

He beareth not the sword in vain: for he is the minister of God, a revenger to execute wrath upon him that doeth evil—so wrote Paul in Romans 13 of the emperor's policemen.

Et prout vultis ut faciant vobis homines et vos facite illis similiter, wrote Luke in 6:31—"And just as you wish others to do for you, do also the same for them."

I decided to let Shakespeare settle the matter: *If you prick us, do we not bleed? If you tickle us, do we not laugh? If you poison us, do we not die? And if you wrong us, shall we not revenge?*

I don't even know why I bothered with the internal debate. I had made up my mind when I gazed into Cathy's eyes, and I confirmed my decision when I found Paulie sitting on the car hood, having a swell time at the expense of the Dannes.

"Fire and brimstone," I said aloud. "Today's homily—fire and fucking brimstone."

Sharren wouldn't approve. Most of the people I knew and cared about wouldn't approve—Cathy Danne might even be among them once she had time to think about it. I didn't care.

Forty minutes later, I was in the lobby of the Pioneer Hotel. I did not know the young woman behind the reservation desk, but she knew me.

"Mr. McKenzie," she said, "Sharren Nuffer asked me to give this to you."

I took a folded sheet of paper from the woman's hand. It contained a list of the Libbie City Council members and where I might find them.

"Thank you," I said.

I headed for the door. The woman called to me.

"If you're hungry," she said, "our brunch lasts until eleven."

I stopped and looked through the arched doorway into the dining room. It was packed. I recognized some of the patrons from last night's fire. I had no doubt that the fire—and the murders of Tracie Blake and Mike Randisi—were the main topics of conversation of the diners. Except for Perry and Dawn Neske, who apparently had other things on their minds.

I saw them sitting across from each other in a booth against the far wall, laughing over plates heaped with eggs, hash browns, flapjacks, ham, bacon, sausage, assorted fruits, and muffins. He reached across the white linen tablecloth and took her hand. She leaned toward him, said something, and smiled. He smiled back. A moment later, she pulled her hand free and cupped it beneath a cube of cantaloupe that she forked into Perry's mouth. He responded with a strawberry that Dawn ate from his fingertips.

Huh, my inner voice said.

Apparently my presence was a huge shock to her, because Linnea covered her mouth and stared when I entered Munoz Emporium. "I'm telling," she said behind the hand. She reached for her red phone as I walked past. A few minutes later, Chuck Munoz found me in the housewares department.

"Can I help you?" he asked.

"I'm looking for a kitchen timer," I said. "Something with a double-A battery. Oh, here we are."

I took two small timers off the shelf.

"Anything else?" Munoz asked.

"Do you have any small glass bottles?" I held my thumb and forefinger two inches apart. "About this big, maybe an inch around."

Munoz led me three aisles over to where there were plenty of empty jars of various sizes, including canning jars. It took me two minutes to find the size I needed.

"Anything else?" Munoz said.

"Are you trying to get rid of me?"

"Why would I?"

"Because I remind you that the woman you disliked so much was murdered yesterday."

"I didn't—I liked—" Munoz closed his eyes. When he opened them, he said, "I liked Tracie very much. She was a friend of mine. We had our problems because of the mall, but we would have gotten past it."

"Not if the mall had been a success. Not if you were put out of business."

"What are you saying?"

"Did you know Mike Randisi?"

"No. I knew of him, but I didn't actually know him. Why? What are you saying?"

"Rush disappearing, Tracie's murder—they take care of a lot of problems for you."

"What are you saying?"

"Stop repeating yourself, Chuck. You sound ridiculous."

Munoz opened his mouth like he wanted to speak, and then quickly shut it.

"The Imposter disappeared after about 9:00 P.M. Tuesday before last," I said. "Where were you?"

"You're not a cop. You don't get to ask me those questions."

"Then we'll have Big Joe Balk ask them."

"I was here until 10:00 P.M.," Munoz said.

Wow, that was the second time using the sheriff's name scared someone, my inner voice told me. *Balk must be some badass.*

"Are you open until ten?" I said.

"We're open until nine in the summer. I was doing inventory."

"Alone?"

"Yes."

"So we have just your word for it."

"What are you say—"

Munoz cut off his sentence abruptly. I filled the void.

"After ten?" I said.

"I went home."

"Witnesses?"

"No."

"Where were you last Friday night?"

"I worked until nine, and then I went home."

"Alone."

"Goddammit."

"I'll take that as a yes."

"You have no business asking me these questions."

"I'm making it my business to find the Imposter and to catch whoever killed Tracie Blake. It better not be you."

"It's not."

"Then you should be willing to help."

I had heard Munoz's long, weary sigh before. He sounded like a man who was firmly lodged between a rock and a hard place. Putting him in that position gave me pleasure.

"What do you want to know?" he said.

"Tell me about your relationship with Tracie."

"We were—intimate."

"For how long?"

"A few months."

"And then?"

"It ended."

"Why?"

"I don't know. She never told me. We were together and then we weren't. A while later I learned that she had taken up with someone else."

"Who?"

"Chief Gustafson."

"That must have stung."

"It did."

"When she started supporting the mall, that must have stung even more."

"I couldn't believe she would betray me like that."

"I could see why you would be angry."

"Angry? I was a helluva lot more than angry. I could have killed both of them."

"Did you?"

Munoz took a step backward.

"What am I saying?" he said. "No, I didn't kill them. Of course not. It was just a figure of speech. I could never—no. I didn't kill anyone."

Sure sounded convincing to me.

Spiess Drug Store wasn't actually a drug store because it no longer filled prescriptions.

"Our pharmacist left," Terri Spiess said. "He decided he couldn't make a living here, and he left. Can't really blame him, but it leaves me in a tough spot. I've been trying to hire a pharmacist ever since—no luck. If something doesn't happen soon . . ." She shook her head as if she were afraid to imagine the possibility.

Spiess was another of Libbie's many beauties. Her hair was black, straight, and long, and her complexion was dark, hinting that she had some Native American blood. Her eyes, though, were red, and the wrinkles around them suggested worry.

"Is it as bad as all that?" I said.

"Last year, prescription revenue accounted for sixty-seven percent of our total sales," she said. "Yeah, it's that bad."

"Where do people go for their prescriptions?"

"Most use the clinic. It costs a lot more, and they don't deliver like we did, but what other choice do people have? No pharmacist, no pharmacy—it's that simple."

"Maybe if the mall had gone through—"

"I don't have the money to pay rent in a mall," Spiess said. "More likely they would have moved in a CVS or Walgreens, and that would have been the end of that. This store has been here almost as long as the town, and now . . ." She shook her head some more. "The way things are going, the town might not be here much longer, either."

I remembered what Miller had told me. "It's the county seat," I said.

"What makes you think the county will survive? Twenty years ago we had nearly five thousand residents. Now it's down to barely three. Besides, we're the county seat in name only. The school is here, and so are the library, public works, the assessor's office, and natural resources. On the other hand, human services, the sheriff's department, the courts, county administration, all that's up in Mercer. People like old man Miller keep talking about consolidation. They think that everything is going to move here, that we'll be the town left standing when the smoke clears. C'mon. We're nearly a quarter million dollars in debt. No one's going to be consolidating with us. We're the ones that're going to be consolidating. We'll be consolidating with Mercer."

"The state could step in."

"Why would it?"

"I don't know."

"It would be damn nice if you could find all that money, Mr. McKenzie. It won't do me any good, but the town . . ."

"Did you have any dealings with Rush?" I said.

"Very few. Once he learned about my situation, that I had no money for him, he stayed away."

"What about as a member of the city council?"

"I just sat there and listened and nodded like everyone else."

"You knew the password for—"

"I heard you were looking into that. McKenzie, everyone knew the password, and if they didn't they could have figured it out easy enough. I mean, we used the same password for all of our accounts, for everything. You want to mess with our Web site the way those high school kids did last October? Just type in LIBBIESD1884. Seems to me that we could have avoided a lot of problems if only we had shown a little imagination. Listen, it's Sunday. Sunday is my day for staring at my books and feeling sorry for myself. Is there anything else I can do for you?"

"As a matter of fact, I could use some hydrogen peroxide, an eyedropper, and a thermometer."

The owner of the only hardware store within fifty miles said he was selling out.

"Business has been falling off for years," he said. "Now this. I never ran for city council, you know. I was appointed when Manny DeVine quit. He was the pharmacist over at Spiess Drugs, and one day he decided to hell with it and left town. Old man Miller

thought I'd make a reliable rubber stamp, so he appointed me—
our charter let him do it. Councilman George Humphrey, I kind
of liked the sound of that. Now—now they're going to blame me
for everything that's happened, for losing the money. Me and
Bizek. I don't need that shit."

"Why blame you?"

"I was a true believer. I thought it was a great idea, the mall,
and I talked it up, talked it up even when guys like Chuck Munoz
and Ronny Radosevich said it would ruin business in downtown,
when Jon Kampa said we should be more careful. Now all that
money's gone. You know what? I'm not even going to the next
meeting. Screw it."

Humphrey rang up my purchases—an acetone-based paint sol-
vent, a roll of electrical tape, rubber gloves, and a pair of protective
goggles—and put them into a brown bag printed with the name
of his store.

"Anything else?" he said.

"Did you have any dealings with Rush outside of the city council?" I asked.

"A lot of dealings. I told you, I drank the Kool-Aid. I believed
every word that bastard said, even put up fifty thousand of my own
for a spot in the mall. That hurt, let me tell you. That's it, though.
I'm done. Kaput. Fini. I'm cutting my losses. I'm selling the store to
the first chump who comes along with money in his jeans. Hell, I
might not even wait for a chump. I might just shutter the doors
and walk away."

"That'll leave your friends and neighbors in a tough spot, won't
it, since you have the only hardware store around?"

"McKenzie, you're not listening. I don't give a shit."

There were two cars and a pickup parked in the lot of Schooley's
Auto Repair. The front ends of all three were smashed in.

"What happened?" I asked.

Schooley tapped the hood of the first car.

"This one ran into a tree," he said. "Can you believe it? There are like three dozen trees in all of Perkins County and the kid finds one. Got his license like two weeks before the accident. Old man is fit to be tied. This one"—he pointed at the pickup—"I don't know what happened here. Owner comes in and says fix it. He's going to pay out of his own pocket; says he's not going to bother his insurance company. I don't know what that means, but it can't be good, can it?"

"Probably not."

"This one hit a deer."

Schooley stopped next to a very nice 2009 Nissan Altima Rogue S—at least it used to be nice before the deer smashed its front right quarter panel all to hell. The passenger side fender had collapsed against the tire, shredding it as well. From the look of the damaged rim, I guessed that the owner had tried to drive it for a few miles anyway. The windshield was also broken. Lines like a spiderweb flowed from a single impact crater on the passenger side. Some of the glass at the point of impact was stained with what I strongly suspected was blood.

"It belongs to the banker," Schooley said. "He's really angry, and I don't blame him. Had me tow it in Wednesday a week ago and told me to fix it, but I can't fix it until I get the parts, can I? I used to work with a guy who was pretty reliable at getting me what I needed, only he went bankrupt. Now I need to go through these other parts guys, except they only ship up here once a week to keep costs down, and I missed the last shipment. Wasted a week. It's harder and harder to do business, I'm here to tell ya. I should get the parts tomorrow, but that doesn't make Kampa any happier. I don't suppose you need any work done."

"Sorry."

"What do you need?"

"I need some battery acid."

Schooley glanced at my car.

"Not for the Audi," he said. There was alarm in his voice.

"No, no, no. Something else."

"Are you going to do some tanning?"

Tanning? my inner voice said. *What the hell is tanning?*

"I thought I'd give it a try," I said aloud.

"Yeah, a lot of people around here come in looking for the sulfuric acid they put in batteries for their projects. What kind of fur?"

"I thought I'd start small."

"Goat?"

Why not?

"Yeah," I said.

"I hear you," Schooley said. "If you don't know what you're doing, just starting out, it's always best to go with something inexpensive. I knew a guy, ruined a perfectly good antelope. Now, if you tan the deer that Kampa killed . . ."

"Maybe I should. What happened to it?"

"Hell if I know. Probably still in the ditch up on White Buffalo Road. So, tell me, what recipe are you using? Pickle tan?"

"That's what was recommended to me."

"Gotta be careful with that. Sulfuric acid works fine if you keep it to about eight ounces per two gallons of water. The salt—that's what you gotta watch out for. What kind of salt are you using? Rock salt?"

"That's what was recommended."

"I wouldn't risk it."

"Why not?"

"Rock salt doesn't dissolve all that well. It's gonna be rough, gonna tear up your fur. Want my advice?"

"Yes, I do."

"Use about two pounds of nonionized salt. It dissolves much better in water; it'll treat the fur a lot less harshly, I'm here to tell ya."

"That's good advice," I said. "I appreciate it."

"No extra charge. I'll be right with ya."

Schooley went inside his shop to retrieve my acid, which confirmed a theory that I've believed since I was a kid—if you speak and act confidently, you can get away with the most amazing bullshit.

The final city council member I wanted to see shut down his riding mower when he saw me walking toward him across his enormous lawn.

"Lookin' for someone?" he said.

"I'm McKenzie."

"The real deal this time, huh? I'm Len Hudalla."

He offered his hand, and I leaned across the riding mower to shake it.

"I heard you were making the rounds," Hudalla said. "Figured it was only a matter of time before you got to me. Learn anything interesting?"

"One or two things."

"Old man Miller says to cooperate, so I'll cooperate. I gotta tell ya, though—I don't know squat."

I asked him a few questions anyway. Turned out he was right.

"T' be honest," Hudalla said, "I kinda hope you don't find the money. It'll give us an excuse to fire that asshole Gustafson."

"Why would you want to do that?"

"Sonuvabitch arrested my kid Friday night."

"For what?"

"DUI. Sonuvabitch was waiting outside the Tall Moon Tavern. Kid comes out after closing, gets in his car, starts it up, drives fifty yards, and the chief's all over his ass. He was just hiding down the road in the dark, lookin' to bust someone, and he gets my son. Fuckin' two thirty and I have to go down to the jail and bail the kid out. Wayne's there, pleadin' the kid's case, sayin' he didn't pour 'im more than two drinks. Gustafson didn't care. I didn't even get home until nearly five. What kind of law enforcement is that?"

"Beats the hell out of me," I said.

In South Dakota it was legal to buy hard alcohol in a grocery store, and Ed Bizek took advantage of the law. His cart held a case of bottled beer, and he was intent on selecting whiskey from a surprisingly broad assortment of brands when I came upon him.

"Looks like you're a boilermaker man," I said.

Bizek glanced at the basket I held in my hand and smirked. The basket contained two large plastic jugs filled with distilled water. In self-defense, I said, "You're supposed to drink eight glasses of water a day."

"If you say so."

I wanted to see how he would react to the news, so I was blunt when I delivered it.

"I saw Dawn and Perry Neske at breakfast this morning. They were behaving like newlyweds."

"I hope they're very happy together," Bizek said. There was no emotion in his voice. He set a bottle of whiskey in his cart and moved toward the front of the store. I followed.

"I take it Dawn's gone back to her husband," I said.

"Is this any of your business, McKenzie?"

"No, but I have questions that still need answering."

"No one cares," he said, meaning he didn't.

"Tracie Blake cared."

That stopped him.

"Tracie." He said the name as if it were an act of devotion, his head down, his eyes closed. When he opened his eyes again, he said, "What kind of town is this? What have we become? First the Imposter and then Tracie and Mike and now the Dannes. Who lives in a town like this?"

"People," I said. "Just people the same as everywhere else, I guess."

"I used to like this town. I used to love this town."

"Tracie said it was a fine place to live if you had someone to grow old with."

"Tracie said that?"

"It was pretty much the last words she spoke to me."

Bizek took a few moments to consider Tracie's theory. From the expression on his face, I guessed that he believed it, too. Finally he said, "What do you want, McKenzie?"

"You knew the password to the bank account—"

"Not that again."

"Did you ever tell anyone about the money in the account—"

"No."

"Did you ever tell anyone the password—"

"No. I'm not stupid, McKenzie. Besides, I'm lousy about things like that. I can never remember passwords or account numbers. I have to write that stuff down and keep it in my wallet. Tell me something? Are you any closer to finding the Imposter and the money?"

"I'm not sure."

"Can you be sure by, say, Thursday?"

"What happens Thursday?"

"That's when the next city council meeting is scheduled. That's when we have to 'fess up about how much money Libbie has lost, although, hell, I think most people are starting to figure it out already."

"George Humphrey said he won't be there. He said he's leaving town."

"That figures. Dawn will probably leave, too."

"Did she say so?"

"Not in so many words. The last time we were together . . ."

I could see the pain reaching Bizek's eyes, and I was afraid that he might break down. I didn't have time for that, so I prompted him to keep talking.

"What did she say?" I said.

"She said that she wanted to give her marriage another chance. She said—"

"When was this?" I said.

"Friday night, about—it was early. Perry works the second shift, gets off at two in the morning, so usually she stays later, only this time, after we—after we—she got dressed and she said it wasn't going to work out."

The tears began to flow silently down Bizek's cheeks, and I wondered, what did he think was going to happen? Men and women cheat on their spouses all the time, yet they seldom leave them. It's the ones who get cheated on that do the leaving, and the cheaters are nearly always surprised when they do.

I left him standing there and went to the checkout in the front of the store.

I had parked my Audi on the shoulder of the county road and was emptying the distilled water out of the plastic jugs into the ditch when my cell phone started playing "Summertime."

"Hello, Chief," I said. "I was just talking about you."

"Oh yeah?"

"A guy named Hudalla wants to stick a knife in your back."

"He can get in line. McKenzie, I finally got hold of the manager of the rental car company down in Rapid City. He's still pissed off."

"About what?"

"Seems they couldn't start the Imposter's rental."

"Why not?"

"Someone opened the fuse panel under the hood and removed the fuses that controlled both the fuel pump and the ignition."

"I'll be damned."

"You were wrong. The car didn't break down. It looks like someone purposely stranded Rush at the lake."

I poured a quart of motor oil into each of the plastic jugs and then filled them to the brim with unleaded gasoline. After topping off the Audi's tank, I went inside Miller Big Stop. The young man behind the cash register seemed surprised when I paid cash. I don't know why. I had paid cash for everything I bought that day.

"Hear about the excitement we had yesterday?" he asked.

"What excitement?"

He waved in the general direction of Mike Randisi's place. "Man and woman got themselves shot just over to the farm over there."

"Oh yeah?"

"Naked as jaybirds, they were. I heard they were in bed doin' it when someone came in and shot them both."

"Does the sheriff have any suspects?"

"Not that I heard, but if it was me, I'd be lookin' to see who they were sleepin' with besides each other, that's what I would do."

I left as soon as he counted out my change. I might have told him to keep it—I've done it before—only I didn't want to give him anything to remember me by.

It was so quiet and the call so unexpected that I jumped when I heard the opening notes to "Summertime" again. I read the name on the display.

"Hey, sweetie," I said.

"Hi, McKenzie," Victoria Dunston replied.

"How was the soccer tournament?"

"We got our butts kicked."

"So basically your athletic career is following the same path as your father's and mine."

"So far. McKenzie, I did what you asked. I looked for high school teams called the Raiders in Chicago and for about a hundred miles around Chicago. There are a bunch of them, including teams called Red Raiders and the Purple Raiders—Wells Academy, Robeson, Glenbard South, Ashton-Franklin, Grove, Bolingbrook. It's a long list. Do you want me to recite the whole thing?"

"No. I'll have to get them later. I'm a little busy right now."

"Okay," she said. "There's something else, though. I checked. There's a Taste of Chicago that's just like Taste of Minnesota except much, much bigger. Guess where they hold it?"

"Grant Park."

"Yep. Is that helpful?"

"It is, but—can I get back to you later?"

"Absolutely."

I hung up and resumed staring out the windshield of my car.

Church lived in a small clapboard house on the wrong side of the tracks that divided Libbie in half, not far from the water treatment plant. The house needed work, and so did the garage and lawn. On the other hand, the Ford F150 pickup parked in the driveway was gleaming, its black body newly washed and waxed. Even the tires sparkled in the hard sunlight. I watched the house from a safe distance through a pair of binoculars that I kept along with my guns under the false bottom of the Audi's trunk. I had removed and loaded a 9 mm Beretta as well. It was sitting on the seat next to me. Even so, my inner voice pleaded with me—*Let's keep our crimes to a minimum, shall we?*

I agreed to that request. Yet I refused to listen when my inner voice told me that what I was about to do was wrong.

This isn't justice, it's revenge.

So?

It's illegal. It's against the law.

The law doesn't work out here.

You're not that person.

Yeah, I am.

I set the binoculars aside and gripped the steering wheel. My hands were icy cold, yet sweating at the same time—go figure. According to my expensive watch, which, among other things, had a timer, Paulie arrived at exactly 8:13 P.M. He parked his battered Dodge Stratus on the street and walked across the spotty lawn to the front door of the house. He walked in without knocking. At 8:42 he and Church emerged from the house. Church carefully cradled a small brown paper bag in one arm as if he were afraid of dropping it as he walked to the pickup. In his free hand he carried a twelve-gauge double-barrel shotgun. Paulie moved toward the Stratus. Church called to him. Paulie paused and pointed at the bag. Church laughed at him. Finally they both boarded Church's F150; Church set the bag on the seat and placed the gun on a rack attached to his rear window. They drove away without coming anywhere near me.

I sat and listened to the quietness, straining to hear any sound resembling a truck engine or human voices. I heard only the sound of the never-ceasing wind. I waited fifteen minutes, partly to make sure Church didn't return for something he forgot and partly to give the sun time to set—this was the kind of thing best done in darkness, I told myself. While I waited, I patted the double-A batteries in my pocket. For safety's sake, I had removed them from the kitchen timers. I would return them when I was ready to set the bombs.

CHAPTER FOURTEEN

I parked in the lot of the Tall Moon Tavern as far away from Church's F150 as I could get. So far, everything had gone according to plan. Even the traffic had obeyed my will. No one had driven past the Audi that I left on the shoulder of the county road earlier while I made my way in the dark through the drainage ditch to the parking lot. No one entered or left the tavern as I opened the door to the pickup and placed my package on the floor, or as I retreated back to the Audi. As for the contents of the brown paper bag that Church left on his front seat, even that worked to my advantage. My only fear now was that Chief Gustafson had decided to take Sunday night off, that he wasn't waiting in his usual spot down the road in hopes of nabbing a DUI violator.

I pressed a button on the side of my watch, and a blue light flared. I watched the second hand sweep around the dial. The timer told me there were twelve minutes to go.

You're cutting it awfully close, my inner voice said.

"I wouldn't have it any other way," I said aloud.

It was a lot quieter inside the Tall Moon Tavern this time around. It was just as crowded with men and women seated at tables, in booths, and at the bar. Yet no one was laughing; they didn't seem to be enjoying themselves as they had the first time I had gone there.

Even the jukebox was silent. I wondered if they were in mourning. This was Tracie's ground, after all, the place where everyone knew her name.

I made my way to the bar, stepping between two empty stools. The bartender, Jeff, the one who had seemed so enamored with Tracie, reached me in seconds.

"Ringneck Red Ale," I said.

He spun around, opened a cooler, produced a bottle, and levered off the cap. Seconds later the bottle and a glass were placed in front of me. While Jeff worked, I studied the crowd in the faded mirror behind the bar. An awful lot of people seemed to be studying me as well.

"The pool table," Jeff said. He spoke quietly, his lips barely moving, as if he were afraid someone beside me might hear him. I took a sip of the ale from the bottle. As I did, I turned my head so I could see the table in the mirror. Church was standing behind it. He was chalking a cue. Paulie was sitting on a stool off to the right, a stick in his hand as well. They were both grinning like bad poker players who had drawn to an inside straight. No doubt they were thinking about the brown paper bag on the seat of Church's pickup truck. Silly boys.

"Where's Wayne?" I said.

"Men's room," Jeff told me. He hunched himself over the bar and spoke in a tone so low the other customers couldn't hear. "He's— well, he's upset about Tracie Blake. He was sweet on her, you know."

"I know."

"You were a friend of Tracie's, so I'll tell you. The night she died, she left early after speaking to someone on her cell. Wayne asked where she was headed. She said she had a date. Wayne was unhappy about it. He didn't say anything while she was here, just smiled, you know Wayne, but he called her a few names after she left, you know the kind of names I mean."

"Did he do anything about her leaving?"

"Nah. Wayne's not the kind to throw a tantrum, at least not in public. He took off for an hour. I thought he might have gone to visit Mike Randisi, but I guess he just wanted to blow off some steam or something. He was fine when he came back."

"When was that?"

"About ten. I remember because he started buying rounds for some of the regulars, which he doesn't do too often, you know? Stayed until last call and then closed up. Usually I close up. He seemed happy enough when I left. Next day he heard what happened to Tracie. He hasn't been good company since. I think they're haunting him a little bit now, the names he called her. Shhhh."

The *shhhh* warned me that Wayne had emerged from the restroom and was making his way to the end of the bar. There was a shot glass waiting for him there, and a half-filled bottle of J&B. I got the impression that he had been sitting there a long time.

"You've got some balls coming here, McKenzie," he said. "I'll give you that."

Jeff turned his head so Wayne couldn't see and mouthed a single word to me—"Tracie."

"I am so sorry for your loss," I said.

"Balls," he said again.

I was genuinely concerned that I had offended him somehow.

"Why do you say that?" I said.

He gestured with his head toward the pool table. "Church has been talkin' loud. He's been sayin' how he's going to kick your ass if you showed up." He raised his voice for everyone to hear. "Ain't that right, Church?"

"Soon as I'm done with this rack," Church said.

"Don't hurry on my account," I said.

Church smirked at that. Paulie set his cue against the wall and started to make his way toward the door. I knew exactly where he was going and why. I glanced at my watch. It was too soon.

"Hey, Paulie," I said. "Sit your ass back down."

He stopped. Confusion clouded his eyes. He looked back at Church for clarity. Church jerked his head. Paulie continued toward the door.

"I said sit down." I slipped out from between the stools, making it clear that I was prepared to intercept him. Paulie stopped again. Again he looked to Church for guidance.

"You got a problem, McKenzie?" Church said.

"I'm going to beat you to death, you gutless piece of crap, and I don't want shit-for-brains here sneaking up on me from behind while I do it."

The bar was as quiet as a movie theater during a Kate Winslet film. Patrons watched us intently, and I thought this was probably as much entertainment as some of them had had in years.

Church tossed his cue stick down on the green felt. He circled the pool table and came toward me. I noticed he wasn't moving quickly, and his eyes—they flicked back and forth, watching the audience watching him. Clearly he didn't want to fight, yet he was afraid of losing face if he didn't. I waited for him. The limp was gone, and he flexed the fingers of his broken hand. When he reached a spot on the warped floor that he thought was close enough, he stopped and lifted his hand, giving everyone in the tavern a good look at the white cast.

"It's going to be an unfair fight, but I'm not afraid of you," he said. "That's your speed, though, ain't it? Sucker-punch a guy when he ain't looking; fight a guy who's got but one hand."

I felt my muscles tighten, felt my eyes grow wide at the insult. This was the part of the program where I was supposed to call him a liar, call him a hypocrite, remind him of all the cowardly crimes he had committed against people like the Dannes, and I would have. There was a clock on the wall behind Church that was made to resemble the logo of a St. Louis beer company. If it was accurate, I needed at least another ninety seconds. Only Wayne gave me the time I needed when he slammed his shot glass down on the bar top. He hopped off his stool, reached around the end of the bar, and came up with a small baseball bat with tattered and dirty white tape wrapped around the handle.

"You fucker," he said.

I didn't know if he meant Church or me until he turned toward the big man and raised the bat. I came up behind him as quickly as I could and grabbed the barrel of the bat and pulled it down.

"No, no, no," I chanted.

"Let it go," Wayne said.

"It's my party," I told him.

Wayne yanked the bat out of my hand and waved it at me.

"Church bullied Tracie," he said. "He insulted her cuz she wouldn't have anything to do with him, and I let him. I let him."

Wayne glared at Church.

Church waved his cast like a flag and took two steps backward.

Paulie skipped to the front door.

The bar patrons took a collective deep breath.

The bomb exploded.

There wasn't a loud bang. It was more of a whooshing sound as the kitchen timer set off the makeshift detonator, which in turn ignited the gas and oil in the plastic jug, splattering the cab of Church's pickup truck with both.

"Oh my God," someone shouted.

I glanced at my watch. The bomb had gone off a good thirty seconds before I thought it would. I held the watch to my ear. *You need a new battery*, my inner voice said.

People rushed to the windows of the bar.

Paulie stood in the doorway, a look of terror on his face.

"You said it was safe," he said. "You said it wouldn't go off."

"Shut up," Church told him. He ran toward the door.

"You said it wouldn't blow up until we lit the fuse."

"Shut up." Church shoved Paulie hard against the door frame. "Shut the fuck up." He shoved him again. Paulie fell out of the bar. Church followed. He kicked Paulie while he was down. "Shut up," he repeated.

A half-dozen patrons followed Church and Paulie out of the tavern. A few of them rushed to move their vehicles away from the F150. The two nearest the pickup managed to start and drive their cars off just as the Molotov cocktail that Church had prepared and left in the brown bag on his seat exploded. The bang it made wasn't quite as thunderous as it is in the movies, yet it was loud enough to make everyone duck and powerful enough to shatter the windshield.

A siren screamed from down the county road; red and blue lights flicked in the darkness. A moment later, a City of Libbie police cruiser turned into the parking lot and came to a screeching halt beneath the light pole. The light at the top of the pole was a pale and sickly thing compared to the brilliance of the fire. The car was still rocking when Chief Gustafson jumped out.

"Do something," Church said. "Save my truck."

The chief didn't even try. Instead, he forced his way to the head of the crowd, turned, and spread his arms wide as if he were herding small, dumb animals.

"Everyone get back," he said. "C'mon now, step back, everyone step back."

Somehow he managed to force the crowd to retreat about ten paces. That was as far as we would go. The fire compelled our attention despite the danger.

Fumes from burning plastic, rubber, metal, and the various synthetic materials that went into making the vehicle wafted over the parking lot. Jeff was standing next to me. He took a deep breath, probably not a wise thing to do.

"Don't you just love that new car smell," he said.

It took hardly any time for the flames to reach the gas tank. The truck didn't explode—that only happens in the movies. Instead, it made another loud whoosh as the gas simply ignited. That was followed by several loud popping sounds. I thought the shotgun shells going off might have caused it, but I was mistaken. It was the tires melting.

Church was screaming. He made several efforts to get closer to the vehicle—I had no idea what he was trying to accomplish. Each time, the heat pushed him back. Most of what he had to say was unintelligible. Only the words "Call the fire department" were loud and clear.

"I did," the chief said. "They can't come. They're already on a call."

"What call?"

"It's your house," Gustafson said. "They said it was completely engulfed in flames."

"My house?"

"I'm sorry," the chief said.

"My house!"

Church continued shouting, mostly obscenities, until he doubled over and began to gag as if he were about to be sick. I don't know if the fumes got to him or it was something else. For a moment, I felt sorry for him. Then I thought about Rick and Cathy Danne, and all of his other victims, and the feeling went away.

He saw me out of the corner of his eye.

"You did this," he said. "You did this."

Church rushed at me. Wayne stepped in to block his path. Church pushed him away. Wayne swung his baseball bat and hit him squarely on the point of the hip. Church went down with an agonizing scream. Chief Gustafson crossed the gravel lot and yanked the bat from Wayne's hands.

"Are you crazy?" he said.

"He insulted Tracie," Wayne said.

"You did this, you," Church said.

"Me?" I said. "What did I do?"

Church tried to rise from the ground. The chief bent to give him aid. "He did this," Church told him.

"What are you talking about?" I said. "You're the one who had a gasoline bomb in his car, not me. Ain't that right, Paulie?"

Paulie was standing near the door of the tavern, both arms clutching his stomach where Church had kicked him. He looked as confused as ever.

"What about it, Paulie?" I said. "Everyone heard what you said."

"What did you say?" the chief said.

"Shut up," Church said. "Paulie."

"I didn't say anything," Paulie said.

Jeff stepped next to him. "Yes, you did, when the fire started. The fire started, and you were talking to Church."

"No."

"What did he say?" the chief asked.

"He was looking at Church," Jeff answered. "When the fire started in the truck, he looked at Church and he said, 'You promised that it wouldn't blow up until we lit the fuse.'"

"That's right," one of the bar patrons said.

"I heard him say it," said another.

"Shut up," Church said. "You got rights."

The chief put a hand on Church's chest and eased him backward. After he made room, he stepped between Church and Paulie. Paulie shook his head.

"I didn't do anything," he said.

"Talk to me, Paulie," said the chief.

"I didn't do anything."

"You're a liar," Wayne said. "We all heard you."

"No."

"It was McKenzie," Church said. "He did it. He set the fire. Oh, you bastard."

"That's crazy," I said. "Why would I do that?"

"To get even."

"For what? What have you ever done to me?"

Chief Gustafson kept his hand on Church's chest, even while he stared at Paulie.

"I'm going to give you one more chance to tell me the truth," he said.

"I didn't do anything," Paulie said.

"All right, you're under arrest."

"No."

Paulie tried to run. Wayne and another guy grabbed him by the arms. The chief tucked the bat under his arm and made a slow and deliberate production out of producing his handcuffs. Paulie stared at them as if they were dental instruments.

"No," he said. He squirmed, but the two men held fast.

"You have the right to remain silent—"

"But I didn't do anything."

"Anything you say can and will be used against you in a court of law—"

"It wasn't me."

"You have the right to have an attorney present—"

"It was Church," Paulie said. He would have pointed at him, except Wayne and the other bar patron had his arms pinned. "He had a Molotov cocktail. He was going to smash it on McKenzie's car like he did against Danne's house last night."

"Shut your fucking mouth," Church said. He lunged for Paulie, but the chief kept him back.

"It was all Church," Paulie said. "I just watched."

"You lying bastard," Church said. "You threw the bomb." He held his hand up, the one covered with a cast. "I lit it, but he threw it."

"I don't know how things work in South Dakota," I said. "In Minnesota, that is what prosecuting attorneys refer to as an excited utterance, and according to the U.S. Supreme Court, it's admissible as evidence."

"You bastard," Church screamed.

This time it was me he charged. The chief intercepted him again, grabbing him by the shoulders, spinning him down to the gravel, and slapping the cuffs over his wrists behind his back as quickly and efficiently as ever I've seen.

Don't you just love it when a plan comes together? my inner voice said.

There were six full-time deputies, two part-time deputies, and an administrative assistant working for the Perkins County Sheriff's Department, and Big Joe Balk called them all in. Mostly it was a matter of crowd control. Balk had Church in one holding cell, Paulie in a second, Wayne in the third, Chief Gustafson dozing in the interrogation room, and eleven other witnesses scattered throughout the county courthouse in Mercer. The county attorney, who ran for the office unopposed, and his assistant, neither of whom had ever prosecuted a felony in their lives, were desperate to keep everyone separate until they took their statements.

Personally, I didn't think prosecution was going to be much of an issue. Starting from the moment Chief Gustafson called the sheriff for assistance, Paulie talked. He talked about how Church smashed a Molotov cocktail against the Dannes' house the night before and how he planned to do the same to my fancy car—that was his word, "fancy." He spoke of seven other fires as well, including the bombing of Christopher Kramme's plane shortly after he returned to Libbie with Tracie. He said how this was all Church's doing, that it was Church's standard mode of revenge against all who wronged him in one manner or another, and how he didn't want to help but Church made him. Later, after the county attorney set up a tape recorder and video camera in a small office and read him his rights for a third time, Paulie said it all over again. Meanwhile, Church kept his mouth shut, demanded his rights, demanded an attorney. That was until he learned that Paulie was spilling his guts in front of a camera, and then he couldn't help himself; he started talking, too.

"Sounds like a slam dunk to me," I said.

Big Joe Balk leaned back in his chair and regarded me carefully from the far side of his desk.

"Do you realize, there hadn't been a single murder, rape, armed robbery, or aggravated assault committed in Perkins County in three years before you came along?" he said.

"I'm sure that's because this is such a law-abiding community."

"Tell me something, McKenzie—when I investigate the fires in Church's home, in his car, and I will investigate the fires, what do you think I'll find?"

"I think you'll find that a confessed serial arsonist, who has been linked to at least eight fires in the past few years, yet had always managed to evade arrest despite the best efforts of the Perkins Country Sheriff's Department, accidentally burned down his own property because he improperly handled the materials he was using to build his firebombs."

"Is that what you think?"

"That's what I hope."

"Paulie said that you wanted Church to meet you at the Tall Moon Tavern at nine o'clock last night. Why would you want that?"

"I'm sure Paulie is mistaken. I had no reason for wanting to see Church."

"Why were you there?"

"To get a Ringneck Ale. I like it."

"You can get that anywhere."

"I didn't know that. I'm new here."

"Uh-huh. So you weren't attempting to lure Church to the Tall Moon so you could burn down his house?"

"Certainly not. Why would I do such a thing?"

"To get a little vigilante justice for all the fires Church set."

"Why would I do that? He never burned anything I owned. 'Course, if you disagree, you should consider that charging me with arson might compromise the county attorney's case against both Church and Paulie. I've been told that confusion is a criminal defense attorney's best friend, and additional arson arrests might cause plenty of confusion. Instead of copping a plea, Church and Paulie could even try their luck at a trial, and who knows what an energetic defense lawyer might do to the amateur prosecutors you have working for you. What do you think?"

"I think I should throw your ass in jail."

"A lot of people say that." I got up from the chair and headed for the door just in case he was serious. "I'll see you around."

"Wait a minute."

I held my breath while I did.

"There were fingerprints on Mike Randisi's gun that didn't belong to him or to Tracie."

The sheriff knew I'd handled the gun, so I felt safe in asking, "Were they mine?"

"No. I ran your prints. Your prints are on file, did you know that?"

"I knew that."

"Of course. You're an ex-cop."

He gave the "ex" a little more emphasis than I liked, but I said nothing.

"Any thoughts of who they might belong to?" the sheriff said.

"Not yet." I held my thumb and index finger about an inch apart. "I'm that far away from putting it all together."

"Putting it together, or taking it apart?"

I had nothing to say to that.

"I'll be watching you, McKenzie. You try something like this again, what you did last night . . ." Big Joe Balk stared at me for five hard beats, then said, "Go home."

I didn't know if he meant go home to my hotel in Libbie or go home to St. Paul, and I didn't ask.

It wasn't a long drive from Mercer to Libbie, it just seemed that way. Partly it was because of the unending darkness. I did not see a single light besides my own headlamps from one city's limits to the other, not even the light of a farmhouse or ranch. It was so cold I had to roll up my windows, and then I had to turn on my defrosters when the windows began to fog up. Mostly what made it such a long trek, though, was my conscience. I was wrong to set up Church the way I did, to destroy his house and pickup, and I knew it. I knew it before I did it.

"What the hell am I doing?" I said aloud.

I used to be a cop, a good cop, I think, for well over eleven years. I quit when I became independently wealthy. I was going to take care of my father; we were going to travel. Dad died before we had much of a chance. Still, I have no regrets about pulling the pin. Only the thing is, I liked being a cop. I liked helping people. I saw a lot of terrible things when I was in harness; I was forced to do some of those terrible things myself, yet I always slept well at night. When my head hit the pillow and I looked back on the day, no matter how lousy the day had been, I could always say, "The world's a little bit better place because of what I did." It made me feel good; it made me feel useful.

After Dad passed, I had money but no plans for it, not to invest it, not to spend it, not to give it away. It was just there, making my life simple and easy, yet not particularly fulfilling. I began to feel restless and out of place. To relieve the boredom and discontent, I started doing favors for my friends, and friends of friends—favors they couldn't do for themselves. They were small favors at first. Gradually they became bigger and more dangerous. Yet they gave some meaning and significance to my life. And fun. Nina once compared me to a Wild West gunfighter, a white knight, and the Scarlet Pimpernel all in one breath. Certainly, it was a more interesting way to spend my time than working nine-to-five. Mostly, though, I did the favors to be useful. I did it to help make the world a better place. At least, that's what I told myself. What should I tell myself now? I wondered.

Is the world a better place because I burned down Church's house, because I blew up his truck? Yeah, he's off the streets; he won't be hurting anyone in the near future. Really, though, didn't I merely substitute one asshole for another?

As for Libbie, it could blow away like a tumbleweed tomorrow and it wouldn't bother me a bit. I came here for payback—Nina was right about that, too. I came here to get even with the man who used my name.

So where does the better world come in?

Have I ever made the world better?

Maybe I should heed Big Joe Balk's advice, I told myself. Maybe I should go home to St. Paul. The difference between right and wrong seemed much more apparent there. Or was it that I never doubted myself there?

I continued to follow the onrushing, unchanging road.

Damn, it was a long drive.

Evan sat in an overstuffed chair, his chin resting on his chest, his arms crossed beneath his chin, his legs extended and crossed at the ankles, looking as if he were at the airport waiting for a plane and not expecting it anytime soon. I startled him when I opened the front door to the Pioneer Hotel. He leapt out of the chair and rubbed his eyes nervously. Probably he had been sleeping and wasn't supposed to, I told myself.

"McKenzie," he said.

"Hey."

"I've been waiting for you."

"You have? Why?"

"Sharren," he said and paused. During the pause all kinds of terrible things came to mind.

"What about her?" I said.

"Sharren told me that if you had another late night, I was supposed to feed you something from the kitchen."

I expressed my relief in one long exhale. "That's okay," I said at the end of it.

"It's no trouble," Evan said.

"It's late, and I'm not that hungry."

I moved toward the staircase, but Evan blocked me.

"You need to eat something," he said.

"I'm fine, really."

"You don't understand."

"What don't I understand?"

"Sharren—Sharren has taken a keen interest in you."

"That's kind of her."

"If you don't eat something after she told me to feed you, she's going to give me hell."

"Well, we can't have that."

Evan seemed relieved as he led me to a chair. I slipped off my sports jacket, folded it, and set it on an empty chair across from me before sitting down.

"Don't move," he said. "I'll be right back."

True to his word, he returned within minutes with a stein of beer. "Drink this," he said.

It sounded more like a command than a request. I took a sip. Evan smiled.

"I'll be right back with your sandwich," he said.

I took another sip of beer, then another. It had a slightly bitter taste but altogether wasn't bad. I wondered if it had been brewed in South Dakota like Ringneck. I would have to ask Evan when he returned, I told myself. I drank until the glass was half empty, then balanced it on my knee, telling myself that I would finish it with my sandwich. I closed my eyes . . .

CHAPTER FIFTEEN

I opened my right eye. It was daylight, and I was lying on my stomach on the ground and staring at a plant I couldn't identify. I raised my head slightly and attempted to open my left eye. The lid was clotted with blood and remained closed. I touched my cheek just below the eye and winced. It was swollen, the skin taut and painful. I explored gently with my fingers. No shattered cheekbones, no broken eye socket—so I had that going for me. After some effort, I managed to roll onto my back. I rubbed the dried blood out of my left eye and opened it. The sky was vivid blue and cloudless. I tried to sit up. I felt a deep pain in my left side, clutched my ribs, and sagged back down. A sudden chill gripped my entire body; my teeth began to chatter violently; I felt nauseous. I waited until the symptoms subsided and tried sitting up again, twisting as I did, leaning on my left forearm, using my right hand for support. My head throbbed, and I had a nasty taste in my mouth. With some effort, I managed to kneel. The dirt beneath my knees was dry and hard-packed. Around me were more of the unidentified plants. They had narrow stems about seven inches high with thin, flat leaf blades and short bristles at the top. There were tens of thousands of them, and they stretched to the horizon. The horizon seemed to be a hundred miles away in all directions.

"Uh-oh," I said.

Holding tight to my ribs, I managed to stand. If anything, it made the horizon seem farther away.

"This is very bad."

If you were to put me on *Who Wants to Be a Millionaire, Jeopardy,* or any of the other TV game shows that test your knowledge, I would probably fail miserably. On the other hand, if you gave me a little context by, oh, I don't know, abandoning me on a prairie in the middle of nowhere, suddenly I'd be able to access all the pertinent information stored in my head. It's like my grasp of languages. I studied French for seven years yet can barely speak a word unless I'm on a beach in Martinique or a boulevard in Paris, and then I can speak it quite well. I don't know why my brain works that way, it just does. I tell you this so you'll understand why, at that precise moment in time, I knew exactly how much trouble I was in.

The Great Plains consist of four hundred and seventy-five thousand square miles of barely populated land, of which over half are range and pasture land, and I seemed to be stuck in the very middle of it. 'Course, a hundred and fifty thousand of those miles are in Canada. I didn't know where I was, but it wasn't Canada.

How would you know? my inner voice asked.

I examined my wristwatch. It was 8:32 A.M. . . .

How do you know it's morning?

The sun is rising . . .

How do you know it isn't setting?

Dammit, it's morning. The sun is rising.

All right. Relax. Take a deep breath.

I did, and immediately felt a stabbing pain in my left side that caused me to clutch my ribs again. Once the pain lessened, I coughed up some phlegm and spat on the ground at my feet. The saliva seemed clear to me.

What does that tell you?

I'm not bleeding inside.

Oh, yeah, like you would know.

I went back to my watch. It was 8:34 A.M. I knew for a fact that I had been in Libbie at four fifteen. That meant I was just over four hours away from where I was. Figure a vehicle traveling at seventy miles per hour out of town, and forty miles an hour over this rough terrain, at the very most I should be about two hundred twenty-five miles from Libbie.

Which tells you what?

I'm not in fucking Canada!

"How the hell did I get here?" I said aloud

The answer was obvious enough—Evan. He drugged me. I remembered that the beer he gave me had a slightly bitter taste. Chloral hydrate tasted bitter. Chloral hydrate was the first depressant developed for the specific purpose of inducing sleep. Add it to alcohol and you have what the Victorians called a Mickey Finn. It works in a relatively short period of time, figure thirty minutes. I went down quicker than that, which means either he gave me a lot of it or the lack of food in my system accelerated its effects.

Why would he do it?

He wouldn't unless someone told him to, paid him to.

Sharren Nuffer?

I didn't think so. Evan used Sharren's name because Sharren had fed me late Saturday night. He knew this because he poured me a Ringneck. Only Sharren wasn't working Sunday. I was aware of that, yet I didn't call him on it. Why not? How come I didn't remember about the taste of chloral hydrate last night?

It was late. You were tired. Tired people make mistakes.

I moved my fingers gingerly up and down my rib cage and then across my face. Someone had kicked me while I was down, while I was unconscious. Someone who didn't like me at all.

It was Dewey Miller. He owns the Pioneer Hotel. Evan works for him.

"Ahh, Mr. Miller," I said aloud. "This time I think you have pushed your luck too far."

Now what?

Despite the pain, I stretched my body. Then I brushed the red-brown dirt from my bare arms, my rust-colored polo shirt, and my blue jeans. It would have been nice to have my sports jacket with the cell phone in the pocket, but I doubted I'd have coverage out there anyway.

I was in for a long walk; there was no doubt about it. The question was, which direction? I slowly spun in a tight circle, examining the skyline as best I could. I saw no transmission lines, no water towers, no power or telephone poles, no fences, no roads. There was not a single tree anywhere, not a river or lake, not a bump of high ground to break the monotony of the limitless horizon.

"I guess they don't call it the Great American Desert for nothing," I said.

I set off, walking in a large circle, scrutinizing the ground intently. I found no tire tracks, from a car or a truck or an ATV.

"How the hell did I get here?" I said. "I didn't fall from the sky."

I circled again, moving more slowly this time, more carefully, examining the prairie grass as well as the ground, looking for bent stems, anything to indicate where a vehicle might have come from or in which direction it went, anything to follow. I failed.

Oh, this is not good.

Would you stop saying that?

I reached down and pulled up a stem of grass. Next, I removed my watch from my wrist. I held it horizontally, pointing the hour hand directly at the sun. I took the blade of grass and placed it halfway between the hour hand and the numeral twelve. This gave me the north and south line. Due east was at ten fifteen.

"That way," I said.

Why that way?

"It's the direction home."

The way my father taught it to me, you pick a point in the distance and walk directly to it, then pick another spot in the distance and walk to that. This way you're always moving more or less in a straight line; the strength of your right leg—I was right-handed—wouldn't push you into a circle. Yet I came to realize that I could not follow those instructions here. I could not walk with an eye to a far goal because there was no way to measure the distance I was closing anymore than I could with a mirage. There simply were no reference points. The land was without water, without trees, without rocks, without discernible hills; there was nothing to help you determine where you've been or where you are going. I began to feel like I was on a gigantic conveyor belt and the earth was rotating at walking speed beneath my feet so that I gained no ground.

I stopped and used my watch to align myself again.

Dammit.

What?

My watch was set to Daylight Saving Time, not the natural arch of the sun. I was hiking northeast.

Does it matter?

Of course it matters.

I reset my watch, turning the hands back an hour, and realigned myself. I decided that I could no longer look to the horizon, so I concentrated on what was nearer my feet—a tuft of grass fifteen paces in front of me, a shrub twenty paces in front of that. All the while, I scanned the horizon, searching for a fence line, a silo, any kind of man-made structure that might lead me out of the wilderness.

A jackrabbit appeared. He was about two feet in length and gray, with those distinctive long ears pointed straight up from his head. The ears twitched while he watched me, a contemptuous expression on his otherwise placid face. I stamped my foot and said, "Hasenpfeffer," which is the name of a German stew made with marinated rabbit. Either he was an uneducated rabbit or he didn't fear the implied threat. After a moment he hopped away, moving in no particular hurry.

I bet he knows where he's going.

I figure there are three modes in life. There's action mode, during which the present and the immediate future are all that concern me. It's the mode I slide into when I'm working, doing all those favors for people, setting up arsonists like Church. In action mode, there is little room for reflection; everything moves with extreme speed; vision narrows to only those people and things within reach. It's an intense living in the moment. Time stands still. True, immediately afterward, time becomes a living thing again. It sweeps forward at its own deliberate pace. One can anticipate the future and all the responsibilities that it entails—to family, to friends, to oneself—and be weighed down by them. It is like coming down from an immense high. Still, I liked it.

Then there is intellectual mode, where most activities take place inside the head. This is where I spend most of my time—reading, listening to music, going to ball games, enjoying a few beverages with the boys, whipping up gourmet meals for my friends, attempting (badly) to emulate Tiger Woods on a golf course, studying the habits of the ducks that live on the pond in my backyard, working out, taking martial arts training, practicing with my guns, solving puzzles like where the Imposter came from and where he went. It's simply the exploration of life, of keeping yourself open to its countless surprises. I liked this, too.

Then there is where I was now—plodding mode. I was simply

moving forward, step by step, hour by hour, into an unknown future, trying to maintain a straight line and hoping for the best. There was no cheering, no cursing, no real thought. I was merely putting one foot in front of the other and trusting, hoping, that eventually I would get somewhere worth going. I think this is how most people go about their day-to-day lives. It is what Oliver Wendell Holmes meant when he wrote, "Alas for those that never sing but die with all their music in them."

"Hell with it," I said aloud. "I have never lived like that; I'll be damned if I'm going to die like that."

To prove it, I started singing, mostly tunes from the American Songbook, until it became too exhausting to walk and sing at the same time.

Hours passed. My legs became sore, especially my ankles. You'd think a guy who's played hockey thirty weeks out of the year since he was five years old would have stronger ankles, but there you are. My feet were beginning to ache as well, and I was sure I was developing blisters; my sneakers were not designed for this kind of travel.

I halted and tried to calculate my progress. It was impossible. A backward glance showed me nothing. The prairie was like the ocean. There was no end to it, no edge lined with mountains or coastal waters or lush forests. Near seemed the same as far out there.

I reminded myself that a man in fairly decent shape walking briskly should cover as much as five miles an hour. Only that's over a flat surface, and despite what you might have heard, the Great Plains are not flat; at least they aren't as flat as a football field or a baseball diamond. There were plenty of low, rolling hills to contend with. Plus, the damn vegetation. Along with the wheatgrass— see, I remembered what it was called—there were other prairie grasses to grab my shoes, pull at my legs, and slow my pace. There was a brown-colored grass that was several inches higher than the wheatgrass that reminded me of knitting needles. Another grass grew in dense mounds eighteen to twenty-four inches high with slender blue-green stems that sometimes turned a radiant mahogany red. Then there were a few grasses that I actually recognized—sunflowers and golden rods.

Okay, you're not walking briskly, but you are walking steadily, I told myself, even though every step caused my ribs to throb with pain. Call it four miles an hour.

C'mon.

Three and a half, then. Make it—I studied my watch some more—twenty-six and a quarter miles since I started. That's pretty damn good.

Except that you haven't eaten anything in twenty-two hours, or drunk anything since the cups of coffee you had last night at the Perkins County Courthouse. Except that you're slowing down—admit it, you're slowing down a lot. Except that you have no idea how much farther you need to go.

Shuddup.

Remember all that distilled water you poured into the ditch yesterday? What a waste.

Shuddup.

Once I got it into my head, I couldn't shake the thought away—the threat of dehydration. Fluids, in the form of sweat, were going out, yet nothing was coming in. What's more, my sweat—which was supposed to cool my body—was being dried before it could fulfill its mission by the hard northwest wind that simply would not stop blowing. It was like standing in front of a huge fan for nine and a half hours. The symptoms became too pronounced to ignore—dizziness, headache, stomach pain, nausea, and an unpleasant taste in my mouth. True, these were also the symptoms of chloral hydrate working itself out of my system. Still . . . Add to it the unrelenting sun. If it wasn't a hundred degrees, it was close to it. I had turned up the collar of my polo shirt, yet it did little to protect my neck. I could feel my skin burning there, as well as on my arms and on the right side of my face.

If dehydration doesn't kill you, sunstroke will.

Whine, whine, whine, whine, whine . . .

I was following my shadow now, the setting sun at my back, the shadow stretching so far in front of me that I could barely see where it ended. Then it disappeared, swallowed by a night that seemed to fall as swiftly as a hammer on an anvil. With it came a wave of cool air that engulfed me and settled around me as if I had just walked into a refrigerator. I had never felt air go from hot to cold so quickly.

I could go no farther, so I sat on the prairie. Hunger clawed at my stomach, yet that did not concern me nearly as much as the parchedness of my throat or the dryness of my tongue as I ran it across my chapped lips.

There were so many times when I should have died and I didn't.

"Hey," I told myself. "Don't talk like that. If you think you're going to die, you'll find a way to make it happen. Instead, do you know what you're going to do? First thing in the morning, you're going to walk a little ways until you find a road. Then you're going to hike down that road until you find a farmhouse or hitch a ride with a local. Then you're going to find a phone, make a few calls, go home, get cleaned up, and then you're going to take Nina to Paris."

I settled against the hard ground; the earth was warm against my back. I cupped my hands behind my head and stared up at the night sky. I watched as it slowly turned from a sorrowful blackness into an extravaganza of light. I recognized the North Star immediately, as well as the Big Dipper. That was it. I didn't know the constellations; I wished I did. Orion, Andromeda, Hercules, Pegasus, Cassiopeia—I knew the names, but not where to find them. An astonishing woman named Renée, who was far too good for the likes of me—just ask her family—had attempted to introduce them to me. Alas, something always seemed to distract us from our stargazing. Oh, well.

Staring up at the starry, starry sky, I had a revelation.

"You gotta believe," I said aloud. "You just gotta believe."

It wasn't a particularly profound thought, I know. Yet it worked for the '69 Mets. It worked for my '87 Twins. It worked for the '07 New York Giants. It would sure as hell work for me.

My eyes closed reluctantly. I slowly fell deeper and deeper through the layers of sleep, sliding effortlessly from dozing to the half-awake confusion that followed to sleep that resembled a coma . . .

It was a slumber so deep, so profound, that I needed to crawl out of it in stages, reconstructing the events of yesterday, the boredom, the pain, the hunger and thirst, the never-ending walking across the never-ending prairie. The light increased very slightly, flitting across my closed eyelids, then sprang upon me like the opening of a window shade in a dark room.

I was curled into the fetal position and shivering. The cool nighttime temperatures had created dew that covered everything. Why it didn't wake me I couldn't say; my clothes were drenched. I uncoiled my body and slowly, painfully stood. It was day in the east, yet still night in the west, and the sky in between varied by degrees from purple to violet to the purest aquamarine. The colors of the dew-soaked grass and shrubs also impressed me—a mosaic of silver, green, blue, red, yellow, and gold. The wind continued to blow, and the air was full of scents I had not encountered before.

I stretched, and the effort reminded me that my ribs were probably broken, that my legs and feet were tender, that my stomach was empty. I stripped off my wet shirt and sucked the moisture out of the material. Afterward, I bent to grab tufts of grass, squeezing the dew off of them and licking the water off of my hands. It took about ten minutes to quench my thirst. When I was ready, I used the sun and my watch to realign myself and started walking east. My shoes and the cuffs of my jeans became even more soaked as I hiked through the wet grass, making travel more difficult than before. There wasn't a single tree—not one. Nor could I discern any visible roads, fences, or power lines. Yet my spirits remained high.

You wake up, live through the day, go to sleep; then you do it all over again. There's a kind of victory in that, I told myself.

I had an exquisite view of the eastern half of the sky, clear and perfect, stretching to the horizon with nothing, nothing at all, to interrupt it. The perpetual wind blowing from the west and north pushed my back, urging me along, even as it turned the landscape into a waving sea of grass and drove cumulus and cirrus clouds across the sky, the shadows of the clouds sliding along beneath them. There was a dragonfly and, later, a squadron of Monarch butterflies. I also saw plenty of animals that had eluded me the day before—badgers, gophers, prairie dogs, more jackrabbits.

"Don't mind me," I told them. "I'm just passing through."

No one could possibly mistake it for Eden, yet the Great Plains had a kind of austere beauty, at least in the morning. I began to like it, although I did so against my better judgment. For the first time, I could appreciate why immigrants might travel across continents and oceans to get there. It was a country with both a glorious and appalling past. It was here that intrepid pioneers, lured by a Homestead Act that promised free land to anyone who would live on it and improve it, withstood loneliness, drought, blizzards, dust storms, and unyielding soil to help forge a nation. It was also here that men, who measured civilization by the color of their skin and advanced weaponry, pushed Native Americans off their ancestral homes and herded them onto reservations. It was a land of outlaws and legendary lawmen, of boomtowns and busts, of builders and destroyers and dreamers. It was also a land with a precarious present and dubious future.

I had no idea what would happen to the Great Plains.

To be perfectly honest, I didn't care.

All I wanted to do was get off them.

That was becoming increasingly unlikely.

It was against my own intellectual inclination to linger in the past—the dark land, a poet once called it. Yet, without a clear destination, I was becoming more pessimistic with every thirsty step. I found myself thinking less about what was in front of me and more about what was behind. Normally my memories were happy ones. Oh, the stories I could tell. Now they were filled with grieving—the death of my father and before that the death of my mother, who had become little more than an image to me, an impression of beauty and strength that could very well be more a manifestation of my imagination than actual memory. Regrets, too, things I had done that I wish I hadn't, things I had said that I wish I could take back, which were actually fewer in number than those things that I had left undone and unsaid that now made me sad.

No, no, no. Stop it. Get out of your head.

Easier said than done. I became obsessed with the notion that if I died out there, no one would ever know what had happened to me. Without my wallet, no one would even know who I was, assuming someone stumbled upon my body, which seemed unlikely.

Stop it. Just stop it.

I've been here before, I told myself. Just the other day, Miller's minions locked me in that damn trunk. Things looked bleak then, too. Remember? What did I do about it? I got tough, that's what I did. There was a nun, my sixth-grade homeroom teacher back at St. Mark's Elementary School, Sister John Evangela. Do you know what she used to tell us? "You can live for forty days without food, four days without water, and four minutes without oxygen, but you can't live four seconds without hope." Well, guess what? I had hope, and plenty of it.

"Hear that, bitch?" I spun in a circle, making sure the Great Plains knew I was talking to her. "You ain't putting me down. A little heat, a little wind, a couple of miles of empty country? C'mon, is that all you got? It didn't stop the pioneers, did it? It didn't stop them, and they had ornery Indians to deal with, too. It isn't going to stop me, either. Get used to the idea. Great American Desert, my ass."

That's telling her.

Despite my defiance, dehydration and hunger were taking their toll. I was no longer sweating; I wiped my brow with my thumb, and my thumb came away dry. My pace had dropped off dramatically; if I was making two miles an hour now, I was lucky. It was becoming harder to walk in a straight line. It was becoming harder to walk, period. Just breathing the furnacelike air in and out had become a burden. Hell, I decided, was a place where you found yourself under a relentless, unmoving sun in a land that did not change, where the wind never stopped blowing.

I stumbled and fell, not for the first time. I rolled onto my back and looked up at the sky. A bird with a long, curved bill circled above me.

"You gotta be kidding," I said.

I thought about it—I really did. I thought about just lying there, about giving up. Only I couldn't do it. No voice spoke to me; I wasn't visited by images of my dead parents or friends or Nina or some ethereal creature sent by God. I just couldn't do it—quit, I mean. I got up and I started walking. I had no idea if I was heading east or not. It didn't seem to matter anymore. All that mattered was that I remain on my feet.

What we have here is a stand-up fight with Death, my inner voice proclaimed.

Damn, that's heroic, I thought.

Except that you're losing.

It was when the sun was as low as my heart, when I was sure that I was slipping away, that I first saw it, something white moving in the distance. It came and it went, and for a few moments I was convinced I was seeing things.

It was heading toward me, so I started toward it.

After a while, I saw that it was a horse.

There was a rider on the back of the horse.

The rider was a young woman.

The young woman was beautiful. Her hair was the color of wheat and neatly tucked beneath her wide-brimmed cowboy hat, the hat tied beneath her chin to keep it from falling off. She wore a blue cotton short-sleeve shirt tucked inside worn blue jeans. Her eyes were blue. Her soft face and arms glistened with sunscreen.

She reined up in front of me.

I kept walking until I was standing next to the white horse. I ran my hand over its neck, patted it.

"You're real," I said.

"Are you all right, mister?" the young woman said.

She slid out of the saddle and dropped to the ground. She unwound the strap of a canteen from the pommel of her saddle. She unscrewed the cap and offered the canteen to me. I took the canteen and drank. I tried to drink slowly.

She asked me what I was doing out there.

I stopped drinking just long enough to tell her that it was a complicated story.

She asked if I needed help.

I told her that I did.

I drank some more of the water and handed the canteen back.

She suggested that I wasn't from around there.

I asked if it would be too much of an imposition for her to take me to Libbie.

"Who's Libbie?" she said. "Is there someone else out here?"

"No, Libbie—Libbie, South Dakota. It's a town."

"Mister, this is Montana."

But not Canada, my inner voice said.

"I better take you to our place," the young woman said. "Can you ride?"

I told her that the only time I was ever on a horse was during a vacation in Colorado.

She showed me how to mount the horse. I sat in back and she sat in front, holding the reins. She told me to hang on tight and I did. I hung on for dear life.

We set off at a trot.

"Our ranch is just a few miles over the rise," she said.

Rise? my inner voice said. I didn't see any rise, but I took the girl's word for it. I asked her name.

"Angela," she said.

No one is going to believe this, my inner voice told me. *Saved from a slow and probably agonizing death on the Great American Desert by a beautiful young woman named Angela riding a white horse. Hell, I don't believe it.*

"May I ask how old you are?" I said.

"Seventeen."

Well, of course she is.

"Are you in high school?" I said.

"I start my senior year in September."

"What are you going to do after that?"

"I'd like to go to college. I have a list of about a dozen schools I'm going to apply to. Except times are tough, you know? Where I go, if I go, depends on how much scholarship and grant money I can scrape up."

"Well, don't worry about it."

"Why not?"

"I know an eccentric millionaire who will guarantee you a full ride to any school you can get into."

Angela turned in the saddle to look at me.

"Why would he do that?" she said.

It wasn't a particularly funny question, yet it made me laugh just the same.

CHAPTER SIXTEEN

A ngela halted the pickup in front of the Pioneer Hotel and put it in park. As I slid out of the passenger seat, she jumped out of the driver's side and sprinted around the truck to my side. I didn't need her help. A full day in the comfort of her family's ranch house, being ministered to by both Angela and her mother, had set me up nicely. Even the sunburn didn't hurt anymore, unless someone hugged my neck like she was doing now.

"Thank you, McKenzie," Angela said.

Her eyes were as bright, wet, and shiny as they were when I had H. B. Sutton transfer fifty thousand dollars into her father's money market fund. He thought that was a sufficient reward for saving my life, despite protests that I considered my health and well-being to be worth considerably more than that. 'Course, now that I had his account numbers, I figured I could deposit a couple more bucks when he wasn't looking. Call it a tip for letting me use his razor.

"Thank you, Angela," I said and hugged back.

"I'm glad I met you."

I laughed at the remark. Just about everything she and her family said Wednesday and Thursday morning while I was recuperating from my two days on the plains had cracked me up.

"Believe me," I said, "the pleasure was all mine."

I smiled when she went back to the pickup, smiled some more when she drove off, and smiled again when I turned and faced the front door of the hotel. No one in Libbie knew what had happened to me except for the people who arranged it. While I was convalescing at Angela's ranch, I made calls to Nina and the Dunstons and Harry. They told me that both Big Joe Balk and Chief Gustafson had made inquires when it became clear that I had disappeared. After assuring them that once again rumors of my demise were greatly exaggerated, I made them all promise not to reveal that I was alive and well. Surprisingly, Harry seemed most annoyed by what was going on; even more so than Nina, who pretended—I knew that she was pretending—to take it all in stride. I reminded Harry that the FBI field office in Minneapolis covered all the counties in South Dakota, and then I explained why he should care. That brightened his disposition considerably. I glanced at my watch. I expected to see him in a few hours.

"This is going to be fun," I said aloud.

Sharren Nuffer was in her usual spot behind the registration desk, her glasses balanced on the tip of her nose. When she saw me, her eyes grew wide and her entire face became one enormous smile. I was happy to see it. It confirmed my hypothesis that she was guiltless in my abduction. She threw her cheaters down and circled the counter.

"McKenzie," she said way too loudly. I silenced her with an index finger quickly pressed to my lips. She hesitated for a beat and then continued toward me until her arms were wrapped around my shoulders and her cheek was pressed hard against mine.

"I thought you were gone like Rush," she said. "I thought you were gone."

"Not me," I said.

"Oh, you're hurt. What happened to your eye?"

"Don't worry about it."

"But I do. I do worry. After you disappeared—I found your sports jacket draped across a chair, and you weren't in your room, so I called the police, the sheriff—"

"Where is my sports jacket?" I said. I didn't need the coat; I needed the cell phone in the pocket. While at Angela's ranch, I also made a call to Greg Schroeder and told him what I wanted and why. Only to make it work, I needed my cell.

"They took your coat," Sharren said. "They searched your room; they confiscated your belongings; they impounded your car. The sheriff, they say he found guns hidden in your trunk. A lot of guns. They thought—they thought the worst. McKenzie, what happened?"

"Yeah, about that. Where's Evan? Is he working?"

"Yes, Evan, he's tending bar. Why, McKenzie? Why?"

I pressed my finger against my lips again.

"Stay here," I said.

"McKenzie?"

I marched through the lobby, under the arch leading to the dining room, and around dining room tables and chairs toward the bar in back. Sharren followed despite my order, but I knew she would. My legs were heavy and stiff, reminding me that I seldom seemed to be in as good a shape as I thought I was. My ribs ached, too, but then they hadn't stopped hurting, not even for a moment, since I found myself on the Great Plains. I tried to ignore the pain.

Evan was behind the stick, brushing his fingers through his blond hair with his fingers. He was busy speaking to a girl who looked like she graduated from high school yesterday and didn't see me until I stepped between two stools and rested my elbows on top of the bar.

"McKenzie," he said. He pronounced my name as if it were a particularly deadly virus and stepped away from the bar as if I were a carrier; bottles on the shelf behind him rattled and fell when he backed into them.

I glanced at the girl and the cocktail in front of her. In South Dakota, an eighteen-year-old can drink alcohol if it's done in the immediate presence of a parent, guardian, or spouse over twenty-one years of age. I threw a thumb at Evan.

"Is this your old man?" I said.

The girl said, "What?"

"You should leave. Leave right now."

The girl glanced first at Evan and then at Sharren. They both looked frightened, and suddenly the girl became frightened, too. She slid off her stool and headed for the exit as fast as she could without actually running. I gestured with two fingers at Evan as if I wanted to place a drink order.

"C'mere," I said. I deliberately kept my voice light and nonmenacing.

"McKenzie—"

"It's okay."

Evan very slowly, very cautiously inched to where I stood at the bar.

"Closer," I said. I was speaking in a whisper.

Evan turned his head as if he were straining to hear.

"McKenzie, it wasn't me," he said.

"What wasn't you?"

"McKenzie . . ."

As soon as he was close enough, I lunged forward, grabbed him by his shirt and his upper arm, pulled him over the top of the bar, and threw him as best as I could onto a round table. The table collapsed under his weight. I clutched my left side.

Dammit, that hurt, my inner voice said.

Evan shook his head and tried to rise from the barroom floor. I moved to his side, grabbed a tuft of his blond hair, yanked his head up, and punched him in the jaw with all my strength. A vast pain rippled all the way up my arm from my knuckles to my shoulder. A spray of blood jetted from the side of Evan's mouth, and he sagged against the floor. I shook my right arm.

That hurt, too.

It probably hurt him more, I told myself.

One can only hope.

Sharren was taking quick, short steps in Evan's direction. She seemed to be trembling. I held up my hand to keep her from coming nearer.

Evan was slumped onto his side. I gripped his shoulder and rolled him over so I could see his face, so he could see mine.

"I'm going to ask you once and only once—"

"Don't hurt me," he said. Blood splattered from his mouth as he spoke. "Don't hurt me anymore."

"Evan—"

"It wasn't me. It wasn't my fault. He made me do it. I'm not responsible. You can't blame me. I was just following orders. I was just doing what I was told. McKenzie—"

"Whose orders?"

"Don't hurt me."

"I'm calling the police," Sharren said.

"Go 'head," I said.

"No," Evan said.

"No?" Sharren said.

"Evan doesn't want the cops," I said. "He doesn't want to be an accessory to kidnapping and maybe attempted murder, too. Do you?"

Evan shook his head.

"Whose orders?" I repeated.

"He said you wouldn't leave town of your own free will so you had no one to blame but yourself for what happened."

"Who?"

"Mr. Miller."

"Yeah, that's what I thought. Is he the one who kicked me?"

Evan hesitated before he answered. "Yes."

Maybe he did, maybe he didn't; maybe it was both of them, my inner voice said. *Does it matter?*

"Not one damn bit," I said aloud.

"Huh?"

"Evan, you're getting off easy." From the look in his eye, I don't think he believed me. "I don't know how badly hurt you are, only it could be considerably worse, trust me. At the very least, I could send you to federal prison. At the very least. Do we understand each other?" He nodded. "Fortunately for you, I happen to be in a good mood. I'm in a good mood because in a couple of hours a lot of bad things are going to start happening to a lot of bad people. If you speak to anyone, tell anyone I'm back, especially Miller, some of those bad things are going to happen to you. Understand?"

He nodded his head again.

"Say it," I said.

"I understand," Evan said.

I turned and started for the exit. Sharren called after me.

"McKenzie, where are you going?"

"To the hospital."

Nancy Gustafson did everything a doctor would have done. First, she examined my eye, even though it was my ribs that were killing me. Next, she pushed on my chest to determine where I hurt—which hurt like hell, by the way. She watched me breathe and listened to my lungs to make sure air was moving in and out normally. She listened to my heart. She checked my head, neck, spine, and stomach to make sure there weren't any other injuries. All the while, she said reassuring things like "A blow that's hard enough to crack a rib is hard enough to injure your lungs, spleen, blood vessels, a lot of other body parts."

Then there were the inevitable X-rays. She secured mine to a light box and pointed. "Look," she said.

I followed her finger from my perch on the examination room table. There was a fracture no thicker than a single strand of hair across two of my middle ribs.

"I bet that hurts," Nancy said.

"It does," I said. "What can we do about it?"

"Very little, I'm afraid. There's no cast or splint. The ribs will have to heal on their own. It should take about six weeks. The best we can do is make you as comfortable as possible while you wait."

"How?"

Nancy cut four long strips of two-inch-wide adhesive tape. She placed two of the strips directly over my damaged ribs, stretching the tape from my sternum to my spine. The other strips were placed on either side of the ribs.

"The tape should help decrease your pain a bit by restricting the movement of the ribs," she said. "We don't want to wrap around the entire chest because that'll restrict breathing. Breathing is important. You want to take deep breaths, and you want to cough every once in a while. It'll hurt. It'll also prevent secretions from pooling in the lung; it'll prevent pneumonia, so man up, okay?"

Man up? How about a little compassion, lady?

"In the meantime, I'll give you something for the pain."

"I don't need any drugs," I said. To prove it, I winced and groaned as I pulled on my rust-colored polo shirt.

"That's very heroic of you, McKenzie, except we're talking ibuprofen, not narcotics."

"Thank you."

"You're welcome. Tell me something? Concussions, broken ribs, black eyes—does this sort of thing happen to you often?"

"I'm just looking for an excuse to spend time with you."

Nancy smiled at that.

"Since I have you here, may I ask a question?" I said.

"Certainly."

"Did you prescribe sertraline for Mike Randisi's agoraphobia?"

"Yes, with the approval of a doctor, why?"

"Mike told me that he couldn't force himself to come into town to get his prescription filled, and since Spiess Drug Store can no longer fill prescriptions, can no longer deliver drugs to customers like it used to, I was wondering—where did Mike get his meds?"

"He got them from us."

"How?"

Nancy stepped backward. Suspicion clouded her face.

"You sound like you're building up to something, McKenzie," she said.

"Your husband told Sheriff Balk that he was with you when Mike and Tracie Blake were killed. At first, I thought he was using you to give himself an alibi. Now I know that he already had an alibi. He was processing a DUI at the time with plenty of witnesses to back him up. That means he wasn't protecting himself. He was lying to protect you."

"He did that?" Nancy said.

"He thought you killed Mike and Tracie. Why would he think that?"

"I don't know."

"You delivered Mike's meds, didn't you? You drove out to his place and gave them to him."

"Yes, I did. It's called being neighborly. You should try it some-time."

"Were you having an affair with him?"

"McKenzie—"

"He seemed like an awfully nice guy. Didn't take him long to charm Tracie, that's for sure."

"It wasn't like that. We were friends, we talked, but no, we weren't having an affair."

"Friday night, the night he and Tracie were killed, you didn't go home after your shift, did you?"

"No."

"Did you go to Mike's? Did you find Tracie there? Tracie stole your husband, and now she was with your friend. The gun was sitting on the kitchen counter. Did you pick it up?"

"No, no, McKenzie. You're wrong."

"That's not what your husband thinks, or else why would he risk his job and more to give you an alibi?"

"He believes Mike and I were sleeping together, but we weren't."

"Then why does he believe it?"

"I wanted him to."

"You wanted him to believe you and Mike were having an affair?"

"Yes."

"Even though you weren't?"

"Yes."

"Why?"

A voice behind me answered.

"It was easier than telling him the truth."

I twisted on the examination table. Sharren Nuffer stood in the entrance to the suite. Nancy spun to face her, too. She hesitated just for a moment and moved to Sharren's side. They hugged like two people who had just escaped a horrific traffic accident. When they finished, they both turned to face me, holding hands, standing straight and still like gunfighters, legs apart, weight evenly balanced, a ferocious expression of defiance on their faces.

"Oh," I said.

"You look disappointed, McKenzie," Sharren said.

"I am."

Nancy said, "Who would have thought you'd be another heterosexual male intimidated by—"

"Oh, don't give me that crap," I said. "I don't give a damn about your sexual orientation. You two lied to me. Both of you. I'm starting to feel like Diogenes wandering around with my lantern held high in search of an honest man and finding only—God, I can't believe you lied to me."

"What are you talking about?" Nancy said.

"All that nonsense about your husband and Tracie Blake. The noble, long-suffering wife—you played the part well, you know? Tell me, who started cheating first? You or him?"

Sharren said, "McKenzie—"

I cut her off.

"And you. What was it you told me? 'I was married three times and not once did I cheat on my husband.' What do you call this?"

"Eric Gustafson is not my husband," Sharren said.

"Yeah, that makes all the difference in the world."

"Why are you angry at us?" Nancy said.

"Be honest," said Sharren. "You weren't angry at Eric or Tracie or Dawn Neske or Ed Bizek. Why are you mad at us if it isn't because we're gay?"

"Because I like you," I said.

"You like us?" Nancy said.

"Of course I do."

"Then why did you accuse me of murder?"

"I didn't accuse you of murder."

"You said I shot Mike and Tracie."

"I did not. I already knew who shot Mike and Tracie. I asked those questions to make sure I was right. I had to know why your husband lied. Now I know. Dammit, you guys."

"Does this mean that we're not friends anymore?" Sharren said. There was a smirk on her face as if she expected an insult and was all set to reciprocate.

"That night in the lobby of the Pioneer, when you gave me the sandwich," I said. "You told me that you finally found someone you couldn't live without. Remember?"

Nancy smiled as if she had just heard the best compliment.

"Why didn't you tell me about you and Nancy then?"

Sharren looked at Nancy. "It's a small town," Nancy said. Sharren nodded as if it were a conclusion they had both reached long ago.

"I don't care. If you're in love, you should be together. It's that simple."

Yet even as I said the words, I flashed on my relationship with Nina.

It's never simple, my inner voice said.

I slipped off the examination table and winced some more. Nancy rushed to my side. I guess she thought I might collapse from the pain. I found myself smiling in spite of myself.

"Libbie, South Dakota," I said. "Rules, regulations, and respect."

"I've always wondered who came up with that motto," Sharren said.

"Someone with a sense of irony," I said.

"Maybe it was just wishful thinking," Chief Gustafson said.

This time he was the one standing in the entrance to the examination suite. Sharren and Nancy glanced at each other with the same alarmed expression. Like them, I wondered how long the chief had been standing there and how much he had heard. He didn't offer a clue. Instead, he said, "I heard you were back in town, McKenzie. Do you want to tell me what happened to you?"

I glanced at my watch. Time was starting to slip away.

"I'll explain on the way," I said.

I wedged past the chief into the corridor.

"Wait a minute," the chief said. "Where are we going?"

"I'm going to identify the Imposter. I'm going to show you what happened to him. After all, that's why I came here. Where's my Audi?"

"Your Audi? It's in the lot at headquarters."

He said "headquarters" like there were police precincts scattered all over the place.

"We'll take my car," I said.

"Just so you know, I confiscated all of your guns," the chief said. "I locked them in the vault in my office."

"All of those weapons are legally registered—"

"Including the Colt submachine gun with the 40 mm grenade launcher?"

"I have a carry permit, too."

"In Minnesota you have a carry permit. This is South Dakota."

I glared at the chief for a couple of beats. He glared right back.

"Fine," I said. "You drive. Oh, by the way, I need my cell phone."

CHAPTER SEVENTEEN

When we arrived, the bison hanging above the front entrance to Grandma Miller's bar and grill was committing the sacrilege of singing the old Louis Armstrong standard "What a Wonderful World"—if you call what he was doing to the song singing. If I could have reached, I would have punched it right in the mouth.

We had paused at the cop shop to retrieve my black sports jacket and cell. By the time we reached Grandma Miller's, most of the lunch crowd had already drifted out, and there were plenty of empty tables and booths inside. The chief and I paused next to a sign that read PLEASE SEAT YOURSELF while I scanned the dining area. Sara Miller was policing a table near the corner. She smiled when she saw us, gave a wave, and gestured at the table near the center of the room.

"Remember," I said. "You promised."

"I remember," the chief said.

We made our way to the table while Sara took the dirty dishes into the kitchen. We were sitting when she returned.

"Hi, McKenzie," she said. "Chief."

"How are you doing, Sara?" I said.

She smiled brightly. I think she was still getting used to her new name.

"I'm doing well. I really am. What happened to your eye?"

I flashed on her father.

"It ran into something," I said.

"Sorry to hear that." She pulled an order pad from her apron pocket. "What would you gentlemen like?"

"Information," I said.

"Information?"

I pulled an empty chair away from the table and beckoned her to sit.

"What is it, McKenzie?" She was looking at the chief when she spoke the words.

I gestured again, and reluctantly she sat.

"What is it?" she repeated.

"It's about Rush," the chief said.

"Rush?" she said.

I gave the chief a hard look. He read my face and directed his gaze out the window at the highway.

"Listen, sweetie," I said. "Nothing bad is going to happen to you. Nothing at all. Right, Chief?"

The chief nodded and said, "Yes. I promised."

"But Sara, I need you to tell us the truth. It's important."

Sara nodded her head and folded her hands on top of the table. I think she knew what was coming.

"The night that the Imposter disappeared," I said. "Tuesday night. You called him, didn't you? You called his hotel room from your home."

Sara nodded.

"You told him to meet you at Lake Mataya."

Sara nodded again. Her hands began to tremble, and tears formed in her eyes.

"Why?" I said.

"I wanted—because of what he did to me, I wanted—I wanted to kill him."

The chief's entire body flinched, yet he continued to stare out the window, continued to remain silent.

"You didn't kill him, though, did you?" I said.

Sara shook her head vigorously. Tears fell and splattered against the tabletop. She gripped her hands more tightly. The chief exhaled as if he had been holding his breath.

"It's okay," I said and patted her hands. "No one thought that you did."

"I was so angry," Sara said. "After what happened at the hotel; the way he laughed. It was already all over town, and other people were laughing, too. Even my father laughed. And he accused me, my father accused me of, of—you know what he accused me of. He said I damaged his reputation. His. I hated him. Rush. I hated Rush and I wanted—I wanted . . ."

"It's okay," I said again.

"No, it isn't. Being that way; wanting to kill someone. I still shake when I think of it."

"Everyone has black and evil thoughts. Everyone knows lust, malice, envy, greed, hate. There is no shame in owning these—these what? Instincts? The shame is giving in to them, giving them dominance. You didn't."

"I wanted to. I wanted . . ."

Sara's tears flowed more freely, yet I noticed that she had relaxed her hands.

"What happened?" the chief said. His voice was gentle. He didn't look at either of us.

"I . . ."

"It's okay," I said.

"I called Rush like you said. I asked him to meet me at the

lake; I didn't know any other place where I wouldn't be seen. He asked why. I told him—I told him that since everyone already thinks we slept together we might as well—we might as well . . ." Sara sighed deeply. "I told him to meet me in the clearing. There's a clearing in the trees about halfway around the lake. I don't know if you've been there."

"I've been there."

"I told him to meet me in the clearing, and I waited. When he arrived—when he arrived, I pointed the gun at him."

"What gun?" the chief said.

"My father's, one of my father's guns. He laughed at me just like he did in the hotel room. He said—Rush said I must be kidding. Then he stopped laughing. I don't know why. I didn't say a word to him, nothing at all. I just started walking toward him with the gun, pointing the gun at his face, and he started backing up. There's a kind of low bench, a bench made of the trunk of a tree, and he kept backing up until his legs hit the bench and he tumbled over. He fell over and he covered his head with his hands and he started—he started begging, I guess. He said he was sorry. He said . . ."

Sara sighed again.

"I wanted to shoot him. I couldn't. I couldn't make my finger squeeze the trigger. I tried so hard. Then I started crying. I was crying because I felt so helpless. I was crying louder than Rush was. Then I ran away. I ran back to the car and I drove home."

"It's okay," I said.

"McKenzie, why do you keep saying that?"

"Because it's true."

I rested my hands on top of hers, and she smiled slightly.

"At what time was this?" the chief said.

"Ten o'clock," Sara said.

"Were there any other cars in the parking lot?"

"Cars? No. Well, there was Rush's car and mine, that was all."

"Did you see anyone else?"

"No, Chief, I didn't. I'm sorry. I'm sorry about everything. Are you going to arrest me?"

The chief grinned. He turned his head and looked her in the eye for the first time.

"There's no law against not shooting someone," he said. "Not even for not shooting a louse like Rush."

"Thank you."

"Sara," I said, "when you went home, did you tell your mother what happened?"

"I wasn't going to say anything," she said. "I was so embarrassed and hurt and—only I couldn't stop crying. She came into my bedroom and hugged me and asked me what was wrong and it just came out—everything—including what happened at the hotel, what really happened. She said the same thing you did."

"What?"

"It's okay."

And then she took the blame, my inner voice told me. *She said that she lured the Imposter to the clearing, substituting a tree branch for the gun because, let's face it, who would believe that she'd be unable to squeeze the trigger?*

"I like your mother," I said aloud. "I didn't before. Now—she's all right. Tell her I said so. Tell her I said, 'Pretty good for an Edina girl.'"

"I don't know what you mean."

I didn't think it was my place to explain it to her, so I simply shrugged as I pushed my chair back and rose from the table.

"You'll have to ask her," I said. I gestured at the chief with my chin. "Are you ready?"

"Yeah," he said. "I'm ready."

"Is that all?" Sara said. "Is that all you wanted to know? Is that why you came here?"

"Yes," I said.

"I don't get it."

"Neither do I," said the chief.

"Patience," I said. I glanced at my watch. "Patience."

Dawn Neske was wearing a thin, filmy red short-sleeve robe that ended just above her knees, and nothing else that I could see, when we opened the door to her apartment.

"Did you forget something?" she said. She saw the chief and me standing behind her husband in the doorway and quickly pulled her robe tighter. "Perry, geez."

"They stopped me in the corridor," Perry said. "They wouldn't let me go to work."

We pushed our way deeper into the apartment and closed the door. The rooms were sparsely furnished, and I noticed that there were several boxes stacked against the walls. Either the Neskes were just moving in or getting ready to move out.

"I should get dressed," Dawn said.

"Don't bother on my account," I said.

Dawn pulled the collar of her robe up and glared at me. "What do you want?"

I fished the cell phone out of my pocket and dialed up the photograph that Greg Schroeder had sent me. I showed the video display to Dawn.

"Is this Nicholas Hendel? Is this the man who called himself Rushmore McKenzie?"

Dawn nodded. I pivoted toward Perry and held up the video screen for him to see. He looked at the face on the screen, glanced at Dawn, and edged closer to the front door. The chief deliberately made a loud thud as he leaned against the door, his arms folded across his chest.

"Is this Nicholas Hendel?" I said again.

"Yes," Dawn said.

"Are you sure? It's a high school yearbook photo. A few years old, not very good—"

"It's him."

I glanced at Perry. He shrugged as if he didn't know whom I was talking about.

"Where is he?" Dawn said.

"I'm not exactly sure, but I have a good idea."

"Where?"

"You took an awful chance coming to me, Dawn. Did you really think that if I found Nick, I wouldn't also find his sister?"

"His sister?" the Chief said.

I dialed up another photo and held it up for everyone in the room to see. It was Dawn, the photo taken six years earlier when she was in high school. I spoke to her.

"You told me that you and Perry worked in a call center in Franklin, a town just down the road from where you lived. A database search for Nicholas Hendel revealed that at least one person by that name had lived in Ashton, Illinois. While he was here, Nicholas made a slip. He told someone that in high school he had been a Raider." I made air quotes around the name. "He also left a clue that suggested he was from Illinois. So we checked all the high schools in Illinois and discovered that the nickname for Ashton-Franklin was the Raiders, Ashton-Franklin being a consolidated high school drawing from towns just a few miles apart. Yesterday, I had an investigator take a look at the Ashton-Franklin yearbooks. When you think about it, it was all really quite simple."

I gave a triumphant glance at Chief Gustafson.

"Was that what you had in mind when you dragged me here?" I said.

"I had nothing to do with that."

"Of course not."

"I knew it," Perry said. He was speaking to his wife. Dawn slowly sat in one of the few chairs in the apartment and lowered her head. "I knew this would happen. I told you so."

"I thought you didn't know who Nicholas Hendel was," the chief said.

Perry looked at the door the chief was leaning against, wishing he were out the door and down the street.

"You were Nick's shills, both of you," I said. "You helped set up the town for him, picked Mike Randisi as a target—because of your job, Dawn, you knew about his agoraphobia. You slept with Ed Bizek to keep close to the money. It was his wallet that you told me about, the one you searched; that's where you found the account numbers and password."

"We have the right to—"

I interrupted Perry before he could say any more.

"Shut the hell up," I told him. "You pimped your wife for money. That means you don't get any rights. Not from me. So you just stand there and shut up."

Dawn looked like she was about to say something, but I cut her off, too.

"Please don't," I said. I glanced at my watch. "Honest to God, we haven't got the time."

"Time for what?" Perry said.

"I said shut up."

I moved close enough to Dawn to see the goose bumps on the flesh of her bare arms and thighs.

"It's all true," I said. "Isn't it?"

She lifted her head to look at me.

"We didn't steal the money," she said. "We don't have it."

"I know you don't."

That caused Chief Gustafson to push himself off of the door.

"They don't?" he said.

"Nope. They have no idea what happened to Hendel or where he went. They don't know what happened to the money, either. That's why Dawn came to me, why she took the risk of giving up her brother's name. They were hoping I could find out. Isn't that right?"

"Yes," Dawn said.

"Did you hear from your brother the night he disappeared?"

"He left a voice mail message," Dawn said. "Nick told us that his car broke down at the lake and he needed a ride. But Perry was working and I . . ."

"You were with Ed Bizek."

"Yes. We didn't hear the message until the next morning. Later we heard"—she glanced briefly at the chief—"that Nick had skipped town with the money, only that didn't make sense."

"That's because you never gave him the password, did you?"

Dawn shook her head.

"But you see—" She turned in the chair to face the chief. "We didn't do anything wrong. We didn't take the money. We don't know what happened to Nick. We're innocent."

"Hardly innocent," I said. "How long did it take you to put the scam together, anyway?"

"Two years," Dawn said.

"That long?"

Despite my threats, Perry started talking again. "It took us a while to figure out how to put it all together. Creating a company, the Web site, recruiting actors to play investors—it was really complicated."

"I'm sure it was," the chief said.

"Perry, geez," Dawn said.

"Tell me something," I said. "Please. Why me?"

"What do you mean?"

"Why did you pick my name?"

"I liked it."

"You liked it?"

"Yes. I liked the sound of it, Rushmore McKenzie. I read it in the paper in the Twin Cities. It was right after you helped find the gold that the gangsters hid back in the 1930s. We were there with Nick to work out our plans before he came to Libbie. We went on-line and discovered that there was enough information about you so that people would know that you were legitimate and that you were trustworthy, enough so that people would be satisfied without digging any deeper. We were always afraid that if people dug deeper they would learn things that would prove that Nick wasn't you. Only they never did. One more thing, something important—there was a description of you online that matched Nicky, but no picture of you."

"As simple as that," I said.

"As simple as that," Dawn said. "Except—" She smiled briefly and shook her head. "If we had taken the trouble to dig deeper, if we had found out who you really were, we would never have used your name."

"Okay," I said. I tried to hide my disappointment. All this time I had expected, I had hoped, that something momentous had gone into the selection process. Instead, it was pure chance. How did the country-western song go—if it wasn't for bad luck, I'd have no luck at all?

"What are you going to do?" Perry said.

The chief looked at me as if he were waiting for an answer.

"Contact your officers," I told the chief. "Have these two escorted to the sheriff's department in Mercer."

Dawn hopped out of the chair so quickly that the top of her robe fell open, letting me know exactly what it was that Ed Bizek had seen in her.

"What charge?" she said.

"Hold them as material witnesses," I told the chief. "The county attorney may charge them with conspiracy to commit fraud or he might not, but it's likely he'll need them to build his case."

"What case?" the chief said. "Against whom?"

"Against the person who stole all that money, of course. Hurry up, will you? We're running out of time. Oh, one more thing. Call Sheriff Balk and ask him to meet us."

"Where?"

By the time we arrived at the lobby of the First Integrity State Bank of Libbie, the free donuts left for the customers were stale and the coffee was burned. There were several customers queued up at the teller cages and another sitting in a chair across the desk from a customer service rep. I sat on the cotton sofa beneath the chandelier and propped my feet on the polished coffee table. The older woman sitting across from me was reading a magazine. She peered at me over the top of her reading glasses. I had no doubt that she was silently questioning my mother and father's parenting skills.

The customer sitting at the desk finished his business, and while he was slipping out the front door, the service rep moved to the lobby area.

"Mrs. Franklin?" he said.

The woman dropped her magazine on the table and stood. She stared at the rep. The message in her expression was unmistakable.

"Sir," the rep said. "Please remove your feet. This is a bank, not a living room."

I removed my feet. The woman smiled in triumph. She followed the rep to his desk. As soon as her back was turned, I propped my feet back on the table, crossing my legs at the ankles.

"Comfortable?" the chief said.

I examined my watch.

They're late, my inner voice said.

A few moments later, Jon Kampa joined us, his eyes sweeping

first over me, then the chief, then back to me again. He was no happier that I was abusing his furniture than the old woman had been but said nothing about it. He adjusted his red tie. It was the same tie that he wore when we first met, the same charcoal suit.

"What can I do for you gentlemen?" he said.

I glanced at my watch again.

Dammit, Harry.

"You could confess," I said, "but in a few minutes, it really won't be necessary."

"What are you talking about?" Kampa said.

"You looted the city's account. You killed Nicholas Hendel. Nick Hendel was the Imposter's real name, by the way. You probably didn't know that."

What surprised me was that Gustafson seemed more surprised by my revelation than Kampa. The chief turned a deep crimson and started breathing in and out as if he had just completed a marathon. Kampa, on the other hand, didn't display any emotion at all. He spoke as if he had been practicing the phrase—"I will not answer any of your questions without my attorney present."

"That's okay with me," I said. "I don't have any questions."

From his expression, the chief, on the other hand, had many, many questions.

"Think about it," I said. "The Imposter was last seen alive at about 10:00 P.M. According to your report, Kampa said that the city accounts were looted at about midnight. Now I have been told since I started this investigation that just about everybody had access to the account numbers and password. I don't believe that's entirely true. For example, the Imposter didn't have access. He didn't have the password. His accomplices didn't steal the money, or they wouldn't have taken the risk of trying to help me find Hendel; they were just as surprised when he disappeared as you were. Who does that leave? It leaves the one person who knew that

Hendel wouldn't be around to ask what happened to the money; the one person who knew that, because he had disappeared, Hendel would be blamed for looting the account."

I pointed at Kampa.

"The man who killed him," I said.

"You can't prove anything," he said.

"It's not my job to prove it. It's theirs."

By then, finally, the front door of the bank had flown open, and a dozen men and women dressed in suits entered, spreading out across the interior like a SWAT team, moving swiftly to the cashier cages and to the computers on top of the desks. Kampa took half a dozen quick steps toward the door. The chief grabbed him by the collar and dragged him back beneath the chandelier. More suits poured into the building. The old woman screamed. A man standing near the cashier cages raised his hands into the air. Apparently he was surrendering to a tall, silver-haired man who found a spot in the center of the bank and addressed the bank employees and customers in a loud, formal voice.

"My name is Daniel Hasselberg," he said. "I am with the Federal Deposit Insurance Corporation. The FDIC has just taken control of First Integrity State Bank of Libbie. Please remain calm. All of your deposits are safe. Nobody is going to have any problems with their money." He paused for a moment, then added, "It's going to get a bit crowded in here."

Kampa squirmed against the chief's grip.

"This is my bank," he shouted.

Hasselberg studied him for a moment.

"Are you Jon Kampa?"

"Yes."

"It's my bank now."

I saw a familiar smile from behind Hasselberg's back. Harry moved around the government official and joined us beneath the chandelier, letting his credentials lead the way. He spoke first to the chief.

"Good afternoon, Officer. I'm Special Agent Brian Wilson, Federal Bureau of Investigation."

"Chief Eric Gustafson, Libbie Police Department."

"Geezus, Harry," I said from the sofa. "You're a half hour late. If I had known you were on government time . . ."

"Did you do this?" Kampa said. "Did you call the FDIC?"

I gave him my best "Who? Me?" shrug. "If your bank wasn't in trouble, why would you steal all that money?" I said.

"Oh, stop it, McKenzie," Harry said. "The FDIC was already on it. After we spoke yesterday I made a few calls. The FDIC was going to close down the bank next month after its audit. They decided to accelerate their plans because they were afraid your accusations would cause a panic. Seems the bank was in trouble because its capital reserves had evaporated and the delinquent loans on its books have more than doubled during the past year. Most of the loans were tied to the housing market. The bank has been quietly up for sale for months, but there have been no takers."

"That explains motive," I said.

Harry nodded at Kampa, who was still being held by the chief. "Who are you?" he said.

The chief answered for him. "This is Jon Kampa. He owns the bank. He's my prisoner."

"What's the charge?"

"Murder," I said.

"You can't prove anything," Kampa shouted.

"You were at the Miller home when Sara called Nicholas Hendel and arranged to meet him at Lake Mataya. I believe you overheard the conversation and followed her out there. I believe you stole the fuses from Hendel's car, stranding him. Hendel called his accomplices for a ride, but neither of them was home, so he decided to hoof it back into town. I believe you ran him down. I believe you killed him with your car so if you got caught in the act, you could always claim it was an accident."

"Believing isn't proving," Kampa said.

"No, it isn't," the chief added.

"Don't worry, Chief," Harry said. "I've seen this before. McKenzie is a music lover. He likes to build to a crescendo."

"The front of your car was smashed in," I told Kampa. "I saw it at Schooley's Auto Repair. You said you hit a deer out on White Buffalo Road, the road leading to Lake Mataya. There's an impact crater and blood on the windshield. A simple test will prove that it's human blood. We don't have Hendel's body, but we do have the next best thing. His sister. What do you want to bet that if we tested her DNA and the DNA taken from the blood sample, we'd come up with a familial match? 'Course, we still have Hendel's hairbrush. It'll take longer to get his DNA off that, but the result will be the same."

"Ta-da," Harry said.

Kampa didn't speak.

"Besides, your vehicle was undrivable," I said. "You needed a tow. So you couldn't have taken the body far. If the chief examines the ground near where Schooley hooked up your car, I bet he finds where you buried Hendel and who knows what other evidence."

Kampa didn't have anything to say to that, either.

"As for the money you stole . . ." I waved at all the suits crowding into the bank and bustling about with laptops and file boxes. "People think computers can do anything. They can't. I bet the FDIC finds the money, and I bet it won't be in the Cayman Islands. I'm making a lot of bets, I know. I bet I win them all."

Harry patted Kampa on the shoulder. "Don't worry, pal," he said. "If you beat the murder rap, we'll have a lot of federal charges waiting for you."

"Jon," the chief said, "how could you have done all this? I would have said you were the most honest man in town."

"Maybe he was," Harry said. "Until his bank failed."

"Show me a completely honest man," I said, "and I'll show you someone who has never truly faced temptation."

"That's so profound," Harry said.

"You like it?"

"McKenzie, you are so full of—"

Before Harry could complete the insult, a commotion near the front door caused all of us to turn. Dewey Miller was shouting.

"What is the meaning of this?" he said. "Who's in charge here?"

"Who are you?" Hasselberg said.

"I'm the mayor of this town."

Harry pivoted at the words and glared at me.

"Not yet," I said.

Hasselberg tried to rest his arm on Miller's shoulder, but Miller shrugged it off.

"I'm with the FDIC," Hasselberg explained. "We have seized this bank. The deposits are safe; you might want to tell your citizens that. We have arranged the sale of seventy-five percent of First Integrity's assets to a bank in North Dakota. We'll try to collect as much of the remaining outstanding loans as possible ourselves."

Kampa moaned loudly at that and slumped down in the chief's arms; the chief had to make an effort to keep him upright. "My family," he said. I don't know if he was in anguish over his wife and children, if he had any, or the generations of Kampas that had built and maintained the bank these many decades.

"We're going to be out of here as fast as we can," Hasselberg said. "All of this will be just a blip in your history."

"I have questions," Miller said. I wondered if they were about the town or his holdings.

"Please ask them," Hasselberg said.

While they spoke, Sheriff Balk arrived.

"What's going on here?" he asked.

"Ahh, Sheriff," Hasselberg said. He extradited himself from his conversation with Miller. "We would like to hire some of your deputies to assist with crowd control. Of course, we'll pay overtime."

While they spoke, Miller surveyed the chaotic scene in the bank. Eventually his eyes found me. I gave him a Victoria Dunston microwave. He didn't wave back. He didn't react at all, not even to display his disappointment. He was totally without guilt, I decided. Without conscience, shame, remorse, regret, empathy, sympathy— there was no compassion or tenderness in his heart.

"What about it, McKenzie?" Harry said.

"Later," I said. "I have things to do first."

"What things?"

I drifted to where Hasselberg and Big Joe were having their conversation. As soon as it began to wane, I said, "Excuse me, Sheriff. You and I need to chat." He stared as if he were surprised to see me. "There's the matter of Tracie Blake's murder."

CHAPTER EIGHTEEN

Four in the afternoon and there were only two customers in the Tall Moon Tavern. A man and a woman, no longer young, sitting in a booth near the jukebox, were surrounded by discarded pull tabs, empty beer bottles, and the remains of a pizza-oven pizza. I wondered briefly if this was what they had planned for their retirement or if it just worked out that way—but only briefly. Jeff was standing at one end of the bar, a knife in his hand. The blade of the knife seemed too long and too sharp for the job—he was slicing lemons, limes, and oranges. Wayne was sitting at the other end of the stick, his elbow propped on the smooth surface, his chin resting against his hand. There was a coffee mug in front of him. He called to us.

"Look what the cat dragged in."

The sheriff and I moved across the impossibly warped floor. I settled on a stool at the bar. Big Joe Balk took a chair at a table facing Wayne.

"How are you doing?" I said.

"Fair," Wayne said. "I heard that you disappeared after Church and Paulie got busted. I thought one of their friends might have had a hand in it until I realized that Church and Paulie didn't have any friends. So, what happened to you?"

"I was just checking out the countryside, bathing in the scenery."

"Some of that scenery punch you in the eye, did it?"

"It's a rough neighborhood."

"Well, I'm always happy to see you. You, too, Sheriff. What'll ya have? Jeff, take care of these boys on me."

Jeff wiped his hands on a towel and moved down the bar.

"Ringneck," I told him.

"I'm good," said the sheriff.

"Not drinkin'?" Wayne said.

"I'm working."

"Can't even offer you a cup of joe?"

The sheriff shook his head.

"Shit." Wayne picked up his mug, took a long sip, and set it down again. "Shit," he repeated.

Jeff served the Ringneck and went back to his fruit. He didn't look at Wayne, or me, or anyone else for that matter. Just a fly on the wall.

"Well, shit," Wayne said again. "If I had known you boys were coming, I never would have climbed back up on the wagon. Hey, Jeff. Pour me a shot."

Jeff didn't look, didn't move; just stood there, slicing lemons as if it were the most important task a man could perform.

"C'mon, Jeff," Wayne said. "I need it."

Jeff ignored him some more.

"Hell," Wayne said. "You tellin' me a man can't get one last drink before he goes to prison?" He drained what was left of his coffee and slammed the mug on top of the bar as if he didn't care if it shattered or not.

"Take your time," Sheriff Balk said. "We're in no hurry."

"That's damn white of ya, Big Joe," Wayne said. "It truly is. But I guess there's no sense puttin' it off. I want to tell you, though— McKenzie, I want to tell you—I'm sorry. I really am, man. Hittin' you with my bat like that—see, Sheriff, I'm confessing. You won't have any trouble with me. McKenzie, hitting you with the bat, that was wrong, flat-out wrong, and I'm sorry. I thought you were stepping out with Tracie, and I got all jealous, and then I find out that it wasn't even true. Then the way you did Church, that was beautiful, man. You're a stand-up guy, McKenzie, and I'm sorry I went after you."

I raised the Ringneck in salute. "Don't worry about it. I forgive you." I took a sip of the ale and set the bottle down.

"Yeah, only Big Joe, he ain't the forgivin' sort," Wayne said. "Are you, Big Joe?"

"Vic won't press charges, what am I supposed to do about it?" the sheriff said.

"What do you mean?"

"We didn't come for that," I said. "You hitting me in the head with a baseball bat, there are worse crimes. Not many, but some."

"We came about Tracie and Mike," the sheriff said.

"No, no, no," Wayne said. He slipped off his stool, and for a moment I thought he might fall to his knees; he steadied himself by gripping the bar. "You can't believe—no, McKenzie. No, Sheriff. I didn't have anything to do with that. You gotta believe me."

"We do believe you," I said.

"Relax," the sheriff said.

"Relax?" Wayne said.

"Tracie and Mike were killed after 2:00 A.M., killed right after closing time," I said. "They were killed while you were at the Libbie cop shop trying to convince Chief Gustafson to drop the DUI charges against Councilman Hudalla's kid."

"That's right," Wayne said. "That's right."

"Besides, you didn't know Tracie left the bar that night to see Mike. You thought she had gone to see me."

"That's right."

"Jeff knew, though. He told me so the night Church's truck accidentally caught on fire. Didn't you, Jeff?"

Jeff didn't move, not even to look up from the cutting board.

"You said a lot of things about Wayne that night, Jeff," I said. "You said he was furious when Tracie left on her date with Mike. You said he insulted her, called her names. You said he went off in a huff but later came back happy. You gave me as many reasons to believe that Wayne killed Mike and Tracie as you could without actually accusing him. I thought that was odd. Do you think it was odd?"

"I think it was odd," said the sheriff.

"Did you, Jeff?" Wayne said. "Did you say those things?"

Jeff didn't say if he did or didn't.

"Where were you that night, Jeff?" I said. "You said you got off early; said that Wayne was in such a good mood that he closed up. Where did you go after last call? Jeff?"

Jeff stared at the lemon on the cutting board, the knife poised above it.

"It's just a hunch, Jeff," I said. "I could be wrong. I could be way, way out there on this one. During the ride over, the sheriff said you could sue my ass for slander if I accused you and I was wrong. Am I wrong, Jeff?"

"Whoever shot Mike and Tracie left his fingerprints on the gun," the sheriff said. "If they aren't yours, Jeff, you could take a lot of money offa McKenzie. I'll even testify on your behalf."

"Jeff?"

"Do I need to get a court order to take your fingerprints, Jeff?"

"Say it ain't so, Jeff," Wayne said.

Jeff's head came up slowly. He looked at the sheriff. He looked at Wayne. He looked at me. Then he threw the knife at the sheriff.

I ducked at Jeff's arm motion and spun off of the stool. I didn't see the knife in flight, but I heard the sheriff's painful cry, and I saw him wrench his left shoulder back and spill from his chair.

Jeff rounded the bar and ran to the door. I went to the sheriff. He was lying on his side and gurgling angrily. I gently rolled him on his back. The knife was four inches deep and protruding from the upper part of his armpit. It didn't seem to have sliced any major arteries.

"Not so bad," I said.

"Fuck you, McKenzie," the sheriff said.

I reached across his body and yanked his handgun from its holster. It was a Glock 17, the primary sidearm used by the St. Paul Police Department while I was there. I never liked the Glock, was never comfortable with the grip.

"What are you doing?" the sheriff said.

"Wayne, call the sheriff's department," I said. "Call them right now. An ambulance, too. Did you hear me, Wayne?"

"Yes," Wayne said. He went running for the phone behind the bar.

"That's my gun," the sheriff said.

"This is what comes from confiscating my grenade launcher," I said.

I went to the door. The couple sitting in the booth stared at me mutely. They could have been watching reruns of *Walker, Texas Ranger* for all the excitement they showed.

"McKenzie, wait," the sheriff said.

I did wait, but only long enough to be sure that it was clear.

I stepped out of the tavern into bright sunlight, the Glock leading the way. I shielded my eyes as I surveyed the parking lot. I saw the sheriff's cruiser and a battered pickup that I guessed belonged to the older couple. There was a seared and blackened area in the corner of the lot where Church's vehicle had burned. No Jeff. I circled to my right, carrying the gun with both hands, staying close to the building. I heard movement. I quickened my pace until I was at the corner of the tavern. I peeked around the corner. Jeff was rummaging in the back of an SUV parked alongside the building about twenty paces away.

"Stop," I said.

He paused, looked at me, then pivoted away from the SUV. The gun in his hands looked like a Magnum. It sounded like a Magnum. When the chunk of the building just above my head exploded, raining shards and slivers of wood on my head and against my face, that sealed it.

I swung into a Weaver stance just as I had been trained to do—my feet shoulder-width apart, my right foot back from my left foot, knees locked, right arm extended at shoulder level with a slight bend in the elbow, my left hand supporting my right hand, my left arm bent at the elbow, the elbow close to my body, my body turned at a forty-five-degree angle, my head bent slightly to align the gun sights on the center of Jeff's chest. I squeezed the trigger slowly.

Click.

What the hell?

I scurried back around the corner of the building just as Jeff threw another shot at me, this one sailing wide.

I pulled back the slide.

Are you kidding me?

Sheriff Balk had been carrying his Glock without a round in the chamber.

You gotta be kidding me. Who are you, Barney Fife?

Maybe that's why he told me to wait, I told myself.

Geez, McKenzie, running around without first checking to see that the gun was loaded—could you be more careless?

I chambered a round and edged back along the corner of the building, keeping low. I took a quick peek and pulled my head back before Jeff could use it for target practice. He was in the SUV. I looked again, taking my time. He was starting the engine. I rose up, using the corner for cover, and went into the Weaver stance again. I pumped five of the Glock's seventeen rounds into the engine.

Jeff poked his Magnum out of the window. He was point shooting, shooting one-handed from the shoulder, and he was using his left hand. I figured the odds of him breaking his wrist with the recoil were considerably greater than they were of him hitting me. I hopped back around the corner just the same. I might be careless, but I'm not an idiot.

I heard the shot; I had no idea where the bullet landed. I also heard Jeff shout, "Dammit."

I shouted back, "I bet that hurt."

"Leave me alone."

"Give it up, Jeff. You've got nowhere to go."

I heard the ignition of the SUV cranking, but the engine refused to turn over. I carefully glanced around the corner again. Jeff was still in the vehicle, his head down, staring at the console, the gun held carelessly outside the window and pointed more or less at the ground.

"It's over," I said.

Jeff lifted his head, an expression of pure panic across his face. I didn't like the expression. Panic made him dangerous.

"Think, Jeff. Think."

Only Jeff wasn't thinking past his gun. He raised it, trying to point it at me.

I fired two rounds into the SUV's front tire. The tire exploded, and the front end of the vehicle listed hard to the left. I ducked back behind the corner before Jeff could get another shot off.

"Think about it, Jeff," I said.

"I'll kill you," he said.

I heard the door to the SUV open. He was coming.

Sonuvabitch.

I spun around the corner and went into a kneeling position, my right knee firmly planted on the ground, my left knee up, my left foot flat, my left elbow resting against the front of my knee. I sighted along the short barrel.

Jeff seemed surprised to see me. He was carrying the Magnum low with both hands. When I came around the corner he started to raise it.

"Stop it. Stop it now."

The voice came from behind Jeff.

It belonged to Big Joe Balk.

He had circled around the tavern from the other side.

He was holding a standard-issue twelve-gauge Remington pump-action shotgun, the stock hard against his right shoulder. I saw the blood from his left shoulder saturating his uniform. The knife had been removed, and for a brief moment I could imagine him pulling it out himself.

Geezus.

The sheriff was pointing the shotgun at the back of Jeff's head, but he was speaking to both of us.

"Drop the guns," he said. "Drop 'em. I mean it. I'll kill you, Jeff. I've done it before, I'll do it again. You know I will. Drop the goddamn guns."

"I didn't mean to do it," Jeff said. "I wasn't going to hurt anyone. I was just going to mess with them, joke with them."

"Drop the guns," the sheriff said.

"I went over there and the back door was unlocked and I went inside and I heard Tracie laughing and I yelled, 'Sounds like a party,' and Mike came into the kitchen. I was joking but he was angry and he started yelling and the gun was on the counter and we wrestled over it and it went off and then Tracie came running out and started screaming—I didn't mean to shoot her. I didn't."

"It's over," I said.

"Drop your guns," the sheriff said.

Jeff raised the Magnum.

He raised it slowly.

My finger tightened around the trigger of the Glock.

The sheriff screamed, "No, no, no."

Jeff hesitated.

One beat.

Two beats.

Three.

He dropped the Magnum.

"You, too, McKenzie," the sheriff said.

I deactivated the Glock and set it gently on the ground.

Nothing in his experience had prepared the Perkins County attorney for the crime wave he suddenly had on his hands. The arson charges against Church and Paulie were one thing—but three murders? Fraud? And whatever the hell was going on at the First Integrity State Bank of Libbie? When he ran for the job, he thought all he'd have to do was attend county commissioner meetings twice a month and try to keep the elected officials from doing something stupid when they let out the snowplowing bids. He certainly didn't sign on for this. So he called the South Dakota state attorney general and asked for help. The AG said it was on its way.

At least that was what Sheriff Balk told me while I watched Nancy Gustafson carefully stitch his shoulder while he lay on an emergency room gurney. I didn't know the extent of his wound, only that the stitches would have to do until he could get to a real hospital; Big Joe was expected to spend the night in Libbie before being transferred to Avera St. Luke's Hospital in Aberdeen the next morning.

"You'll be here when I get back, right?" he said.

"Sheriff, I have one more thing left to do, and then I'm going home," I told him.

"Your testimony—"

"I'll come back for that."

"You'd better. I'd hate to have to come down and get you."

"You could always send bounty hunters. Speaking of which . . ." I patted the sheriff's foot. "Take care, Big Joe."

"You, too."

I paused at the door and looked back at him. The sheriff had told Jeff that he had killed someone once, and I wondered about that. I also wondered about his Glock.

"I still can't believe that you carry a piece without a round in the chamber," I said.

"I never thought it was necessary," he said. "Before you came along, McKenzie, this was a peaceful community."

The city council meeting was being held in a large conference room inside the Libbie government building across the street and down the block from the Libbie Medical Center. Although many people were starting to drift away by the time I arrived, the room was still crowded. Most of the citizens had satisfied expressions on their faces. Whatever spiel the mayor was giving them seemed to be working. I heard the end of his remarks as I entered the room.

"Our tax money will soon be returned to the city," Miller said. "The funds that the various businesses invested will soon be returned to Main Street. The future of the City of Libbie remains secure."

A smattering of applause followed.

Most of the people were sitting in rows of folding chairs in front of the conference room tables. The tables were arranged in a V pattern, the arms of the V extending toward the audience. Two city council members sat behind the tables—Len Hudalla and Terri

Spiess—one on each side. There was a nameplate for George Humphrey, but he was absent, and the space reserved for Tracie Blake was left empty. Ed Bizek also sat behind the table. All things considered, he seemed surprisingly subdued to me. Dewey Miller sat at the base of the V, making it seem as if everything funneled toward him. He saw me enter the city council chambers, and a kind of quizzical expression colored his face.

"What are you doing here, McKenzie?" he said. "You're not a citizen of Libbie."

I ignored him and marched purposefully along the aisle between the wall and the rows of chairs toward the conference tables.

"What business do you have before this council?" Miller said.

I edged past the arms of the V and moved to Miller's chair.

"What do you want?"

As I approached, Miller brought his arms up like a boxer fending off body blows. I pushed his arms apart and grabbed him by the collars of his shirt and suit jacket. I yanked him off of his chair, surprised by how easy it was—he was a big man, after all.

Must be adrenaline, my inner voice said.

I half threw, half pushed Miller toward the aisle. He stumbled, nearly fell, yet managed to keep his feet. As I approached him, he spun about and tried to hit me with a long roundhouse right. I ducked under the blow, using his momentum to spin him back toward the aisle, and shoved him hard. He bounced off the wall and back into my hands. I grabbed him by the collars again and started pushing and dragging him along the aisle.

"Stop it, stop it," Miller said. "You're insane."

Half the people in the room were on their feet, including all of the city officials. They screamed, they shouted, they demanded to know what the hell I thought I was doing, yet no one moved to help Miller. Maybe they thought I really was insane and were afraid to interfere.

"We can do this the easy way or the hard way," I said.

Miller grabbed an empty chair as we passed and swung it around, hitting me in the kneecap. The pain was enough to cause me to release my grip. I bent to clutch my knee.

The hard way.

Miller tried to hit me again. I slapped his fist away from my face, and it passed harmlessly over my shoulder. I grabbed the lapel of his suit jacket. He tried to escape by spinning away and pulling his arms free from the sleeves of the jacket. The jacket came off, and I tossed it down on the floor. Miller ran up the aisle and nearly reached the door before I grabbed him again by the collar. I yanked backward. I heard the shirt rip and saw several buttons fly off. Miller waved his arms as he fell back toward me. I leaned forward, catching him, then reversing his momentum, and shoved him out of the conference room door.

Miller was shouting many things now, yet they all amounted to the same thing—"Let me go." Eventually he added, "I'll kill you."

You had your chance.

He turned in my grasp and tried to gouge my eyes, scratching my cheek instead. For an old man, he certainly was feisty. I moved my head away and yanked down hard on his shirt, pulling him off balance. He lurched forward and put his hand out, using the wall outside the conference room to remain upright. He turned again. The shirt tore in my hand as he edged away. Miller saw the advantage in this. He pulled on one end of the shirt as I pulled on the other until the shirt separated into two pieces. He swung his arm up and down until the sleeve slid off, and I fell backward against the wall.

Miller ran out the door of the government building, which was where I was taking him anyway. His upper torso was pale and fleshy; his muscles were flaccid. His fat legs generated no speed. It was easy to run him down. He screamed and twisted, his fists flailing at me and hitting only air. I took hold of the remains of his shirt and deliberately yanked it off.

The obscenities were spilling fast and furiously from Miller's mouth, along with questions—what, why? A crowd was gathering, and it was asking the same things.

I curled my fingers around the back of his belt and propelled him into the street, steering him in the general direction of the bank. He attempted to run again, and I had to hang on to keep him from escaping. His weight was too much, though, and the belt slipped from my fingers. Miller fell forward, splashing against the asphalt, scraping his elbows. I reached for him.

"C'mon, Miller," I said. "You're making it harder than it needs to be."

Miller rolled onto his back and lashed out at me with his feet. His heel caught me in the upper thigh. He tried to kick me again. I caught his foot. He pulled it back. His shoe came off in my hand, and I tossed it behind me, nearly hitting one of the citizens who had followed us out of the government building. Miller shrieked and tried to spike me with his other shoe. I caught it and yanked it off as well, taking his black sock with it.

Miller rolled onto his knees and started crawling forward. I grabbed his belt again and helped him along. The crowd following us seemed to swell in size as we closed the distance to the bank. Some of the people were telling me to leave the old man alone. Others were laughing. Miller heard the laughter. The obscenities increased in volume and included everyone around him, even his supporters.

I used his arm and belt to pull him upright. He spun his massive body around. An elbow jabbed my fractured ribs. Pain went through me like a jolt of electricity. I pressed my left elbow against my rib cage even as I brought my right hand up. I wanted to slap him down. If he had been twenty years younger, I would have.

Instead, I shoved him. He moved several steps backward, lost his balance, and sat on the pavement.

"Why are you doing this?" he said. "I never hurt you. I never hurt anyone."

Does he actually believe that? my inner voice said. *Is he that much of a sociopath?*

I grabbed his wrist. He pulled it away and tried to kick me again. I seized his pants cuff. He kept kicking at me. I pinned his leg under my arm.

"Boxers or briefs?" I said.

I couldn't bring myself to beat up an old man, but humiliate him the way he had humiliated me when his minions dragged me nearly naked from my bed—yeah, I could do that.

I reached for his belt buckle. Miller clawed at my hands, scratching them with his fingernails, yet I managed to open the clasp. Horror colored his face.

"What are you doing?" he said.

I opened his pants and started to yank them down. He clutched the waistband. I slapped his hands away and tugged. Miller screamed. I kept tugging. He kicked at me. I grabbed both cuffs and wrenched the pants off of his hips, his thighs, and his knees, until he was dressed only in white cotton briefs. He shrieked like an animal in pain. The sight of his ashy body caused some in the crowd to howl with laughter. I got the distinct impression that Miller had made many enemies over the years and they were now having a wonderful time. I didn't like them any more than I liked Miller.

"The emperor's got no clothes," someone said.

Humiliation burned in Miller's eyes. He started to beg. He used the word "please" for the first time since I'd known him.

I grabbed his wrist and forearm and pulled up. Miller resisted, but not very much. Up ahead I saw Harry step through the front door of the bank. He walked to the curb and stood watching us, his hands behind his back, looking like a football referee waiting for the TV time-out to expire so he could start the game.

Miller was weeping silently, yet he hadn't given up. He pulled his arm from my grasp and tried to run again. It took some effort to gather him in my arms; I nearly tackled him. Miller made a long wailing cry. He attempted to speak, but his words were unintelligible. I pushed Miller toward the bank. His resistance diminished until he saw Harry waiting for us. For the first time he realized what was happening. He said he had made a mistake. He said he was sorry. He offered me money. He offered more money. He said he would give me anything. I thought about Victoria Dunston and what she had said.

The people who hurt McKenzie, they're still out there and they'll probably hurt other people, too, unless someone stops them. If McKenzie doesn't stop them, who will?

You're making the world a better place, I told myself, as I gave Miller a hard shove. I pulled on Miller's arm and heaved his massive body the remaining yards to where Harry stood in front of the bank. I forced him into a sitting position at Harry's feet. I was pointing when I said, "Special Agent Wilson, this man drugged me, beat me, kidnapped me, transported me across state lines, and left me to die on the Great Plains. I would like to press charges."

"It's about time," Harry said.

Miller sobbed.

Michelle Miller slowly made her way to his writhing, nearly naked body. She looked down at her husband and shook her head.

"I want you to remember something, Dewey," Michelle said. "You're the one who insisted on putting an immorality clause into our prenuptial agreement. At the time I thought you meant adultery, but I think this qualifies, too. You'll be hearing from my divorce lawyers."

"Man, that's cold," Harry said.

"Couldn't happen to a nicer guy," I said.

JUST SO YOU KNOW

There are some astonishingly good criminal lawyers in South Dakota.

The couple that Miller hired made me look like a vengeance-crazed lunatic on the witness stand and portrayed Evan both as the most maniacal villain since Charles Manson and the greatest traitor since Judas Iscariot. After he rested his case, the federal prosecutor told me that he didn't like our chances at all. Then the arrogant sonuvabitch decided to testify, insisting on telling the jury his side of the story even though Miller's attorneys stipulated to the judge that they had strongly advised him against it. After sixty minutes, with his attorneys cautiously leading him, Miller had the four men and eight women practically weeping at the injustices he had suffered. After two and a half hours of the prosecutor's systematic interrogation, they were ready to convict him of everything from Lincoln's assassination to the disappearance of Amelia Earhart. He's currently serving one hundred and fifty-six months at the Federal Correctional Institution in Littleton, Colorado, while the appeal process runs its course. I was a little disappointed at the court's generosity; I thought he should have received a much longer term. Yet at Miller's age thirteen years could easily amount to a life sentence. We'll see.

Pleading guilty and agreeing to testify against Miller didn't help Evan much at all. He was sentenced to a hundred and twenty months in the Federal Prison Camp at Yankton, South Dakota. At least he'll have someone from home to chat with—Jon Kampa.

Kampa's attorneys were nearly as effective as Miller's had been. They managed to convince a Perkins County jury that Nicholas Hendel was a thief after all, that he had attempted to defraud the community and steal all of the jury's hard-earned tax money, and would have succeeded if Kampa hadn't heroically tried to stop him, killing Hendel more or less by accident. The jury reluctantly convicted Kampa of second-degree manslaughter, and the judge, his judicial reasoning influenced by the fact that Kampa had been an upstanding community leader and that this was his first criminal offense, sentenced him to four years. The Feds, on the other hand, hammered him. They convicted Kampa of a dozen counts of bank fraud and embezzlement and gave him a twenty-four-year jolt—and then insisted that he serve his federal sentence before he was released to the custody of the South Dakota Department of Corrections to begin his state time.

Dawn and Perry Neske were never charged for their crimes and left Libbie immediately after testifying in the Kampa case.

Jeff wasn't so lucky. He was convicted of second-degree murder in the killing of Tracie Blake and first-degree manslaughter in the death of Mike Randisi. He is currently residing at the South Dakota State Penitentiary in Sioux Falls. He won't be eligible for parole for about thirty-seven years.

And yes, he'll also have friends from home to visit with. Church and Paulie both pled guilty to two counts of "reckless burning or exploding"—I am not making this up—and threw themselves on the mercy of the court. Church in particular bemoaned the fact that he was now homeless and without personal transportation. Fortunately, the problem was soon rectified when he and Paulie both drew seven-year sentences.

This all took about a year out of my life as well, while I provided evidence in five—count 'em—five criminal court proceedings, actually testifying three times. Yet somehow I managed to fulfill the promise I had made to myself on the great, windswept plains of Montana. I took Nina to Paris for three glorious weeks. I didn't even whine when she refused to let me buy a Royale with cheese at the McDoo on the Champs-Elysées—what they call McDonald's in France—claiming it was tacky even by my standards. During our second day visiting the Louvre, I actually got down on one knee inside the Near Eastern Antiquities exhibit and proposed yet again, figuring we had been touring the museum so long that she might say yes out of pure exhaustion. She didn't. I told her it was my final offer, that next time she'd have to propose. I don't know if she was relieved by that or not. She hooked her arm through mine, and we walked back to our hotel where we ordered room service—twice.

Meanwhile, Michelle Miller convinced a court that her husband's criminal acts had violated the immorality clause in their prenuptial agreement. Faced with the ruling, Miller caved, quickly agreeing to a three-million-dollar settlement. Apparently he was preoccupied at the time and didn't want to be bothered with a protracted divorce action. After his conviction, he arranged for management of his many business concerns; the proceeds were to be deposited in a money market fund pending his release from prison. At his death, everything will go to Sara. She said she didn't want it. On the other hand, she confided to me that she was planning to attend the University of Minnesota to study both economics and film. To hell with sound effects. She was going to be a movie producer. I could imagine her using Daddy's dough to finance a film. So could Michelle, and she didn't like that idea at all, but I'm betting on the kid. In any case, Sara Anne and Michelle moved to Edina. Michelle had invited me to visit her—emphasis on "her"—but that's not going to happen. Sara Anne, however, is one of about a dozen people who have my cell number.

I also recently received a nice e-mail from my heroine on the white horse. Angela enrolled at the University of Illinois, where she's studying agriculture and consumer economics. I put her and her family up for the night and bought them dinner when they passed through the Cities on their way to visit the campus.

As for the bounty hunters—it turned out that their names really were Lord and Master; they weren't kidding when they told me that. They worked out of an office in Billings, Montana. At a cost of five thousand dollars in cash—Greg Schroeder gave me a two-for-one deal—a couple of gentlemen were dispatched to the Big Sky State to carefully and emphatically explain to Lord and Master that they were no longer welcome in Minnesota. They were free to pursue their chosen profession anywhere else, but Minnesota was closed to them. Cross the state border and they would be the ones who would be hunted. Names were never exchanged, but I'm pretty sure they knew where the message came from. Probably I should have delivered it myself, but Schroeder talked me out of it. "This is a great country," he said. "It doesn't matter if you're tough or mean as long as you can hire someone who is."

As far as I know, the sign outside the Libbie, SD, city limits still reads, RULES, REGULATIONS, AND RESPECT! Go figure.